RUINED

Ann Barker

CHIVERS

British Library Cataloguing in Publication Data available

This Large Print edition published by BBC Audiobooks Ltd, Bath, 2010.
Published by arrangement with Robert Hale Ltd.

U.K. Hardcover ISBN 978 1 408 47846 2
U.K. Softcover ISBN 978 1 408 47847 9

Printed and bound in Great Britain by
CPI Antony Rowe, Chippenham and Eastbourne

RUINED

For Martin, in the hope that he will continue in his endeavour to 'do a good deed in a naughty world'.

PROLOGUE

Spring 1776

It was not long after her tenth birthday that Jessie Warburton discovered that the man she called 'Papa' was not in fact her father. This discovery did not come as a complete surprise. Over the years, a gradual suspicion had crept into her mind, nurtured from half heard conversations, and from the unconsidered things that her parents had sometimes said during their frequent arguments. She had become used to the scenes, Squire Warburton shouting in his drunkenness, and her mother responding with rather tired sounding sobs. At such times, she had tried to make herself scarce, glad of her old, drab clothes which meant that she was as inconspicuous as a rather tall, slim girl could be.

She had always been aware that she was a terrible disappointment to the man she called father, and vastly inferior to her five little brothers who had all died before they could be properly born. At one time, she had wondered whether the squire would have loved her if she had been pretty and dainty, with blue eyes and golden curls, like Alice the vicar's daughter. The Rev'd John Smedley could often be seen with Alice perched up in front of him on his

1

horse, both of them beaming with delight. Jessie had never seen her father look at her with anything warmer than cold indifference. More often, his expression was one of undisguised hostility. It must have been dislike, she concluded later, that had made him give her that horrible name—the name that made all the children snigger behind their hands, and grown ups, especially Mr Smedley, look at her in pity.

Every so often, Mama would take to her bed because she was expecting another child. At such times, the squire's mood would improve slightly. He would even address remarks to Jessie which were not orders barked in her general direction. Then the baby would be born too soon, there would be another little funeral, and Mr Warburton would disappear to London in a bad humour.

When Jessie was ten years old, her mother was brought to bed once more. Jessie, who had by then perfected the art of blending into the surroundings, was listening unobserved when the doctor explained to the squire that the birth had been particularly difficult. There would be no possibility of Mrs Warburton bearing any more children. Jessie never forgot the squire's words as he had addressed his wife later.

'Damn and blast you,' he had sworn, his tone full of anger and bitter disappointment. He had not even waited until his wife had risen

from her bed to berate her. 'You could give that bloody artist a daughter—you can't give me a son. Damn you to hell!' Jessie, who had been waiting in her mother's dressing-room, had heard the tired murmur of her mother's reply, but had not been able to distinguish the words. 'Yes of course I knew,' the squire said by way of answer. 'Your father paid me to marry you, didn't he? Well it wasn't enough for such a poor bargain.'

From that day on, Jessie resolved that she would never again call the squire 'father'. It was after this that he began to disappear to London on more frequent visits. It was much more agreeable when he was away because there was no shouting and Mama smiled more and talked to her about things instead of crying all the time.

Mr Warburton did return occasionally, but never for long, and when he went away again, some painting or ornament always went with him. Jessie could not remember a time when there had been paintings all over the house, but she knew that that had once been the case. The differently shaded marks on the walls bore silent witness to the fact that pictures had hung there.

There was a painting to which Jessie knew her mother was very much attached. It was of a small girl with a kitten, and Mama had told her that it was very like a sister of hers who had died in infancy.

3

One day, when Jessie was about twelve, she had gone with Mama to pay a visit to the vicarage. Mr and Mrs Smedley and Alice had all been there and, as usual, Jessie sat looking on in wonderment at the way in which mother, father and daughter had talked cheerfully together, without raised voices or contemptuous looks. When they had arrived back at home, it was to discover that the squire had returned on horseback, stayed only briefly and gone out again, this time in the carriage. On hearing this news, Mrs Warburton, shaken by some kind of presentiment, had run upstairs to look for her picture. It had gone, along with several others.

The squire's wife was distraught. Jessie so much wanted to comfort her mother, but only dimly understood what was happening and could not think of the right words to say. All she knew for sure was that when the squire returned, there would be a scene. Her hope was that he would go straight off to London, and that the shouting would be postponed. Unfortunately, she was to be disappointed.

Perhaps Mr Warburton had thought to evade his wife, for the confrontation between them took place in the square, wood-lined hall. Jessie had taken refuge in the library, which opened out from the hall. Her mother's loss had made her think of her own particular treasure, a pink and white shepherdess figurine. She had gone into the library to find

4

it, where she had placed it in the window seat earlier, to be near her while she was reading. She had not closed the door, so when she heard raised voices, she went to peep through the crack to see what was happening, the figurine in her hand. The squire was dressed for travelling in a tricorne hat placed on top of a brown tie wig, a long caped greatcoat and shiny boots. His clothes looked much newer than anything that she or her mother possessed. He was a tall, well-made man with a strong, square face, and rather a high complexion. At moments such as these, before the shouting started, she was conscious of a rush of pride in him, and a feeling of wistful longing that he would like her, rather than regard her with his usual cold indifference.

'Where is my painting, Edgar?' her mother was saying. 'What have you done with it?'

'Not now, Chloe,' said the squire irritably. 'I'm due at Maskill's and you're making me late.'

'Due at Maskill's?' repeated her mother. 'What, pray, is so urgent that you must go rushing over to Maskill's?'

'I'm expected,' was the short answer.

'Oh, I'm sure you are,' said Mrs Warburton scathingly. 'No doubt everyone there is rubbing their hands in gleeful anticipation at the thought of easy pickings.'

'Don't talk about what you know nothing of. A man's entitled to a flutter or two.'

5

'A flutter or two! Our pictures and furnishings are disappearing by the day—by the hour, almost.'

'*Our* pictures? *Our* furnishings? I'll remind you, woman, that the law says everything here is my property to dispose of as I choose.'

'Half of what is here is mine—over half! But you sell it without so much as a by your leave.'

'Why the hell should I say "by your leave" when it belongs to me?'

'That picture was mine! You knew how fond I was of it. What have you done with it? Where is it?'

'What difference does it make to you what I've done with it?' He laughed derisively.

'I could get it . . . redeem it . . . ' Her voice tailed away.

'Redeem it? With what? It's gone—thank God.'

'How dare you call upon the name of the Almighty!' demanded Mrs Warburton, her voice shaking. 'When you squander your substance on your gambling and drinking and women, and leave your wife and daughter to—'

She was not to finish her sentence. Until that point, husband and wife had been standing confronting one another, not touching, the squire slapping his gloves on to his left hand with his right. At her words, Mr Warburton dropped his gloves, and seized hold of his wife by her upper arms, pushing her hard up against the panelled wall. They were now no longer within Jessie's vision, but she could hear very well.

'Daughter! Hell, that's rich. The bastard isn't even mine!'

'Edgar, pray!' came her mother's voice, breathless and fearful.

'Pray, what? We both know it. My mistake was to think that it proved you fertile. I should have let you run after the spineless dauber who painted that worthless piece of trash.'

'If it was so worthless, then why did you sell it?' Mrs Warburton demanded swiftly.

'Because I chose to; and because every time I looked at it, I saw his blasted face.' A gasp following this speech told Jessie that the squire was hurting her mother once more. Without thinking, she ran out of the room, and laid her hand on Warburton's arm.

'Please don't hurt Mama,' she cried.

He swung round, his arm upraised, Jessie stepped back, the figurine fell from her grasp and broke into several pieces on the wood block floor.

The sound gave them all pause. Then the squire stepped back, whirled round and strode out of the house. Mrs Warburton shrank wearily against the panelling, and Jessie, weeping, gathered the precious fragments into her apron and ran outside and into the wood just beyond the garden. She sat down beneath her favourite tree, opened her apron and, still

7

sobbing, laid the pieces on the grass in front of her.

*   *   *

Lord Ilam had not intended to ride such a distance, but at least while he was out of the house, he was not obliged to associate with the cold, hard man who had fathered him. The morning had not begun well. Lord Ashbourne, who had himself insisted that his son should go on the Grand Tour, had done nothing but criticize the ideas and acquisitions that he had brought back with him.

Raphael Stafford Montgomery, Viscount Ilam, was Ashbourne's only son, so in an attempt to secure the succession, his lordship had arranged a marriage for the young man when he was not quite seventeen. The young lady had been of Ashbourne's choice, and was over two years older than her bridegroom and barely known to him. Perhaps the marriage might have worked, given time, but the union was never given an opportunity to succeed, for the young viscountess had died giving birth to their son only ten months after their marriage.

Lord Ashbourne, who had exercised firm control over his son's life from the very beginning, now proceeded to take charge of his grandson's fate too, sending him to a local farming family to be brought up, whilst ordering Raphael's departure to the

Continent. The viscount had had no choice. If he had had a single penny that his father had not grudgingly given to him via his steward, he would have walked away and never come back. He might even have done so anyway, had he not had his own son's needs to consider. Like it or not, his life was constrained by people and events that were quite beyond his power. His father wanted neither his help nor his interest either in the Ashbourne estate, or even at Illingham Hall and in the surrounding land which should properly have been his to administer.

'Now you have fathered a brat, you may go to hell as fast as you please,' the old man had told him that very morning, not even looking up from his desk as he spoke. The only thing that seemed to please Lord Ashbourne was if his son was away in London playing the rake. Of course, that was what a lot of young men did, up to a point. Having it forced upon one was a different matter.

After that interview, Raphael had gone to visit his son, Gabriel, the child whom he had hardly seen since his birth six years before. The child had stared at him uncomprehendingly, then hidden behind his apologizing foster mother's skirts. He might as well go to hell as his father had recommended.

So preoccupied was he with his gloomy thoughts that he had strayed further into the wood before he had realized it. He was about to turn around when he heard someone crying. It was a girl with long, brown hair, dressed in a drab brown gown, and she was bending over something in the grass. Thinking that it might be an injured pet, he urged his mount forward, and spied some pieces of what looked like pottery in front of her. At the same moment, the girl heard the sound of the horse approaching and turned her head, her eyes drowned with tears, her expression fearful. Quite unexpectedly, his heart was touched.

'It's all right. I won't hurt you,' he said gently. 'What's the matter? I'm Raff, by the way.'

Looking up, Jessie saw a man who, even to her immature eyes seemed to be quite extraordinarily handsome. He was tall, dressed in a tricorne and a frock coat, with buckskin breeches and high black boots. He had glossy black hair, tied back with a ribbon, expressive grey eyes surmounted by finely arched brows, a thin lipped mouth which still somehow managed to look generous, and well-shaped cheekbones.

'I'm Jez . . . Jessie Warburton,' Jessie replied, 'And I am very sorry for sniffing, but I've lost my handkerchief.'

Raphael took a snowy white handkerchief from his pocket. 'Here, Jez Warburton, have mine,' he said. She took it, dried her eyes, blew her nose, then looked down at the handkerchief with a doubtful expression on

10

her face.

He laughed. Like his voice, his laugh was low and cultured. 'Keep it,' he said. He crouched down next to her and picked up one of the pieces. 'Ah, that's a shame,' he said, and it seemed to Jessie as if he was speaking as much to himself as to her. 'Meissen, I think.'

'I don't know,' Jessie answered, not understanding his meaning. 'But it was my special thing . . . ' She could feel tears coming into her eyes again.

'How did you break it?' he asked. The breaks appeared to have been clean, with no little fragments missing.

'I didn't break it,' Jessie answered. 'It was my fa—' She broke off. 'I mean, the squire. He isn't my father, and I don't like him. I'm not going to say I'm sorry, either.' She stared defiantly at the young man, as if expecting to be reprimanded.

'I see no reason why you should do so if you don't mean it,' was the surprising reply. 'I don't like my father either, and he really *is* my father. Did you dislike him before, or was this' —he held up one of the pieces of the figure— 'what made you feel like that?'

'He makes my mama unhappy and he sells things,' said Jessie. 'And he gave me a horrible name.' She had never spoken in this way to anyone before. Perhaps the uncritical way in which he had accepted her dislike of her father somehow made her feel that she could trust

11

him.

'I've always thought that Jessica was quite an attractive name,' he responded. 'Or won't people use it? Is it Jessie that you dislike?'

'I wouldn't mind if it was Jessica,' she answered in a small voice.

'What is it then?' he asked her, watching how the brown head drooped. She had a long neck which might become elegant in half-a-dozen years or so.

'It's Jezebel,' she answered, her voice lower, so that even bending close to her, he only just caught it. 'Mama was ill for my baptism. *He* told the vicar that that was my name. He was angry with mama. I don't really understand why, but it was something to do with money.'

'Most of the nastiness in the world has something to do with money,' Raphael replied. 'Anyway, what's the matter with Jezebel?'

'She's from the Bible and she was really wicked,' replied Jessie, annoyed with him for not understanding. 'In the end she was killed and the dogs ate her. Would you want to be named after someone wicked who had been eaten by dogs?'

'Some might think it would be preferable to being named after an angel,' he retorted.

'Is that where your name comes from?' Jessie asked him, wide-eyed.

'That's where all the men in my family get their names,' he responded. 'Anyway, why let one poisonous woman spoil a name for ever? *I*

12

think Jezebel is a pretty name, and to prove it, I will call you Jez from now on. Would you like me to see what I can do with this?'

Jessie stared at him. In all the discussion about names, she had temporarily forgotten about her figurine. 'Can you mend it?' She asked him.

'I can try,' he answered with a shrug. 'I like porcelain. At any rate, it can't be any worse than it is now, can it?'

She looked at him for a long moment, causing him to notice for the first time that now the evidence of tears had faded, she had lovely eyes, with clear whites and irises of a particularly warm brown. After a moment, she shook her head.

He took his cravat from round his neck, carefully wrapped the pieces in it and put the improvised parcel in the pocket in the skirts of his coat. 'I'm not making any promises,' he said, 'but I'll do my best. Whatever happens, I'll let you have it back.'

He was on the point of mounting his horse, had indeed set one foot in the stirrup, when he felt a light touch on his arm. He turned, whereupon Jessie reached up, swiftly kissed him on the cheek, then ran back in the direction of her home. For a few moments, he watched her flying figure, his hand going involuntarily to touch the place where she had kissed him. It was the first spontaneous gesture of affection that he had received in

13

more than seven years. Then he mounted his horse and set off once more in the direction of Ashbourne Abbey.

A week later, a small box was delivered for Miss Warburton. Luckily, neither the squire nor Jessie's mother was around when the box came. Half guessing what it must be, she ran upstairs with it and took it into her room, closing the door behind her. Inside, on top of a neatly wrapped bundle was a note which read:

Dear Jez,
I have done my best. I trust you will approve.
Raff

Jessie carefully unwrapped the linen bundle, gasped with surprise and took out her figurine with hesitant fingers. For a moment, she thought that he must either have wrought a miracle, or else bought another, for it looked perfect. Then, as she examined it minutely, she detected a very tiny crack. He had mended it, just as he had promised, and it was almost as good as new. How clever he must be!

She would keep it in a drawer so that nothing could happen to it again, she decided. But before she put it away, she took out a snowy, freshly laundered handkerchief. It was the one which Raff had given her, and which she had washed and ironed herself. Carefully, she wrapped her precious figurine inside the

14

handkerchief. From now on, she would keep her two greatest treasures together.

CHAPTER ONE

October 1794

'Goodbye! Goodbye! Good luck!' The good wishes of the wedding guests still hovered in the air as Gabriel, Lord Ilam and Eustacia, his new viscountess bowled away down the drive in his lordship's gleaming curricle, which had been polished to a shine and decorated with ribbons and flowers for that very occasion.

Almost inevitably, the ladies were the last to go inside. Most of the gentlemen, having done their duty, soon wandered back in to find the glasses that they had set down and to pick up the conversation which had had to be left off with the departure of the bride and groom. Sir Wilfred, who had been one of the few men who had remained outside—understandably, since it was his only daughter who had just got married—offered his arm to his wife, who was looking a little tearful. After a few dabs at her eyes with a dainty handkerchief, however, Lady Hope soon had herself well in hand. An actress before she had married, she seldom lost control in any situation.

One of the two other men who had remained on the steps was Lord Ashbourne, the father of the groom. Alone amongst the company, he had not raised his hand in farewell, but had simply stood watching the vehicle disappear, an unreadable expression on his handsome face.

The third man turned to the lady who was standing beside him and said, 'May I escort you inside now, Miss Warburton? The sun is pleasant but the breeze is cold.'

Jessie Warburton looked blankly for a moment at the thin featured young clergyman before saying 'Oh. Oh yes, thank you. It is a little cool out here.' She pulled her shawl more closely around her shoulders, her actions a little clumsy, for she had a book in one of her hands.

'What do you have there?' asked the Rev'd Henry Lusty, taking the book from her so that she might adjust her shawl more easily.

'It is a gift from Eustacia,' she told him. The new Lady Ilam had handed it to her just before her husband had lifted her effortlessly into his curricle, amid cheers from the wedding guests. 'Don't forget to read it,' Eustacia had told her firmly. 'It might give you some valuable guidance.'

The clergyman examined it more carefully. *'A Vindication of the Rights of Woman.* Are you sure that this is suitable reading, ma'am?' he asked concernedly.

'Be sure that I will abandon it if I find that it is not,' replied Jessie serenely, as she took it back. They were about to go inside when an elderly lady addressed the clergyman, and he took a few steps towards her in order to answer her. Jessie was going to join him, when she felt a light touch on her arm and, turning, she saw Lord Ashbourne standing just behind her. He was as tall as Henry Lusty, but broader and dressed in the first style of elegance, in a coat of dark-blue cloth with snowy white linen, edged with rich lace. His waistcoat was also white, but embroidered with silver thread, and his knee breeches, which were biscuit coloured, fitted him to perfection, like everything else that he was wearing.

Jessie looked up into his face, and felt her heart lurch, as it had done almost since the first time she had met him nearly twenty years before. Of course, age had left its mark upon him. His hair, which had then been jet black, was now greying slightly at the temples, and there were lines on his face which had not been there when he was in his twenties. Nevertheless, he was still a remarkably handsome man, and there was no sign that his physique had lost any of its vigour.

'What is it, Raff?' she asked him.

He smiled down at her. 'I just wanted to tell you how charming you look,' he said, his voice suave and cultured. 'It's the first opportunity I've had.'

'Thank you,' she replied, trying not to feel flustered. She was not accustomed to receiving compliments about her appearance.

'I believe I detect the unerring taste of Lady

Hope,' he went on. Jessie had recently enjoyed a long stay with Sir Wilfred and Lady Hope. Her ladyship had encouraged her visitor to discard the drab colours and styles to which she was accustomed, and to wear clothes that flattered her more. Today, in a green gown trimmed with gold, she looked much younger than her thirty years. 'In all matters of fashion, you cannot do better than place yourself in her hands, in my opinion.' He took out his quizzing glass in order to survey her costume in more detail.

She had seen Ashbourne look other women up and down, but she had never had such attention directed towards herself before, and she found it a little unsettling.

'Yes, she has been very kind,' Jessie agreed. 'Raff, don't do that.'

'Don't do what?' he asked her quizzically.

'Don't look at me in that way.'

'You don't like the fact that I find you pretty?'

'I would if you meant it,' she responded honestly.

'And you don't think that I do?'

'Everyone knows what manner of man you are. You never mean any of your attentions towards any woman.'

'Well that's certainly tipped me a leveller,' he said bluntly. 'How do you know that?' For a long moment, hard grey eyes met defiant brown ones. Then, abruptly, he said, 'Are you

20

staying here for long?'

'I think that Lady Agatha and I will be returning to Illingham almost immediately.'

Ashbourne glanced over to where Lusty was continuing his conversation. 'Rumour has it that a certain clergyman will soon be following in your wake,' he observed, lowering his voice.

'Then rumour has got ahead of itself,' she replied, turning away from him so that he would not see her startled expression. Mr Lusty had indeed proposed to her the day before, but she had told him that she needed time to think.

'Should I ask him his intentions, I wonder?' he said playfully. 'After all, I am Agatha's brother, and you are her companion. I'm probably the nearest thing to a male relation that you have.'

'Don't you dare do anything of the kind,' she whispered angrily. 'His intentions are none of your business.'

As if on cue, Henry turned. He was dressed in black as befitted his calling. The dark colour emphasized the slenderness of his figure. 'My lord,' he acknowledged, bowing a little stiffly.

'Lusty.' The earl inclined his head. 'This nuptial atmosphere seems very beguiling to me. What do you say? Does it tempt you to take the plunge?'

'The church teaches that marriage is an honourable estate,' answered the clergyman, his disapproval of the nobleman coming

21

through in his voice.

'Why, so it does. No doubt it would rejoice your heart, then, if we were all lining up at your door to be joined in matrimony.'

Since Lusty had no idea how to respond to his teasing manner, Jessie said quickly, 'Don't be so absurd, Raff. In those circumstances, Mr Lusty would have no time to do anything else.'

'How sensible,' murmured the earl.

'I am sure that Miss Warburton can always be depended upon to take the sensible course,' said Mr Lusty.

'That's just what I'm afraid of,' Ashbourne responded in the same low tone as before.

'Which is why I shall go inside now, away from this rather chilly wind.' She curtsied to the earl, and Lusty bowed stiffly, as before. In return, Ashbourne swept them a bow that in another man less polished would have seemed an exaggerated courtesy.

Barely had he straightened from his reverence than he was approached by another lady, dark, handsome, and close to his own age of forty-two. 'Penelope,' he murmured. 'What a pleasure to see . . . so much of you, over the last few days.' He flashed a glance down at her daring *décolletage*.

'How kind of you to notice,' Penelope Gilchrist replied, drawing her shoulders back slightly in order to give him a better view.

'And where is Sir Philip? On the Continent?'

'Oh, indeed,' she answered. 'No doubt in pursuit of the beautiful, the fragile and the expensive.'

'A man after my own heart. May I take you to find a glass of champagne?'

'If you please. Don't expect to find me as fragile as your usual objects of desire,' she went on, her eyes twinkling. 'In fact, I am quite robust.'

'I am delighted to hear it,' he responded, grinning.

Jessie Warburton and Henry Lusty had been delayed in their return to the house by some ladies who were talking animatedly on the threshold. Hearing the other couple's conversation, Jessie stiffened her spine. Deliberately, she addressed Lusty with some idle remark, but did not pay any attention to his answer.

She had always known that Lord Ashbourne was a rake. She had been companion to his older sister, Lady Agatha Rayner, for eight years, since the death of her mother. Brother and sister did not get on, but her ladyship kept herself well informed about her brother's doings, and she was always criticizing his profligate way of life. What was more, Jessie had seen for herself how women tended to throw themselves at him. The suggestive conversation between the earl and Lady Gilchrist had not been the first such exchange that she had overheard. She thought of the compliment that he had recently paid her, and told herself that she was just one in a very long line.

Yet to Jessie, he had always been kind in his way. She still kept the figurine that he had mended carefully wrapped in his handkerchief, and she was reminded of him every time she looked at it. After that first encounter, she had not seen him again until two years later, when he had attended the squire's funeral. She and her mother had not gone to the service, but they had welcomed people back to the house afterwards, and Raff had been amongst the company. She would not easily forget his warm hand clasp, and the way that he had remembered her name, and asked her how she was feeling.

After the funeral, it had been revealed that the squire's debts were so great that the house had to be sold to cover them. It was then that Mrs Warburton and her daughter were offered the use of a cottage on the Ashbourne estate. Jessie had wondered many times since whether Raff had been instrumental in that offer.

Three years after that, she had summoned up the courage to ask her mother about her real father. It had been Raff who had taken the trouble to find out that he had died on the Continent just three years after Jessie was born. Then, a short time later, he had given her a book of artistic prints, containing two by her father. She kept the book with her figurine.

At that moment, Mr Lusty drew her into a conversation with two other people, and her ruminations concerning Rake Ashbourne ceased for the present.

*   *   *

Understandably enough, the party acquired a certain languor after the bride and groom had gone, and it was not long before the guests had made their farewells. The only people who were staying overnight at Woodfield Park were Jessie and Lady Agatha, who as well as being the groom's aunt, was also the bride's godmother and one of Lady Hope's oldest friends. Henry Lusty was riding back to Sheffield, where he served as the bishop's chaplain.

'Such a relief to have Eustacia married so well,' murmured Lady Hope, as she and her husband sat at dinner with their two lady guests that night. 'Although I did not say so at the time, I quite thought that when Morrison jilted her last spring, it would prove to be the end of her prospects.'

Sir Wilfred smiled. 'I think that your son-in-law's character is too strong for him to be swayed by such considerations,' he remarked.

'He shouldn't be too concerned about a bit of scandal,' Lady Agatha observed dispassionately. 'He ought to be used to it with

Ashbourne as his father.'

Jessie paused briefly in her eating, then determinedly carried on.

'I will say this for Ashbourne, and you know that I am the last woman to defend him,' said Lady Hope, 'but he conducted himself impeccably while he was here.' Her ladyship had known Lord Ashbourne when, as Viscount Ilam, he had laid siege to her in her acting days.

'He certainly did,' agreed Sir Wilfred. 'I was glad to have him on hand at the ball and at the wedding breakfast. It was like having another host about. '

Lord Ashbourne had called that day to bid them all farewell, announcing that he was returning to London. 'You are very kind,' he had said in response to Sir Wilfred's invitation to dine, 'but I am expected by Lady Gilchrist today, and I may spend a few days there.'

Enjoying Lady Gilchrist's beautiful fragility, Jessie had thought to herself. Quite involuntarily, she had imagined his lordship's shapely fingers that had so meticulously mended the figurine, caressing Lady Gilchrist's white skin.

Now, Lady Agatha gave a disapproving sniff. 'No doubt he'll be off to the Continent and back to his boozing and wenching,' she said scornfully. 'By the way, have you heard what Ilam has done for me?'

'I think Eustacia told me that he had put a

house at your disposal,' said Lady Hope. 'I thought that you were going to live in the dower house.'

'Yes, I was, but when Ilam went to have a look at it, he found that it needed a lot more work than he had thought at first. Besides, I wasn't much looking forward to living in the dower house. It's too isolated, and will be even more so if Jessie takes it into her head to marry. It will suit me much better to be in the house in Illingham which Ilam has offered to me. Remember I've lived there for half my life.'

No one commented upon this, and a moment or two later, Lady Hope began to speak about the difficulties of living in outlying areas, particularly in the winter. Jessie was not fooled. She had sensed everyone's eyes upon her and knew that they were all wondering about Henry Lusty, who had begun to make his interest plain over recent weeks.

She had not yet decided what to do about his proposal. She had not told anyone about it, apart from Lady Ilam, and while she would never wish the younger woman's honeymoon away, she would have been glad to be able to consult her further.

She could never think of marriage without having Raff at the back of her mind. She knew in her heart of hearts that he would never look her way, but she could not stop thinking about him. Yet she did want to be married and have

27

children. Henry Lusty might be her last chance. He was a good man and not ill-looking. Right now, she felt as if she stood at a crossroad. If only she could be given some sort of sign!

'Raff says that he is going to visit me whilst he is in Derbyshire,' said Lady Agatha. 'Personally, I'll believe it when I see it.'

That will be my sign, Jessie thought to herself. If he fails to visit us, then I will accept Henry Lusty.

CHAPTER TWO

After Lord Ashbourne had bade Sir Wilfred and Lady Hope farewell, he set off in his travelling post-chaise to make his promised visit to Lady Gilchrist. John Pointer, his valet of some ten years standing, travelled with him. A slim, fair-haired man of his lordship's age, he was elegantly if discreetly dressed in sober black.

'An interesting visit, John,' remarked the earl.

'Extremely so, my lord,' the valet responded.

'Lady Hope's still a handsome woman, don't you think? I courted her over twenty years ago, if you remember.'

'A very attractive lady, who knows how to

dress to her best advantage,' the valet agreed.

'She's done Jez Warburton some good, don't you think?' mused the earl.

'Indeed.'

'I've always been fond of Jez. I hope she doesn't settle for Lusty. She could do so much better for herself.' He thought of how Jez had looked at the wedding breakfast. His compliment to her *had* been sincere. He liked her, he was glad that she had had some guidance from Lady Hope, and if he was honest with himself, he had been surprised at how very lovely she had looked. He found it disturbing that she could not believe that he had meant what he said.

For a while, the two men travelled on in a companionable silence. Those who were familiar with the suave, debonair picture that Lord Ashbourne presented would have been astonished at the easy way in which he conversed with his valet. The fact of the matter was that his lordship let his guard down with very few people, not being prone to trust anyone unless he had first proved himself worthy of the earl's confidence: John Pointer was such a man.

'Ilam cut a fine figure, didn't you think?' asked Ashbourne, his tone deceptively casual.

'Certainly,' Pointer answered. 'He is a son to be proud of.'

'As you say.'

Ashbourne closed his eyes and thought

about the past. He had been the only son and the youngest child of Michael Eldred Stafford Montgomery, the 7th Earl of Ashbourne. After his birth, his mother had lingered for a week and had then faded away. His father, never a very paternal man, had detested him from that moment. It had always seemed to be the way in his family that fathers and sons had detested each other. He had certainly hated his.

Strangely enough, he did not hate Ilam. He did not really feel that he knew him. That summer, something unexpected had happened. His son had fallen in love. Ashbourne had only had to see the couple look at each other to know that Ilam's feelings were returned. The cynic in him sneered that such affection would not last. Yet there was something deep inside him that desperately hoped that it would. Miss Hope, or rather Lady Ilam as she now was, enjoyed a very good relationship with both her parents. What if she could teach her husband to love their future children? The thought almost made him catch his breath.

Thanks to a loveless childhood, brought up motherless and largely separated from his sister who was eight years older than himself, he was not used to looking for affection in his home. He and his sister had never been close. By the time he had been old enough to know her, she had been packed off to school, then he had been sent away to Eton, as soon as he was old enough to be accepted. He had hated it from the moment when, as one of the very smallest boys among a milling crowd, he had been sent from his boarding-house to collect bedding, and had found himself one of about fifty others trying to identify what had been allotted to him.

That night, in the room which he shared with three other boys, he lay bitterly cold, and unable to sleep, and heard one of the others crying for his mother. He could not remember his mother, but he did shed a few silent tears for his nurse. When next he went home, he hurried up the stairs to look for her, and found that she was gone.

'What do you need a nurse for, sir?' his father had asked him, barely looking up from the letter that he was writing. 'You're not a baby.'

He had protested; he could not now remember what it was he had said. He remembered the consequence, though. The pain from that beating had stayed with him for many days; and he had never pleaded with his father for anything again.

So deep was he in memories of the past, that it took him by surprise when the movement of the carriage told him that they were turning into the drive of Crown Hall, the home of Sir Philip and Lady Gilchrist. It was a handsome building, only twenty years old, purchased by Sir Philip as somewhere to display the antiquities that he regarded so highly.

As the carriage drew up at the foot of the steps which led up to the columned portico, Penelope Gilchrist emerged, and extended both her hands to him as he reached her side. 'Welcome, Raff,' she said, as he took them and kissed first one then the other. 'It's much too long since you were last here.'

'It must be three years at least,' he replied, as he offered her his arm and they walked together into the marble entrance hall, with its black and white checked floor and high ceilings. He looked about him, smiled down at her then said, 'Now that, I like.'

She smiled back at him roguishly. 'Oh Raff, I'm so flattered,' she murmured as he walked past her to a plinth on which stood a black two-handled bowl with figures of athletes painted on it in shades varying from cream to red.

He did not pick it up, but cradled it gently in his hands. 'Greek?' he asked. 'About 500 BC, I would guess.'

Lady Gilchrist wandered over to join him. 'I believe you are right,' she answered. 'Philip brought it back with him last time he came home. Someone handled the box carelessly at the docks and he nearly had a fit. It travelled the rest of the way on his knee.'

'I believe I would have done the same. It's

magnificent.'

'As well as being beautiful, fragile, and very expensive,' she agreed, laughing. 'Come along. I'll show you to your room, and you can have a look at the rest of Philip's collection. I believe he has acquired some pieces that you haven't yet seen.

*   *   *

After he had left his travelling things in his room, Ashbourne came back downstairs, carrying with him a package which he presented to his hostess.

'It's Meissen,' he told her, as she opened the wrappings. 'I thought it might be to your liking.'

'This is charming,' she declared, turning the pastoral figure around and admiring the delicate green and pink colouring. 'You and Philip may keep your mouldy Greek and Roman pottery. I find this infinitely preferable.'

'You see, I remember your taste,' he murmured.

'As I do yours,' she replied, indicating a tray with glasses and a bottle of claret. 'You did not stay long after the wedding, then.'

He poured wine for each of them. 'I am not so popular with my daughter-in-law's family or with my sister that I felt tempted to stay,' he replied. 'Besides, after the bride and groom

33

have gone these affairs acquire a degree of languor, I find.'

'Your son's wife is lovely,' her ladyship observed. It was one of her attractions that she was able to see qualities to praise in other women.

'Yes she is, isn't she? She has some spirit, too. When we were dancing the other night, I asked her, out of devilment you know, whether she did not think that had she met me first, she might have been tempted. She told me that I was much too pretty for her.'

Lady Gilchrist laughed. 'What she should have said, of course, was that she was utterly besotted with Ilam. Anyone could see it.'

'Yes. The boy is fortunate,' answered Ashbourne, looking down into his wine. 'Any news of when Philip will return?'

Later on, the two of them sat down to a well-chosen dinner, eating in a small parlour rather than in the dining-room. 'It's much easier to keep warm in the winter,' said Lady Gilchrist.

They were both well-travelled people with a wide interest in art and books, and found plenty to talk about. After dinner, they went into the drawing-room together, Ashbourne carrying his glass of port in one hand and the decanter in the other. 'Agatha would be surprised,' he remarked. 'I'm sure she thinks that I spend every dinner that I attend slowly sinking further and further under the table.'

'You used to, didn't you?'

'In my youth,' he agreed. 'That was before I discovered that it didn't drive the demons away; it just brought them back next morning with tiny hammers inside my head.'

'And have the demons gone now?'

'Don't pry, Penelope,' he said in a good-humoured tone that nevertheless held an edge of finality.

In the drawing-room, Lady Gilchrist had found a place for her new Meissen figure on a table which stood against the wall with a mirror behind it. 'It could have been made to stand there, don't you think?' she said. She paused then added delicately, 'You must know that I would be very glad to show you how grateful I am.'

'You are very good, my dear,' he replied, with a graceful inclination of his head, 'but you see, Philip has promised me something very special from Pompeii, so . . .'

'You regard the delights of ancient pottery above . . . ?'

'No, my dear, I value Philip's friendship very highly,' Ashbourne replied frankly. 'I don't trespass on his preserves—as you well know.'

She did not press the matter, but instead began to talk of other things. This had not been the first time that she had suggested a liaison, but, attractive though she was, he had never really been tempted to succumb. His friendship with Sir Philip, formed quite unexpectedly in Greece when they had both been in quest of the same amphora, was of ten years standing, and the nature of his upbringing had meant that he did not easily form attachments. He had therefore no intention of sacrificing one of the few that he valued for a romantic romp which, although it would no doubt be stimulating in its way, experience told him would prove to be all too brief.

*   *   *

On the day of his departure, he stood at his bedroom window in his shirt sleeves looking out at the rain lashing down into the garden. He himself had been married on such a day as this. Not for him the glorious October sunshine that had seemed to offer a blessing to his son's union with Eustacia Hope. He had been married to Laura Vyse in the chapel at Ashbourne Abbey on a day when the heavens had opened and powerful winds had ripped through the countryside. It was almost as though nature itself sensed that the enterprise was doomed to failure. The marriage had been planned by his father for some time, but his intention had been that it would not take place for two more years. It had been brought forward by circumstances for which he, Ashbourne, was largely responsible. As he looked at the patterns the driving rain made on the outside of the windows, he could still see the face of Dora Whitton, the farmer's daughter whose gentle affection had been such a contrast to his father's coldness, and who had given herself to him so sweetly in the first intimate contact that either of them had known . . .

A murmured suggestion from Pointer reminded him that breakfast would be on the table. Turning, he allowed the manservant to help him into his coat. He looked at himself in the mirror. It would probably be the last time that he paid any attention to his reflection before dressing for dinner. He was so used to his astonishing good looks that he never thought about them, and was not personally vain. Now, however, he looked at himself critically, noticing the lines at the corners of his mouth, and the grey at his temples. Laura, his bride, had never loved him. She had, he suspected, been a little in love with his father, and his father with her. Clare Delahay the actress, now Lady Hope, had rejected him in favour of Sir Wilfred. His daughter-in-law had said that he was too pretty for her taste. Lady Gilchrist would have taken him to her bed, only because Philip was away. Even Jez Warburton, who had adored him for years, would probably marry Henry Lusty. Was he destined to be the kind of man with whom women played for entertainment, but who was always rejected eventually in favour of someone else?

Firmly putting this destructive piece of introspection behind him, he took his handkerchief from Pointer and set off down the stairs. Lady Gilchrist was waiting for him in the breakfast parlour, and they sat down together. Ashbourne was not one of those men who favour silence at the breakfast table, and they talked as they ate with the ease of old acquaintances. The conversation turned to some of the items on display at the British Museum. As Lady Gilchrist had not seen some of the latest pieces she was eager to hear the earl's descriptions.

After the meal was over and Ashbourne's belongings had been collected from his room, they stood in the hall to say goodbye, not venturing outside because of the inclement weather. 'I'll come and see Philip when he returns from the Continent,' the earl promised.

'You are welcome to come before that,' Lady Gilchrist told him roguishly.

'You are very kind, but I always avoid temptation if I don't intend to succumb,' he answered, grinning. He was walking to the door with his hat in his hand when a messenger arrived from the village with the post. He gave every appearance of being a drowned rat. 'You cannot possibly expect someone to bring your letters to you in this weather,' said Ashbourne.

'I can and do, for three excellent reasons,' she replied. 'One, I pay him a huge sum of money to do it; two, he can now have a warm by the fire; and three, he is sweet on one of the maids.' She looked down at her letters. 'Here's one from abroad, but it's not in Philip's writing. I wonder, would you excuse me if I opened it now?'

Raff waved his assent. Her ladyship opened her letter, looked down at the writing and murmured, 'No, it can't be.' Then the letter fluttered out of her grasp, she staggered and would have fallen, had Ashbourne not caught hold of her. The butler who had been hovering in the background, hurried forward in concern.

'Your mistress has fainted,' said the earl as he lifted her up in his arms. 'Open the drawing-room door so that I may lay her down on the sofa, and send for her maid to attend her.'

'At once, my lord.'

'And bring me that letter.' If it contained something shocking, it would never do for it to fall into the wrong hands. Having arranged Lady Gilchrist on the sofa, he took the letter which the butler was holding out to him. It only took him a moment or two to overcome his scruples about reading it.

Dear Lady Gilchrist,
It is with the deepest regret that I write to inform you of the death of your husband . . .

'God in Heaven!' muttered Ashbourne. No wonder her ladyship had fainted. He read on. It appeared that Sir Philip had been engaged upon an errand connected with his abiding passion, namely, seeking out pottery, the more ancient the better. He had gone to meet someone who had promised him some Roman pieces from the time of Tiberius. Either the message had been a hoax or someone had not wanted him to make his purchase, or perhaps he had simply been unlucky, for he had been set upon, robbed and murdered.

A faint moaning sound alerted Ashbourne to the fact that Lady Gilchrist was coming round. He laid the letter down on a table and knelt on one knee by the sofa, taking her hand. A moment later, a maid came in with smelling salts. The earl relinquished his place to her and went in search of brandy. At the same time, he ordered Pointer to have his bags taken back upstairs. This was not the moment to leave her ladyship unsupported.

'Is there anyone I can have sent for?' he asked her, when she was fully conscious. 'A relative, or a neighbour, perhaps?'

She shook her head. 'There is no one. I have no close relatives and neither does Philip. My closest neighbours are away from home. Oh Raff, it seems so unfair! Why did it have to be Philip who was attacked?' Her voice broke, and she began to cry.

Without any hesitation, he pulled her into his arms. 'You won't be alone,' he said. 'I'll stay for as long as you need me.'

'Thank you. You're a real friend.' Shortly after this, she went up to her room, supported by her maid. Ashbourne did not see her again that day.

The following morning Lady Gilchrist came downstairs, looking stunning in black. 'I have been thinking about my best course of action, and I have decided to go to Austria. I will not be there in time for the funeral, but I must see for myself where he is laid to rest. I must also deal with . . . with his affairs. I was wondering, Raff . . . could you . . . ? Do you think . . . ?'

'Of course I will,' he replied without hesitation. 'When do you want to leave?'

*   *   *

'It's as I thought,' said Lady Agatha, as she sat opening her post at breakfast one morning. 'He's gone to the Continent.'

'Gone? Do you mean Raff?' Jessie asked, her heart sinking.

'Yes,' answered her ladyship. 'I never did think he'd call upon us. He's gone off with Lady Gilchrist, apparently.'

Jessie remembered the conversation that she had heard them having at the wedding breakfast. To think that she had been deciding which gown to wear in the event that he should

41

arrive at the vicarage! What a fool she had been!

This was her sign. When Henry Lusty asked her for her answer, she would accept.

CHAPTER THREE

In the event, Mr Lusty did not renew his suit until after Christmas. He wrote Jessie several letters, informing her that a variety of matters had kept him from visiting as he intended. He mentioned specifically the very severe weather, the illness of the bishop, who had taken to his bed leaving many things in his chaplain's hands, and the busyness of the festive season. However, he hoped to call upon her in the early spring.

This was not very encouraging, particularly when Jessie had determined to accept his proposal as soon as it came. She managed to keep herself busy, and was given an effective distraction in the return of Lord and Lady Ilam from their wedding tour. No sooner had the happy couple settled in, than an invitation arrived for Jessie to come and take tea, since Eustacia was anxious to tell her friend as much about their honeymoon as was seemly.

The new viscountess greeted Jessie with a fond embrace, and conducted her to the drawing-room where there was a roaring fire.

'Gabriel has gone to visit his foster mother and father at Crossley Farm,' Eustacia said, 'so we may be quite cosy and free from interruption.'

Lord and Lady Ilam had not gone abroad for their wedding tour, but had travelled in England instead, spending a large part of their time in Norfolk. 'Gabriel wanted to inspect new farming methods pioneered by Coke of Holkham,' said Eustacia with a twinkle in her eye. 'I can never distract him from thinking about his acres for long.'

'You must acknowledge that he is very good at tending them,' Jessie put in.

'Oh yes. That is largely down to his upbringing, I think. But we did have a lovely time, and I got the chance to do a little sketching.' She took out her sketch-book and for a time, they were fully absorbed in looking at the drawings of the Ilams' wedding tour, a large number of which seemed to feature the viscount, his hair blowing in the breeze, his shirt moulded seductively to the contours of his body.

'So marriage agrees with you,' Jessie observed.

'Oh Jessie, you cannot believe how much,' sighed Eustacia. 'If only you yourself could—' she broke off, then spoke again. 'How is Henry Lusty? Have you heard from him recently?'

'I do hear from him,' Jessie admitted. 'He is quite a good correspondent, actually.' She paused. 'I have decided that when he comes for his answer, I will accept.'

'Then I will wish you every happiness,' said Eustacia warmly. Neither of them mentioned Lord Ashbourne.

*   *   *

Lady Agatha and Jessie spent a large part of the Christmas celebrations at Illingham Hall. Jessie found these celebrations at one and the same time enjoyable, yet poignant. She had known Lord Ilam for as long as she had lived in Illingham. Never had she seen him so happy. His eyes glowed as they rested upon his new wife, and Eustacia was clearly similarly smitten. There was no doubt that theirs was a love match, although they were both too well bred to embarrass the company by flaunting their affection in public. Certainly no one would have guessed it from the decorous way in which they had kissed beneath the kissing bough, to the loud applause of all present. Had Jessie not been aware of their feelings, however, she would undoubtedly have guessed after wandering unexpectedly into the library, and finding the newly married couple locked in each other's arms, exchanging a far more passionate embrace.

Whatever marriage to Henry Lusty might hold, it would not be a love match. He esteemed and respected her. Plenty of marriages—that of her parents, for instance—

did not have as much. She could not help hoping, however, that the clergyman would never seek to bestow such an embrace upon her. She was sure that she would dislike it extremely. As to what she would feel should Lord Ashbourne kiss her in such a way, she put it firmly from her mind. No doubt he would save such passionate embraces for Lady Gilchrist and her like.

After Christmas, the weather closed in, and there was little chance of travel until the beginning of February. The first thaw brought Henry Lusty, who had no hesitation in renewing his proposal to Jessie, who in her turn, had no hesitation in accepting him.

*   *   *

A few weeks after her acceptance, Mr Lusty appeared in his best black, with his clerical wig well powdered, and was shown in to where the ladies were busy with their needlework. He had clearly taken a good deal of trouble with his appearance. Jessie wondered whether as he entered the room, he thought of times when he had been far less welcome, having called at the bishop's behest in order to ask Lady Agatha to vacate the vicarage for the next incumbent. On one of those occasions, she had even chased him out with a rolled umbrella. This time, however, her ladyship welcomed him with all the graciousness of a monarch

45

receiving an inferior but well-meaning subject, then announced that she needed to speak to the housekeeper and left the engaged couple alone together.

For a moment, they stood looking at each other without the least idea what to say. It was the first time that they had spoken privately since Jessie had accepted his offer.

'It is . . . a fine day, again,' Jessie remarked eventually, her colour a little heightened.

'Er . . . yes. Yes indeed,' Lusty agreed.

'We are fortunate to have such pleasant days in February.'

'Yes indeed. Sometimes February can be very . . . harrumph . . . unpleasant.'

There was a brief silence. Both parties stood with their hands behind their backs as if to ensure that there would be no kind of undesirable contact. Then, as is often the way after an awkward silence, they both began to speak at once. 'Have you . . . ?' Jessie began.

At the same time, Lusty said, 'I have written . . .' They both stopped, and laughed self-consciously; but this little hiatus seemed to dispel some of the tension. 'Pray, speak first,' said Mr Lusty.

'No no,' Jessie answered. 'Your sentence, unless I am very much mistaken, was a statement, whereas mine was a question. A statement should always take precedence over a question.'

'Why so?' he asked, honestly puzzled.

46

'Because your statement might be the answer to my question and I should then be saved the trouble of asking it. Pray, speak first, Mr Lusty.'

'You must call me Henry, my dear. I did say that you might.'

'So you did . . . Henry. Pray, tell me what it was that you were going to say.'

He took a step or two forward, unclasping his hands and putting out one rather awkwardly to take one of hers. She allowed him to do so. His clasp was light, and not unpleasant. 'I have written to my sister, telling her of my good news,' he told her. 'I am almost certain that she will want me to bring you to London for a visit. Why are you smiling?'

'Why, because I was correct in my supposition,' she answered. 'I was about to ask you whether you had written to her. When do we set off?'

He frowned slightly. 'You are happy to go? I had thought that I might need to persuade you.'

'I am a countrywoman, but that does not mean that I am not prepared to go to Town,' she replied.

'I am glad. I must confess, however, that I hope you will be mostly content to be in the country. The life of a parish priest in such a setting as this is the one that I have chosen. I would not want to change.'

'I would not have you change,' she

47

responded honestly, meaning simply that she, too, was happy with country life.

He must have read more into her statement than she had meant, however, for he murmured, 'My dear,' raised her hand to his lips, then stepping closer, pressed a kiss upon her cheek. 'I have always thought your appearance to be perfect,' he went on, colouring a little at his own temerity.

'Even when I looked drab and twenty years older than my real age?' she asked playfully. The copper coloured gown decorated with cream lace that she was wearing was new, and one of her favourites.

'I hope that you are not expecting me to be free with compliments,' he told her, with a hint of severity. 'As long as it is modest, a woman's dress is a matter of indifference to me.' Jessie recalled that when she had first met him, she had been accustomed to dress in drab greys and fawns which did nothing to enhance her appearance. The change in her dress clearly did not please him very much. Briefly, she remembered Raff's openly expressed admiration, but repressed the memory. Henry's stumbling compliments were far more sincere than Raff's practised flattery.

Before she could reflect upon this, he spoke again, this time his tone arch. 'There is one item of apparel that I am very anxious to procure for you, and that must be purchased in London.'

'Mr Lusty, I am sure that buying items of clothing for a lady would not meet with the bishop's approval,' she teased.

'I am speaking of an engagement ring,' he said reproachfully. 'Jessica, my dear, you must not wilfully misunderstand me, you know.'

'I will try not to,' she promised, feeling rather like a person who had told a mildly amusing jest, only to be asked to explain it afterwards.

A few moments later, to Jessie's relief, Lady Agatha returned, judging that they had been alone together for long enough. After having a glass of wine with the ladies, Mr Lusty took his leave, bowing very correctly to her ladyship, and raising Jessie's hand to his lips. 'I will tell you when I hear from Henrietta,' he promised.

'I have to admit, I never thought you'd do it,' said Lady Agatha, when Jessie came back from seeing her betrothed off at the door. The older lady was pouring herself a second glass of wine. 'I quite thought you'd go on sighing after my libertine brother until your dying day.'

'I've been a fool,' replied Jessie calmly. 'Ashbourne is not for me. I must have something of my own.'

'Sensible girl,' replied her ladyship. 'Lusty may not be the most exciting man in the world, but he'll never stray. Unlike my Colin, I daresay he won't gamble away his substance, either, *or* drink himself silly.' Over twenty years before, she had ruined her chances of a good marriage by befriending Lady Hope when she had been the actress Clare Delahay. Her father, in the vindictive fashion that was characteristic of him, had refused to give her his support, so she had seized her only chance of freedom and accepted an offer of marriage from Colin Rayner.

Mr Rayner, a younger son of a minor family, had been a clergyman from necessity rather than choice, but he had never allowed his work to interfere with his pleasures. He had enjoyed dressing up in vestments, and mingling with his congregation, particularly in the tap room of the Olde Oak, where he permitted anyone who was willing to buy him a drink or two, or possibly three. The pastoral care of his flock he had left to Lady Agatha, who usually rewarded those who brought him home on those occasions with a coin or two. Jessie had quickly learned to leave Lady Agatha her dignity by keeping out of the way at such times. It was a mark of how well Jessie knew Lady Agatha that the latter was prepared to be so frank about her husband's shortcomings.

'I am a very fortunate woman,' Jessie agreed, and told herself that she would soon believe it.

*   *   *

That night in bed, she took out her copy of *A Vindication of the Rights of Woman* by Mary Wollstonecraft. Idly turning over the pages, she came across the following lines:

> *Rakes know how to work on [women's] sensibility, whilst the modest merit of reasonable men has, of course, less effect on their feelings, and they cannot reach the heart by the way of the understanding, because they have few sentiments in common.*

How very true! Ashbourne was a dangerous man. He *did* have the power to affect her sensibilities. His light tap on her arm to attract her attention on the steps at Woodfield Park had affected her far more deeply than Henry's kiss on her cheek. A sensible woman could not ignore these facts. Having admitted the truth, however, it did not follow that she must therefore be silly and sentimental. The love that she felt for Ashbourne was not of the stuff of which reality was made. She would put all of that silliness behind her, cultivate an affection for Henry, and only think of Raff as a family friend.

*   *   *

Henrietta Machin wrote back a short time later, and Lusty hurried round to show Jessie the letter.

Words cannot express, my dear brother, how delighted I am to hear your good news. I am very sure that I shall soon come to esteem Miss Warburton as highly as you do yourself. Pray bring her to stay with me in London as soon as possible. Perhaps she might help in organizing Percival's sermons, which demand my most urgent attention.

'Percival was my brother-in-law,' said Mr Lusty by way of explanation. 'He was a clergyman, who sadly died five years ago. My sister is not in affluent circumstances, but she inherited a house in London three years ago and has a small income from our father's estate. She also makes a little money by writing.'

'Writing?' echoed Jessie, intrigued. 'What kinds of things does she write?'

'She is putting together her husband's sermons in a number of volumes,' replied Lusty. 'She also writes moral tales for children and other books of moral guidance.' He reached into the pocket of his coat and brought out a slim volume. 'This is one of her books. I thought that you might like to see it.'

Jessie took the book from his hands. *'Flirtation and its Undesirable Consequences: A Guide for Young Ladies,'* she read.

'That sounds . . . informative.'

52

'I have a number of others in my possession which are equally so,' he answered eagerly. *'Concerning the Folly of Trivial Activity on the Lord's Day* is one. *The Deplorable Consequences of Novel Reading upon the Impressionable Mind,* is another. Perhaps you might like to peruse them on the journey. They would help to make many a weary mile pass by, I am sure.'

'Yes indeed,' agreed Jessie, wondering whether Henry would be observing what she was reading during the whole of the journey.

'I was wondering whether her example might encourage you to write some little tracts of your own,' said the clergyman shyly.

'Only time will tell,' Jessie temporized. 'It seems to me that your sister's work is very wide ranging. There may not be any new subjects left for me to consider.'

CHAPTER FOUR

They set out for London a week later. 'Sadly, I will not be able to stay with you for more than a few days,' Lusty explained to Jessie. 'Duty dictates that I must not be absent from my tasks for too long. I will come to see you in London as often as I can. I have every confidence in my sister's abilities to raise your spirits and the tone of your mind.'

There was a long pause. Jessie straightened her back. 'I was not aware that the tone of my mind was particularly low,' she said, with a touch of hauteur.

'No no, you mistake my meaning,' replied Lusty, colouring a little. 'It is simply that the . . . the connections that you are obliged to acknowledge here are . . . that is . . .'

'You do not need to say any more,' replied Jessie, her own colour heightened. 'I am sure that Lord Ashbourne and your sister move in very different circles.' As soon as she had spoken, it occurred to her that he might think that she was trying to sound superior.

Thankfully such a thing did not seem to enter his mind. 'Yes, you are right,' he answered, relieved.

Ironically, the mail coach in which they were to travel departed from Ashbourne, and to Jessie, it seemed a fitting beginning to her new life. Leaving in the early afternoon from one of the posting houses, it was due to arrive in London at the Swan with Two Necks in Lad Lane at around seven o'clock the following morning.

There were two other occupants of the coach, a merchant who, like themselves, got on at Ashbourne and a thin, depressed-looking lady who had travelled from Manchester. This lady was sitting facing the horses, and although Mr Lusty would have preferred to sit next to his betrothed, he invited Jessie to take the other forward facing seat, and took his place opposite her, and next to the merchant.

'Sixteen hours is a long time to be shut up with strangers,' said the merchant in bluff, northern tones. 'What say we introduce ourselves? My name's Nathaniel Peacock and I'm off to London on a matter of business to do with the cloth trade.'

After a moment's pause, Henry said rather stiffly, 'I am Henry Lusty, an Anglican priest, and this is my betrothed, Miss Warburton.'

'Off to London to be married, are you?' Peacock asked, beaming at the engaged couple as if he had had some hand in arranging the match. 'I don't blame you! Snap her up before some other fellow does so.' He was a well-built man, even a little on the stout side, with a square, weather-beaten face, topped by a brown tie wig.

'We are visiting a relative in the capital,' said the clergyman in cold tones.

'Making sure the family take to her, no doubt,' grinned the merchant, seemingly unaffected by the other man's disapproval. 'They'd have to be mad, or blind, if they didn't.' He smiled at Jessie in a manner that was simply good-humoured, without a trace of flirtatiousness and she could not help smiling back. No one had ever suggested that she ought to be snapped up before. She could feel Henry's disapproval, but determined to ignore it.

'What of you, then, ma'am?' Peacock asked the fourth member of their party.

After a brief hesitation, the depressed-looking lady said, 'My name is Griselda Watson. I am a governess travelling to find a new situation.'

'A governess, eh,' exclaimed the merchant. 'Rather you than me, ma'am. Chase a lot of brats around a schoolroom for a pittance? I'd rather starve.'

'Easier said than done,' murmured Miss Watson under her breath, before opening her reticule to take out a thin notebook with a folded letter inside it. Clearly, she did not wish to continue the conversation.

Mr Lusty had taken advantage of Peacock's attention being turned away from himself in order to extract a volume of sermons from his pocket and, when the merchant turned back, the clergyman was, to all intents and purposes, deeply involved in his reading. Jessie, who had been afraid that her fiancé would press one of his sister's tracts upon her, took out her copy of *A Vindication of the Rights of Woman*, confident that he would be too anxious to avoid conversing with the merchant to examine her reading material.

'Reading, eh?' remarked Mr Peacock. He leaned towards Mr Lusty, in order to examine his reading matter. Rather self-consciously, Lusty leaned away from him, affording Jessie, who was only giving a small portion of her mind to her book, with a rather entertaining tableau. Resuming his place after a moment, Peacock turned his head to look out of the window, and said 'ho hum,' a few times at irregular intervals, to no one in particular. He then began to drum his fingers on the window frame of the carriage in a rhythmic pattern. Looking surreptitiously at Miss Watson, Jessie saw her give way to a tiny smile. She was wondering whether the governess was thinking that had Mr Peacock been a small child, she could have offered to entertain him by suggesting that they should count all the different animals that they saw on the journey.

After another interval, Mr Peacock leaned across once more, whereupon Lusty said, in the tone of a very irritated man who is trying to sound patient, 'It is a book of sermons.' No doubt he hoped that this would be the end of the matter, but it was not to be so.

'Waste of time!' declared Mr Peacock forthrightly.

Even Mr Lusty could not ignore this. 'I beg your pardon, sir?' he exclaimed, outraged.

'Waste of time, reading sermons,' Peacock responded, expanding his point. 'They're meant to be heard, not read.'

'Perhaps originally, but—' Lusty began.

'Heard a fine sermon preached in Sheffield fifteen years ago,' Mr Peacock interrupted. 'I've never forgotten it. 1779, it was. In the open air, too, where everyone could hear it.'

'Indeed,' replied Mr Lusty, his face rigid with disapproval.

'Certainly. It was Mr John Wesley who was preaching that day, and as fine a sermon as any I've heard.'

'I do not dispute that you were impressed at his words, sir,' replied the clergyman. 'But to preach in the open air is very shocking.' Perceiving that this argument would absorb both men for some time, Jessie turned to Miss Watson, who was looking out of the window. 'Do you have a situation to go to, or are you intending to look for one in London?'

The governess turned to face her. 'I am intending to visit an employment agency,' she replied. 'I found myself obliged to leave my situation earlier than I had expected, so I will have to take whatever I can get.'

'Such a pity that women are so limited in the work that they are permitted to do,' Jessie observed. 'Look what Miss Wollstonecraft has to say here.' She pointed out a paragraph.

Women might certainly study the art of healing, and be physicians as well as nurses . . . They might, also, study politics, and settle their benevolence on the broadest basis . . . Business of various kinds, they might likewise pursue . . .

Miss Watson looked at the paragraph that Jessie had indicated and smiled cynically.

'Wouldn't that be agreeable?' she murmured. 'It will never happen in our lifetime, though. Men are much too anxious to have their own way.'

Listening to Mr Lusty and Mr Peacock each arguing his own position with single-minded intensity, Jessie felt very much inclined to agree.

* * *

The Manchester mail lived up to its reputation by delivering its quartet of travellers to the Swan with Two Necks at 7.30 the following morning. The debate between Mr Lusty and Mr Peacock had proved to be quite protracted, leaving Jessie free to enjoy her book in peace, and Miss Watson to give her attention to the scenery outside, until the gathering dusk had put an end to both of these activities.

A short break at a busy posting house at around seven o'clock in the evening had provided them with a meal, very welcome but rather too hastily swallowed because the mail could not wait. After that, they had all attempted to get some sleep. Mr Peacock, obviously a comfortable traveller, had dropped off almost immediately, and then snored in the kind of loud, vigorous manner that might have been expected from one of his general demeanour. Miss Watson had closed her eyes and settled back quietly in her corner. After a

59

few minutes' desultory conversation, Mr Lusty had suggested that he and Jessie should try to get some sleep. She was thankful for the suggestion. She was finding it a little difficult to converse with Mr Lusty, and was hoping that the whole of their married life would not be spent in struggling to think what to say to him. She consoled herself with the thought that shared experiences would surely give them things to talk about.

At length, she had slept fitfully, but their arrival in London had soon roused her. It was her first visit to the capital city, and she was astounded by the noise, the dirt and by the general feeling of being closed in as they passed through streets already busy, although it was still very early in the morning. Miss Watson, she noticed, stared out at the scenery with the jaundiced eye of one who had seen it all before.

On their arrival at the Swan with Two Necks in Lad Lane, they stepped down into the inn yard which, like the rest of London, seemed to be all a-bustle. Mr Peacock bade them farewell in a hearty manner, thanking Mr Lusty for his interesting conversation the previous day. 'There's nothing like a good argument for making a journey go by,' he declared.

While the men were speaking, Jessie turned quietly to Miss Watson. 'We are staying in Sloane Street with Mrs Machin,' she told her. 'Please come and call when you are settled.'

Miss Watson thanked her. 'I will let you know when I have found a position,' she said. Standing in the inn yard, Jessie could see that the governess was younger than she had thought; probably about her own age. Drab clothes did indeed make a difference, she reflected wryly.

She turned to look at Mr Lusty, suddenly thankful for his presence in this large city. What would it be like to be in Griselda Watson's position and have to fend for herself, she wondered? Mr Lusty, she then discovered, was on the point of arranging a sedan chair to take her to his sister's house. As for himself, he told her, he would walk alongside.

'My dear sir,' Jessie exclaimed, after one anxious look at the leaden sky. 'Why do we not take a hackney then we might both ride in comfort?'

The clergyman's face set in lines of rigid disapproval. 'Certainly not,' he said. 'It would be most improper for us to travel together unchaperoned in a closed carriage.'

'Not when we are engaged to be married, surely,' replied Jessie. 'In any case, what if it comes on to rain?'

'A little rain will not do me any harm,' he answered. 'You forget, Jessica, that we are in London now. Gossip is liable to spread like wildfire. There will be time enough for these questionable diversions when we are married.'

As she climbed into the sedan chair that he

61

summoned for her, Jessie reflected that London must indeed be a strange place if its inhabitants had time to remark upon the travelling habits of a country clergyman and his betrothed.

Fortunately, the rain held off until their journey to Sloane Street was over. The journey itself was accomplished quite speedily for the chairmen, two strong fellows, went as fast as the traffic would allow. Mr Lusty kept up with them with some difficulty, and he was still trying to get his breath back as they waited on Mrs Machin's front step for her servant to open the door.

There was some little confusion as they were shown into a tiny parlour, for the maid who had let them in declared that 'missus is still in bed,' giving rise to some very disapproving looks from Mr Lusty, for by then it was past nine o'clock. The confusion was explained, however, when Mrs Machin entered, declaring that she had been up for hours, but that the maid was a little deaf.

'I dare say she did not properly hear what you said,' suggested Mrs Machin as she came forward to greet her brother. She was a small, plump woman of about forty, with dark blonde hair, rather prominent brown eyes and a dimpled chin. She was dressed in sober grey silk, with a crisp white apron and cap. She turned to Jessie. 'This must be Miss Warburton,' she said, smiling politely. 'You are very welcome.' She glanced down at Jessie's gown and seemed to be about to make a comment upon it. Then either she changed her mind at the last minute, or Jessie was mistaken in her supposition, for when Mrs Machin spoke again, it was to comment upon the weather.

*   *   *

In the event, Mr Lusty only stayed for three nights. The day after their arrival was a Sunday, so naturally a journey on that day was unthinkable, particularly for a clergyman. The only travelling that they did was to walk to St George's in Hanover Square for divine worship. Jessie was surprised that they did not attend a church that was nearer, but she didn't mind. She had a true countrywoman's enjoyment of a long walk. On this occasion they were accompanied by Mr Hinder, a young man who lived in lodgings just two doors down. He made his living by doing some teaching and, in response to Mr Lusty's urgent questioning, disclosed that he was thinking of taking orders. Jessie decided that she must be getting older, for this prospective clergyman, with his fresh face and slender figure, hardly looked more than about twelve years of age, although she guessed from his responses that he must be in his mid twenties. He seemed to be an agreeable enough person, however, listening to anything Lusty said to him with rapt attention, prompting the older gentleman to say that he appeared to be a sensible fellow.

'He has been helping me with Percival's memoirs,' said Mrs Machin.

'I thought that it was his sermons that you were collecting,' put in Mr Lusty.

A brief glance passed between Hinder and Mrs Machin before the young man answered, 'Each piece of writing throws light upon the other.'

'Just so,' agreed Mrs Machin eagerly.

The outing to church was a revelation to Jessie. For the past few years she had worshipped almost exclusively at the little parish church in Illingham, which was attended by the villagers as well as by some of the better families, and sometimes Lord Ilam himself, who, since his wedding, was naturally accompanied by his lady. Here, the church seemed filled with fashionable people, some of whom seemed far more concerned to see and be seen than to pay their respects to the Almighty. Mr Lusty, who looked exceedingly sober compared to some of the gentlemen who were attending, was inclined to be disapproving of those present, and critical of his sister for choosing such a place. Mrs Machin, however, whose demeanour throughout had been exceedingly devout, insisted that those who had built the new streets amongst which she was living had not yet been given permission to build churches. 'We are within the parish of St George's so it would not be proper to attend any other church,' she explained. 'Rest assured, dear Brother, when there is a place of worship nearer to my home, I will attend it.'

'I'm sure you will, my dear,' said Lusty with a smile.

On Mr Lusty's last full day in the capital, he took both his sister and his betrothed to visit St Paul's Cathedral. Jessie had been impressed by the size and grandeur of St George's in Hanover Square, but the mighty cathedral, the fourth to be built on that site, almost took her breath away. She spent such a long time gazing upwards at the dome, the columns and the magnificent painting on the ceiling that she feared she would have a stiff neck later.

Mr Lusty was obliged to spend the next morning with some other clergymen whom he had arranged to meet, so Jessie and Mrs Machin occupied their time by getting to know one another a little better. Mrs Machin showed Jessie around her house which, in all honesty, did not take very long because the house was not large, only requiring two live-in servants—Dilly, the maid, and a cook—and some daily help. 'It suits me very well,' said Mrs Machin. 'In fact, a larger place would be a worry to me. My companion, Mrs Smales, is visiting her brother in the City for a while; but if she were here too, we would almost be crowded.'

'It is charming,' said Jessie sincerely. As a single woman, she knew that she would never be able to set up house in London, even if the small allowance from her mother made that possible. One of the attractions of Mr Lusty's proposal had been that she would have a home of her own, and no longer have to depend upon what amounted to Lady Agatha's charity. 'Has Mrs Smales been living with you since your husband's death?'

'Only since I inherited this property,' replied Mrs Machin. 'Her brother is inclined to be sickly, and she is obliged to visit him quite frequently. I should not be surprised if you did not even meet her while you were staying in London.'

Mr Lusty's meeting was over by about eleven, so he came back to escort his betrothed to a jeweller's shop in order to buy her a ring. The shopkeeper brought out a number of trays for their examination, but Jessie stood by her first decision which was to have a ring with a small diamond, a single stone in a very simple setting.

'It pleases me very much that you have chosen the plain and ordinary,' said the clergyman approvingly. 'There is nothing in that ring that would give offence as being too ostentatious for a vicar's wife.' His words made Jessie feel guilty. As she looked at the tiny stone, it was almost as if its modest size made her feel less engaged.

The afternoon being fine, Mr Lusty took his sister and his betrothed for a walk in nearby Hyde Park for, as Mr Lusty said, he would be obliged to sit still in the mail coach from late that evening for a good many hours, so would be thankful to stretch his limbs. He also expressed a desire to look at St George's again, as he had not looked properly on Sunday, deeming sight-seeing inappropriate after attending divine worship.

Their walk took them the length of Brook Street, along which many fashionably dressed people were coming and going. There was an immaculate travelling chaise standing outside one of the houses on the opposite side of the road, and a gentleman was escorting a lady to the door. As the lady turned to make her farewells, Jessie realized that the two people were Lady Gilchrist and Lord Ashbourne. Her ladyship stood on tiptoe and bestowed an affectionate kiss upon her escort.

Henry Lusty stiffened and muttered 'Ashbourne' under his breath, before hurrying his sister and his betrothed along the street at a greatly increased pace.

'Goodness!' exclaimed Mrs Machin, looking back over her shoulder as well as she was able. 'Was that Rake Ashbourne?'

'Yes, it was he,' answered Jessie, whose heart had lurched at sight of him, much to her annoyance. 'He is the brother of Lady Agatha

67

Rayner, with whom I have been residing.'

'And do you know him?' asked the clergyman's widow.

'I see no reason why we should even be speaking about Lord Ashbourne,' said Mr Lusty repressively. 'His activities are not a fit subject for ladies' ears.'

'Nor are the activities of the lady who accompanied him, I suppose,' observed Mrs Machin, rather spoiling the severe effect of her words by adding 'Such a handsome bonnet, though.'

'The bonnet is immaterial,' Lusty declared disapprovingly. 'Let us instead turn our minds and our conversation to higher things.'

None of them spoke again until they reached St George's.

CHAPTER FIVE

Ashbourne had only been in London for a week longer than Jessie. He had accompanied Lady Gilchrist to Austria as he had promised, and once there had found that there was quite a lot of business to be sorted out. Sir Philip had been engaged in some complex negotiations concerning some valuable pieces. The other persons involved were inclined to be obstructive, encouraging Ashbourne to suspect that they might not have been entirely guiltless over the baronet's murder.

He had managed eventually to settle the matter to his satisfaction. Initially, the two men concerned, one Austrian and one Italian, had attempted to pull the wool over Raff's eyes concerning the value of the items involved. On discovering that the earl was just as knowledgeable as his late friend, they had tried to intimidate him, firstly by veiled threats, then by arranging for him to be set upon in an ambush strangely similar to the one in which Sir Philip had met his end.

Again, they had underestimated their man. Raff had taken Pointer with him who, as well as being his valet, had a number of other talents, and had stood beside his master in tight corners on more than one occasion. Two of the rogues had fled rather the worse for wear, and a third had been despatched with his own stiletto. The fourth had been 'persuaded' into disclosing the names of those who had sent him. The next time Raff had confronted Herr Hummel and Signor Vasselli, he had begun the conversation by impaling the desk between them with the stiletto.

Thereafter they had been much more co-operative. They had also been surprisingly indiscreet. Raff, a wry smile on his lips, had left them, taking what was owed to Philip's widow. As soon as he had left, the authorities had entered, ready to take action on what they had heard. Philip's death would not go unpunished.

Raff had wondered whether Lady Gilchrist would want to have her husband's coffin brought back to England, but she had other ideas. 'His passion was travel,' she had said. 'I think it very unlikely that he would ever have settled for a quiet life in England. Let him remain here.'

Her ladyship had seemed to want to stay in Austria for a little while, mingling with those who had known Philip, and exchanging reminiscences. This had suited Raff as he was in no particular hurry to return to England. Their return had to be carefully managed in any case, for the more investigations that Raff made, the more that he found Sir Philip had bought and stored.

No doubt there were many who supposed that Ashbourne and Lady Gilchrist were more than just good friends, but they were mistaken in that belief. Rake though he was, the earl would have been appalled at the idea of making an advance to a lady who was so recently bereaved. He could not forget, however, that her ladyship had as good as propositioned him at Crown Hall, and he wondered whether she might turn to him for comfort. It was not until they were in England once again, travelling back to London in Raff's comfortable chaise, that Lady Gilchrist mentioned the matter.

'No doubt you've been wondering why I

haven't been attempting to lure you into my bed,' she said, with the kind of frankness that is only possible between old friends.

He raised his brows. 'Strangely enough, I haven't,' he replied.

'It's very odd, you know, but while Philip was simply away on the Continent, I had absolutely no compunction about taking lovers,' she observed. 'Now that he is gone, such an action would seem dreadfully disloyal. Does that sound illogical?'

'Completely; but then bereavement makes one say, do and think strange things.'

'You mustn't think that I don't grieve his loss. Of course I shall miss him; but ours was not a love match, and he never really needed me. Besides,' she added with a wry smile, 'I have come to value your friendship too much to risk spoiling it with a fling.'

On their arrival in London, Raff escorted her ladyship to her house in Brook Street before continuing to Ashbourne House in Berkeley Square. 'Do you wish me to come in with you?' the earl asked as he accompanied her to the door.

'There is no need,' Lady Gilchrist answered. 'My servants have been alerted and they all know me and look after me exceedingly well.'

'Let me know when you are ready and I'll come and help you unpack Philip's acquisitions. He seems to have purchased enough to restock the British Museum.'

'You're only hoping to get your hands on the best pieces,' she retorted.

'Of course,' he murmured.

Impulsively she stood on tiptoe and kissed him. 'I would not have had the slightest idea what to do without you,' she said warmly. 'My dear friend, how good you have been.'

'Not so loud, I beg you,' he said, his eyes twinkling. 'My reputation as the Fallen Angel could be damaged beyond repair.'

'Don't worry, I shan't tell anyone,' she assured him. 'When asked about the time I have spent in your company, I shall maintain a discreet silence!'

*   *   *

Once in his house in Berkeley Square, Ashbourne greeted his butler and went up to his chamber to remove the grime of travel from his person and change his clothes. On coming downstairs, he glanced briefly at his correspondence. There were several violet-scented offerings from a lady with whom he had enjoyed an intimate connection before his visit to the Continent. He glanced through the contents of one and his face took on an expression of distaste. The scent was strong, and the lady was far too persistent. They had already made their farewells and he had been more than generous. He dropped the letters on the fire.

He never expected to find love in his connections with his mistresses. His expectation had been that once he had returned to London, he would soon find someone to suit him, at least for a time. His stay in Derbyshire had made him feel restless in a way that was unusual to him. More recently, his involvement with Lady Gilchrist's affairs had left him no time to indulge in the kind of pursuit that he found most stimulating. Increasingly, he had found himself wondering whether his final inevitable triumph in the chase was ever as enjoyable as the chase itself.

There were a few bills which he set on one side to give to his man of business. He was unusual amongst those of his class in that he paid his bills almost as soon as they arrived. Ever since he had ceased to be dependent upon his father following a bequest which had come to him on his twenty-fifth birthday, he had a horror of being beholden to anyone.

Another letter, lengthy and beautifully written, was from an acquaintance who lived in Bath. He read the first few sentences and chuckled to himself. Georgiana was always so amusing. He would reserve the rest until later and enjoy it over a glass of brandy. A short time later, he donned his greatcoat and set out to walk the short distance to Brooks's in St James's Street.

*   *   *

That night, after Mr Lusty had left to catch the Manchester mail, Mrs Machin said, 'I will be taking breakfast in my room tomorrow. You are very welcome to do the same. Just ring the bell when you are ready.'

Jessie, whose only experience of taking breakfast in her room had been at the home of Sir Wilfred and Lady Hope, decided that this would be an agreeable novelty. She was astonished the next morning when she woke up at a little before nine o'clock. The tiredness from the journey must still be catching me up, she decided. She rang for breakfast, and when Dilly came upstairs with her morning chocolate, she apologized rather shamefacedly for waking so late. 'I hope it has not made things difficult for you,' she said.

'Oh no, ma'am,' answered Dilly earnestly. She was a tall, rather thin young woman with a long nose with a red end, and rather straggly mousy brown hair. Jessie had also noted that she did not appear to be at all deaf, as Mrs Machin had declared her to be at their first meeting. 'Missus is often not down before eleven. She likes to read and study in her room before she comes downstairs. What can I get you, miss?'

Reflecting that she would have to find things with which to occupy herself during the mornings, Jessie made her wants known, and settled back to enjoy the very agreeable luxury of reading in bed in the daytime.

Dilly came up a little later with hot water for washing and, after offering to help Jessie dress—which offer she refused—went downstairs again, leaving the visitor to her toilet.

Even after having taken her time over dressing, Jessie was still downstairs a full half-hour before Mrs Machin, so she occupied herself with writing a letter to Lady Agatha, giving an account of her journey, their visit to St Paul's Cathedral and to St George's, and their walk in Hyde Park. After some thought, she decided to mention that they had seen Lord Ashbourne, but only because Mr Lusty might visit her ladyship, mention the encounter and think it odd if she had not referred to it in her letter.

Why had Lord Ashbourne been kissing Lady Gilchrist? She had heard the sad news that Sir Philip had been killed, and had sent a civil note to Crown Hall. She had not received a reply, presumably because the widow had been travelling with Lord Ashbourne. Was (shocking thought) Lady Gilchrist now Raff's mistress? Their conversation at the wedding breakfast had certainly been flirtatious enough. Or did his assiduous attentions mean that they would marry now that she was free?

Scolding herself because it was none of her business, she quickly signed the letter and was on the point of sealing it up when she remembered a glaring omission. Not only had she failed to mention that Mr Lusty had bought her an engagement ring, but she had also forgotten to put it on that morning! Shocked at herself, she determined to start again, this time getting her priorities right. She took up a fresh piece of paper and set about copying down what she had written, this time adding the news about her ring near the beginning. Mr Lusty would certainly have been far more displeased that she had failed to disclose that piece of information than that she had forgotten to mention a brief sighting of Rake Ashbourne!

Unfortunately, her carelessness now meant that she did not have enough paper to finish her letter. She looked around the drawing-room for more, but could not see any. The maid, when asked, disclosed that Mrs Machin always kept some in the book-room, so Jessie decided to go in there and find it. She would not look in any drawers or cupboards, she decided; but if there was any within easy reach, she would make use of it.

Mrs Machin's book-room was not as neat and tidy as Jessie might have supposed. Indeed, there were books lying open on the desk, and on a chair next to it, and others, higgledy-piggledy on a pile, looking as if they were in imminent danger of falling to the floor. Jessie tried to make the pile more secure, and in doing so, she caught sight of one or two titles. *A Treatise Upon the Useful Science of Defence; A Dissertation on the Duty of Mercy and Sin of Cruelty to Brute Animals; List of Covent Garden Ladies; Jockey Club, or a Sketch of the Manners of the Age.* 'What an odd selection,' remarked Jessie out loud, picking up the first volume in order to peruse it. She had not closed the door, so Mrs Machin's voice came entirely without warning.

'How dare you poke and pry amongst my private papers!' said that lady, her voice trembling with indignation, but her expression looking faintly hunted.

'I beg your pardon,' Jessie answered, her colour somewhat heightened, but her voice steady, for her conscience was clear. 'I had no intention of prying.' She put the book back on top of the pile.

'Your actions betray you,' replied Mrs Machin, her prominent brown eyes flashing fire.

'I was only looking at the books,' said Jessie in placatory tones.

'I dare say you will be telling Henry that I am reading improper literature,' said Mrs Machin in a haughty tone that was nevertheless a little breathless. 'Well, allow me to inform you that I am preparing some more tracts about the evils of pugilism and savage sports.'

'That is exactly what I had supposed,' answered Jessie, dismayed that a simple quest for paper should have turned into an argument that threatened future good relations with her sister-in-law-to-be.

'So you now say,' that lady retorted. 'Be very sure that if you say anything to Henry, *I* shall tell *him* that you were poking and prying.'

'I have no intention of saying any such thing to Henry,' said Jessie, starting to feel angry at the injustice of the accusation. 'I only came in search of some writing paper so that I could finish my letter to Lady Agatha. My own is all used up.'

With a grudging gesture, Mrs Machin handed her two pieces of paper, then held the door open for her to leave.

'Thank you,' said Jessie. Then she turned to add, 'I am very sorry for—' It was too late: Mrs Machin had closed the door in her face.

That lunch-time, when they met at the table, Jessie apologized wholeheartedly for unwittingly offending her hostess. Given the cold reception of her earlier apology, she did not expect very much, and was somewhat relieved when her hostess said grudgingly, 'I daresay you did not mean any harm. Let us forget the whole matter.'

'You are very good,' Jessie responded. Her words were received with a gracious inclination of the head. A little later, she found the courage to say, 'I understand from Henry that you are working on putting together a collection of your husband's sermons. That

78

must be very satisfying work.'

'Yes . . . yes indeed it is,' replied Mrs Machin, sounding a little self-conscious. 'Although his handwriting is rather difficult to decipher, so I find that I cannot do too much at any one time.'

'And you have your own writing to absorb you,' Jessie pointed out.

'What?' cried the other lady in an alarmed tone.

'Your tracts on various moral issues.'

'Oh! Oh, yes, of course,' replied Mrs Machin with a sigh. 'Yes, I do need to work on those, and when I do, I must be alone—quite alone. I hope you do not mind?'

'Not at all,' answered Jessie cheerfully, reluctant to damage this new, if fragile accord. 'You will find that I am very well capable of occupying myself.'

CHAPTER SIX

Jessie had spoken the truth when she had told Mrs Machin that she did not mind being left to her own devices. Although she was Lady Agatha Rayner's companion, her ladyship needed her presence for propriety, and not because she expected to be entertained. In fact, Lady Agatha was often busy with her own correspondence and Jessie was quite accustomed to taking herself off to do a little parish visiting, or simply to take a walk around the village, sometimes carrying her sketch-pad with her. She had not inherited her father's artistic gifts, but several people had found her drawings pleasing and the activity gave her pleasure. In addition, she often went into the village school to read with some of the children, and give drawing lessons to those pupils who showed aptitude. She was also accustomed to lending a hand with the housekeeping, usually dealing with the linen cupboard, which duty interested Lady Agatha not at all.

Here in London, however, she found herself in some difficulty. There were no duties for her to perform as she was a guest in Mrs Machin's little house. Her assistance in organizing the linen cupboard might have been welcomed, but she did not feel that she knew her hostess well enough to offer such help. From that lady's reaction to her presence in the book-room, she feared that such a suggestion might be looked upon as interference.

As a resident of the vicarage in Illingham, she could visit people there in the name of the church. Here, she had no such standing in the community. Furthermore, her tentative offers to help her hostess with her husband's memoirs had been firmly refused. Mr Hinder's frequent presence in the house and in the book-room in particular made it very plain that the clergyman's widow had all the help that she needed. Consequently, when Mrs Machin continued to remain in her room for most of the morning, and disappear at other times in order to write, Jessie found herself with rather a lot of time on her hands.

As the days went by, if she was honest with herself, she would be bound to say that she did not think very much of her future sister-in-law's notions of being a hostess. She herself had never had a home of her own in adulthood, but Lady Agatha occasionally had people to stay. Although her ladyship often had many concerns, she would never have dreamed of neglecting a visitor in the way that Mrs Machin was doing.

There was one thing to be said for the current state of affairs, she decided, after leaving the dining-room after breakfast in order to sit in an empty parlour. She was very up-to-date with her correspondence. She had written to Lady Agatha, Henry, Lady Ilam, Lady Ilam's mother Lady Hope, and a married friend who lived in Scotland. To whom else could she write? She had lived a retired life in Illingham for the past eight years. Her parents had both been only children and were now dead. She really knew very few people. There was always Lord Ashbourne, of course.

After a few moments, she came to with a start, realizing that she had been remembering

81

how handsome he had looked on the occasion of Lord and Lady Ilam's wedding. She must think of something else. She had no address for him, and anyway, he was dancing attendance on Lady Gilchrist. She, Jessie, was to be married to Henry Lusty and had no business thinking about other men. A bird in the hand was worth two in the bush. That was a proverb that she had learned as a child. Indeed, she could remember copying it out on a slate in her best writing.

Of course! She could write to Miss August, the village schoolmistress in Illingham. Then with a cry of vexation, she realized that if she wanted more paper she would have to interrupt Mrs Machin. After a moment's thought, she straightened her shoulders and came to a decision. If there was no writing paper within easy reach, she would go and buy some.

She went back up to her room, and when she met Dilly in the hall a few minutes later, she was drawing on her gloves. 'I am going to buy writing paper,' she told her. 'I shall not be too long. Pray tell your mistress where I have gone, and that I shall be back soon.'

'Oh, miss, I don't think you should go,' said Dilly. Her face looked worried.

'Nonsense,' answered Jessie bracingly. 'The day looks perfectly fine. I am not a young slip of a girl, you know. I shall be perfectly safe.'

'I'm not sure that missus would like it,' the

girl protested doubtfully.

Repressing the urge to say that if the 'missus' wanted to prevent her guest from doing things that she did not like, then she would do well to make a bit more of an effort to entertain her, Jessie simply replied, 'I will be back before I am missed. You will probably not even need to tell her that I am gone.'

Once out in the fresh air, she felt better immediately. Sloane Street was only built up on one side, and looking across the road from Mrs Machin's house, she felt as though she was in the middle of the countryside, with green fields, market gardens and even some animals grazing. It was quite difficult to believe that she was so close to such a big city. Then, as she walked on to Knightsbridge, the amount of traffic suddenly increased. She recalled Mr Lusty remarking that much of the south and westbound traffic would use this route, and indeed a fair number of people seemed set upon either leaving London or entering it, be it on foot, on horseback, or by carriage. She glanced across towards Hyde Park, remembering how the three of them had taken a walk there a short time before. Spring had commenced and trees were already looking green. She paused in admiration of a fine horse chestnut, resolving to come and look at it again and perhaps sketch it when its candles were fully out.

Suddenly conscious of being observed, she

looked round and saw a very rakish-looking man watching her with a decidedly predatory expression upon his face. Turning hurriedly, she set off towards the city at a brisk pace and was soon entering Piccadilly.

At first, all her attention was taken up with observing the noise and activity of the city, from the urchins hanging about, hoping to earn a few pence holding someone's horse, to the carts delivering goods, and fine carriages carrying the wealthy from one place to another. The hour was still early for the *ton* to be about, but there was a smattering of well-dressed people visiting shops, looking in windows, or simply getting an airing.

She had set out with the definite purpose of buying writing paper. The notion of looking for one specific shop, however, quite disappeared out of her head, when she saw the wide variety of shops to be found in Piccadilly. After taking what seemed to be a very few paces, she discovered a jeweller, a wine merchant, a hosier, an ironmonger, and a draper. To a woman whose daily diet was just one village shop, enlivened occasionally by a visit to a market town, this was a feast indeed. She did see a bookseller's, but hesitated before going inside. She was rather reluctant to exchange the richness of her present vista for the dark and possibly musty interior of a shop.

As she looked about her, however, it dawned upon her that there were no respectable females walking alone. Gentlemen seemed to be able to enjoy that freedom, but any ladies were all accompanied, and the only women without companions were obviously servants going about errands. Furthermore, she noticed to her alarm that the rakish man whom she had seen earlier was standing on the other side of the road and observing her with interest. She recalled Dilly's concern that she should not go into the city unaccompanied. She was beginning to see why. The man seemed about to cross the road, but most fortuitously, a cart rolled between them, and whilst his view of her was obscured, she darted into the shop, resolving to remain there until the man had gone, if necessary begging the shopkeeper's assistance in hiding her.

As she had suspected, the shop was rather dark, and it took her eyes a moment or two to recover from the effects of coming in from the spring sun. She could hear voices, and she deduced that the shopkeeper must have a customer. Hurriedly she snatched up a book and pretended to read, not wanting to look as if she were eavesdropping.

'Very good, my lord, I'll see what I can do. If the item you're looking for comes in, I'll send you word.'

'I'm obliged,' was the courteous response. 'Good day to you.' Jessie recognized his voice immediately, and her heart gave that familiar painful lurch which was her customary response to Lord Ashbourne. Telling herself crossly that as a betrothed woman she had no business to feel so excited at the sound of a voice that did not belong to her affianced husband, she looked for a bookcase to hide behind. Unfortunately, there was not one tall enough to conceal her, so she was obliged to turn her back to the other occupants of the shop and attempt to give the impression of being thoroughly absorbed. She hoped that this would be sufficient to ensure that she would not be noticed.

'Good day, my lord.' The shopkeeper hastened forward to open the door, and Jessie breathed a sigh of relief. Then the man spoiled her calculations by looking in her direction and adding, 'One moment, madam, and I will be with you.'

Becoming aware of the presence of a lady, Lord Ashbourne turned his head in her direction. 'Well well,' he murmured, sketching a bow. 'And what brings you to London, Jez?'

'Good morning,' replied Jessie, curtsying. 'I am visiting my sister-in-law-to-be.'

He raised his brows. 'Then you are to be married. Is Henry Lusty the lucky man?'

'Yes,' Jessie replied, feeling guilty because she had not told him before, then remembering that she could not have done so because he had been travelling with Lady Gilchrist.

'You should have waited for me, Jez,' he

complained lazily. 'Still, no doubt Lusty would make you a much better husband.'

'He couldn't possibly make a worse one,' she retorted.

'As you say.' He moved gracefully towards her and, with one elegant movement removed the book from her hands. 'Ah, Lucas's *Memoirs of the Loves, Intrigues, and Comical Adventures of the most Famous Gamesters and Celebrated Sharpers in the Reigns of Charles II, James II, William III and Queen Anne,'* he remarked. 'And you read upside down. A remarkable accomplishment.' The famous steeply arched Ashbourne eyebrows soared.

She snatched the book away from him. 'I didn't want to look as if I was listening to your conversation,' she replied.

'I would never have dreamed of supposing it,' he responded. 'For how long are you fixed in London?' He was looking exceedingly elegant in a cutaway coat of emerald green, with leather breeches and knee-high boots. His tall-crowned, wide-brimmed hat he had removed on acknowledging her, and now held in his gloved right hand, along with his cane. His black hair, still only touched lightly with grey at the temples, was caught back with a bow at the nape of his neck. His grey eyes gleamed. With his fine sculptured features, he was, and always had been, the most handsome man that she had ever seen.

'It has not exactly been settled,' Jessie

replied. 'I expect I will return home before Easter.' He did not say anything in reply, and in order to fill up the silence, she went on quickly, 'Mr Lusty—that is, Henry—wanted to buy my engagement ring.'

'Indeed? May I see?' He put out his hand to take hers.

Jessie coloured. 'I do not have it on today,' she said defensively, very conscious that she had not given it a thought before she had come out. 'I did not want to risk losing it in the . . . the street.'

'Very sensible,' answered the earl, looking as if he did not quite believe her. 'And now, I believe I must be going. What may I desire Long to find for you?'

'There is nothing in particular,' replied Jessie. 'I just came in to—' She glanced through the window and saw that the man who had been watching her before was still outside. 'Oh no,' she exclaimed involuntarily.

'What is it?' Ashbourne asked, following her gaze 'Hmm. Now what did you do to attract the attention of Felix Wiley?'

'Nothing at all,' Jessie said quickly, stepping further back into the shop, since Wiley's gaze seemed to be directed towards the window out of which they were looking. 'I was simply walking into town.'

'I'm surprised that Lusty has left you alone here. This part of London can be full of sad rogues, you know.'

'Yes, I know,' answered Jessie, looking directly at him.

He laughed. 'I've never attempted to deny it. Where is Lusty, by the way?'

'With his bishop.'

Ashbourne's brows drew together. 'Then who is accompanying you?'

Jessie straightened, and drew her shoulders back. 'I came alone. A lady of my years does not need a chaperon, surely.'

'Believe me, a lady of *any* years needs a chaperon in this wicked city.' He sighed. 'I'll find a sedan chair and escort you home.'

'Raff, I don't need a sedan chair to walk that little distance,' Jessie protested. 'I'm a countrywoman, remember.'

'I'm not likely to forget it, my dear, when you conduct yourself with such appalling *naïveté*. To be blunt, respectable women don't walk the city streets alone. Nor are they seen hanging on the arm of such as myself. Why isn't your hostess accompanying you? What are you shopping for, anyway?'

Jessie sighed. 'My hostess is—' She hesitated, not wanting to be disloyal to someone to whom she would soon be related. 'She is very busy, so I am left a good deal to my own devices,' she said eventually. 'I was looking for writing paper. I must not neglect my correspondence.'

'Long can supply you with what you need,' the earl told her. 'In the meantime, don't come into town alone again. I'm sure Henry Lusty would not appreciate your destroying your reputation within days of your arrival in the capital.'

Jessie lost some colour. 'It cannot be as bad as you say,' she began, before Ashbourne interrupted her.

'My God, he's coming in here,' he exclaimed, his urgent tone far removed from his usual society drawl. 'Long, take Miss Warburton into the back, and remember you've not seen her in here, particularly in my company. Jez, stay with Long until I come back with a sedan chair.'

Jessie allowed the earl and the shopkeeper to hustle her into the back room. Moments later, they heard the door of the shop open, and then the voice of a newcomer saying, 'Well met, Ashbourne.

You've not seen a wench in here, have you? Nice looking piece, tall, elegant, all on her own, so I thought my luck was in.'

'Wiley,' the earl replied. 'I take it you lost sight of her.'

'Exactly so. Blasted cart came down the road, and then when it was gone, so was she. Thought she might have come in here.'

Jessie could imagine Ashbourne shaking his head. 'I've been here for some time with Long. I'd have seen if anyone had come in.'

'Pity. She quite took my fancy. Good figure and pretty hair. Walk with me to Brooks's. I'm told they've had a delivery of some rather palatable wine.'

The door closed behind the two men, and Jessie heaved a sigh of relief. 'Thank you, Mr Long,' she said gratefully.

'It was my pleasure, miss.' He was a well-spoken, neatly dressed man in a brown wig. 'What part of the country are you from, if I may be so bold as to ask? I may have some books that will interest you.'

'I live in Derbyshire, not far from Ashbourne,' Jessie replied.

'Then if you'd like to take a seat here, I'll see what I can find.' He carefully dusted a chair so that Jessie could sit down, and soon returned with several volumes. 'No doubt you will have read Mr Defoe's *Tour,* but Misson's *Memoirs and Observations* may not have come in your way. There is also a diary of a gentleman from Chapel-en-le-Frith which you might find interesting.'

Jessie thanked Mr Long for his thoughtfulness and, for the sake of courtesy, opened one of the books in front of her. In fact, her mind was elsewhere. Part of her was very annoyed that she had chanced to meet Ashbourne. Had she not done so, then she could have continued with her expedition, none the wiser about the construction that some might have been placing upon her solitary expedition. On the other hand, had Raphael not been around, then Mr Wiley —

and how appropriate *his* name was—would undoubtedly have pursued her into the shop and made himself obnoxious in some way. Raphael was right about her reputation, too. A clergyman's wife, like Caesar's, must be above suspicion. She had to admit, though, that she was rather flattered by Mr Wiley's interest, however unwelcome.

She knew that she was tall, but she had never seen herself as elegant, with a good figure and pretty hair!

She glanced anxiously at the clock in Mr Long's office, and wondered how soon Lord Ashbourne would return from drinking with Mr Wiley. When would Mrs Machin start to worry about her? Jessie had always been accustomed to thinking of Ashbourne as a rake. Would his 'raking' involve feeling obliged to sit drinking with Mr Wiley for the next hour or two? Would he even forget about her completely?

She was just wondering how much she ought to pay Mr Long to close his shop and escort her home when she heard the sound of the shop door, and moments later, Lord Ashbourne strolled in. 'Your chair awaits, ma'am,' he said, with a sweeping bow. 'Long, thank you for your help in this matter. Did you have the chance to peruse those books, Jez, or would you like me to purchase them for you?'

She was about to say that she had no particular desire for the books, and already had a copy of Defoe's account, when she realized that this would be Ashbourne's way of thanking the man for his assistance. Accordingly, she nodded. 'If you please,' she said.

'It has been a pleasure to serve you, miss,' said the bookseller, as he handed her the parcel of books neatly tied up with string, together with an ample supply of writing paper. 'I hope I shall be able to do so again whilst you are in London.'

'Thank you. You have been very kind,' she told him, as she prepared to get into the sedan chair. Lord Ashbourne had already asked for her direction and was giving it to the chairmen.

It was only when they were halfway back, Ashbourne walking alongside the sedan chair, that Jessie wondered how her hostess would react to the sight of her guest being escorted home by one of London's notorious rakes. Would she feel it incumbent upon herself to tell her brother? After her threats to do so when Jessie had entered the book-room, it seemed quite possible.

There was nothing wrong in her accepting Ashbourne's escort, Jessie told herself stoutly. After all, she had known him for nearly half her life, and had been companion to his sister for eight years. It would have been far stranger if he had *not* offered to escort her home. Nevertheless, she could not help remembering guiltily that she should not have been in town alone in the first place; and she was old enough to have known that.

She was still rehearsing the various arguments when the chair stopped outside Mrs Machin's house, and one of the chairmen opened the door at the front so that she could step out. While the earl was paying the men, the front door opened, and Dilly stood on the threshold. She looked a little flustered. 'Please, miss, missus said to ask his lordship inside for some refreshment, as she'd like to thank him for bringing you home.'

Jessie looked at the maid, unable to conceal her expression of astonishment. Given the earl's reputation, and Mrs Machin's close relationship with members of the clergy, it seemed to her that it would have been just as likely for that lady to throw open her doors to Beelzebub himself. Then she reflected with a sinking feeling, that the invitation would very likely be in order to warn the earl not to come near the house or its occupants ever again. Quite how Ashbourne would respond to such a command she could not imagine.

She was just beginning to wonder what her own feelings would be in such circumstances when the earl turned towards Dilly with Jessie's books under one arm and said, 'Thank you, I would be delighted.'

'But surely, you need to get back to Brooks's,' Jessie protested, as the chairmen left.

Not at all,' he responded with a smile. 'I can think of nothing that attracts me more at this moment than meeting a new connection of an old family friend.'

Mrs Machin's house was neat and well-kept, but not fashionable in its appointments, and Lord Ashbourne, in this modest exclusively female establishment, somehow looked more fashionable and more masculine than ever. Dilly, clearly quite overwhelmed at admitting such a well-dressed, titled gentleman, became more flustered, took the books from him, attempted to take his hat and cane, which he had intended to retain as was proper for a brief visit, then released them. In the confusion, his cane fell to the floor and Ashbourne bent to pick it up. Dilly suddenly realized that she should not be permitting a visitor to do this, and bent over herself in order to get it. In so doing, in Mrs Machin's small hall, she found her face rather close to his. Quite forgetting all her training, she gave a little scream and ran back to her own quarters.

'I did nothing!' protested Ashbourne, opening his free hand in a disclaiming gesture. 'You saw that I did nothing.'

He didn't have to do anything; he just had to be, Jessie reflected ruefully as she ushered him into Mrs Machin's presence. That lady was seated with a piece of embroidery on her knee, but at their arrival she laid aside her work and stood up. On her face was an

95

expression of outrage.

CHAPTER SEVEN

'Mrs Machin,' said Jessie tentatively. 'I must beg leave to introduce Lord Ashbourne to you. Raff, this is Mrs Machin, my kind hostess.'

'Your servant, ma'am,' drawled Ashbourne, bowing with consummate elegance.

Mrs Machin took a deep breath. 'Lord Ashbourne, I cannot say when I have been more shocked,' she said, causing Jessie's heart to sink into her boots. Then, to her visitor's relief and surprise, she went on, 'That foolish girl! She has no notion of how to behave! To go off to the kitchen without announcing you!'

'Think nothing of it, ma'am,' answered the earl, taking his hostess's hand and raising it to his lips. 'She was surprised, that is all.'

'You are very generous, my lord,' replied Mrs Machin, positively bridling. 'Pray be seated, and tell me how it is that you have come to meet my sister-in-law-to-be this morning. Miss Warburton, will you be so good as to see if Dilly is getting wine, or if she has neglected her duties in that respect as well?'

As Jessie left the room, she heard her hostess bemoaning the fact that she had no butler who would doubtless have taken the visit of a nobleman in his stride. On her arrival in the kitchen, Jessie found that Dilly was already preparing a tray, so she went back to Mrs Machin's neat drawing-room. Mrs Machin was sitting upright, an air of suppressed excitement about her. Jessie now noticed that although she was dressed in her most usual attire of grey silk, the gown that she had on was embellished by a rather frivolous pink shawl that Jessie had not seen before. Ashbourne was sitting very much at his ease, his hat and cane on the floor next to his chair, one leg crossed negligently over the other. At Jessie's entrance he rose fluidly to his feet, and placed a chair for her, so that she might be part of the conversation.

'My dear Miss Warburton, you should have told me how negligent I was being,' Mrs Machin said reproachfully. 'I have been so involved with my work that I have not thought about your entertainment as I should. Lord Ashbourne has very properly reminded me of my duty.'

'He has?' questioned Jessie, unable to imagine the earl ever doing anything properly.

'Most certainly. What a blessing that he chanced to encounter you this morning. You will always be welcome in this house if for that reason alone, my lord,' said Mrs Machin, beaming. 'And here is Dilly with the wine. Will you pour for us?'

As the earl did so, Jessie tried to work out whether her hostess, the widow of one clergyman and the sister of another had really just invited a notorious rake to run tame in her house. She came to the conclusion that the nature of the day's events so far must simply have addled her wits.

The conversation that followed did nothing to change that impression. Mrs Machin seemed eager to find out all that she could concerning fashionable London society, and once she had asked Ashbourne a question, she waited avidly for his answer. So enthusiastic was she about obtaining information that Jessie felt strongly tempted to ask if she would like to take notes.

Lord Ashbourne stayed for only twenty minutes, then announced that he had engagements in town. 'I hope that your stay will prove to be agreeable,' he told Jessie before he left. 'Indeed, I cannot see how it could be otherwise, with such a kind hostess.'

'You are too generous in your praise, my lord,' said Mrs Machin, beaming. 'Pray return at any time. We shall be more than happy to see you. Our door will always be open.' After he had gone, she added with a sigh, 'What a charming man. He is just as I imagined him to be.'

Feeling very much like saying waspishly that she wondered in that case why Mrs Machin had not asked him to come and live with them, Jessie merely remarked, 'I had no idea that you had ever given Lord Ashbourne any thought.'

Mrs Machin turned bright red. 'I . . . that is to say, he is often spoken about, you know.' Then, in a condemnatory tone that was quite at variance with her manner during Ashbourne's visit and since his departure, she said, 'Such a wicked man!'

'In that case, I wonder that you made him so welcome,' answered Jessie angrily. She knew that she ought to put the earl out of her mind, but she could not stand and listen to him being traduced, especially when the lady who was criticizing him had been fawning over him five minutes before.

'What else could I do when you came dancing in on his arm?' demanded Mrs Machin defensively. 'I do not know what Henry would say if I were to tell him that you were bringing rakes into the house.'

'My dear Mrs Machin,' said Jessie, wanting to remain civil but determined not to put up with this slander, 'you must know very well that I did nothing of the sort. I was quite prepared to say goodbye to Lord Ashbourne at the door. It was Dilly who came scurrying out and, at *your* behest, ma'am, invited him in.'

'I considered it to be my duty to discover what kind of company you were keeping,' said Mrs Machin, her chin lifted high, but her tone more than a little defensive. 'I thought it best to warn him off for the future . . .' Her voice tailed away towards the end of her speech, and her expression became more than a little hunted.

Jessie stared at her for a moment, then said incredulously, 'Warn him off? You all but invited him to run tame in this house. What would Henry say to *that?*'

With that, Mrs Machin's outraged façade disappeared completely. Her figure began to droop, and she seemed to lose at least six inches in height. 'Oh dear, oh dear,' she murmured. 'What on earth am I to do? Henry will be so angry.' Her voice suddenly took on a note of panic. 'You won't tell him *really*, will you?'

'I haven't yet decided,' answered Jessie thoughtfully. 'You will have to tell me what it is you are about, though.'

'About, my dear?' said Mrs Machin in a quavering voice.

'It is of no use to pretend to be so innocent because I am convinced that you are concealing something,' said Jessie firmly.

'Oh dear, oh dear,' said Mrs Machin again. 'I feel a little faint. Might I have a drink?'

'I will send for some tea at once,' answered Jessie.

'Actually, I was thinking of something stronger,' confessed the other lady. She paused. 'There is some brandy in the tall cupboard in the corner of the book-room,' she said at last. 'My husband used to recommend that I take it—purely for medicinal purposes, you understand.'

With one puzzled look at her hostess, Jessie left the room and found the brandy without difficulty, where Mrs Machin had said it would be. There were no glasses immediately visible, but she soon found them. It was while she was putting the brandy on a tray that the door-bell rang. Reluctant to take the strong drink through to her hostess without discovering the identity of the guest at the door, she left the book-room in time to see Mr Hinder disappearing into the drawing-room. Glad that she had waited, she approached the door in order to discover whether Mrs Machin might want some tea brought now that she had a visitor. She was in time to hear Hinder say, in excited tones, 'I have finished the tract on the evils of drink, and what a bore *that* was! I have earned my fee for that one, I assure you. Have you got any further with the latest chapter? The last one had me on the edge of my seat!'

Quite forgetting to consider the propriety of commenting upon a conversation that did not include her, Jessie entered the room, saying, 'Please explain, ma'am. What are you really writing, and how is Mr Hinder involved?'

The two occupants turned to look at her, their faces wearing identical expressions of dismay. Mrs Machin, who had stood up to greet Mr Hinder, sank back into her chair. 'There is nothing for it,' she said despondently. 'I shall have to tell you, I suppose, but I must beg you, please do not tell Henry. What I am doing makes no difference to him, you know, and he really would not understand. Then of course, because of his exaggerated sense of honour or piety or whatever, he would feel bound to tell the bishop, and his chances of preferment would go completely out of the window. Promise you will not tell?'

'My dear ma'am, I have nothing to tell at present,' said Jessie with a touch of humour.

'No, of course not,' agreed Mrs Machin in accents of relief. There was a sigh from Mr Hinder who, while the ladies were talking, stood looking like a rather badly executed statue.

'But,' Jessie went on firmly, 'unless you tell me what all this is about, I will inform Henry that I am convinced that you are concealing something.'

Mrs Machin peered over first one shoulder, then the other, as if someone might have sneaked into the room while they had been speaking. She nodded to Mr Hinder, who tiptoed over to the door, flung it open and looked outside. 'Very well,' she said in a low tone, after Hinder had nodded to signify that the coast was clear. 'I have to admit that it will be a relief to tell you. I am writing a novel.'

'I beg your pardon?' said Jessie, startled. 'What about your husband's sermons—his life's work?'

'That was a ruse,' said Mrs Machin proudly.

'Hector, I believe that Miss Warburton was getting some brandy from the book-room. Will you fetch it if you please?'

'What do you mean, a ruse? Are there no sermons, then? What will you do when the time comes to take them to a publisher?'

'That will be quite easy,' answered Mrs Machin. 'The sermons have always been there, written out neatly in my own hand and tied together in order.'

'You acted as his scribe, then?' Jessie surmised.

'Oh no. I wrote his sermons,' Mrs Machin responded with a note of modest pride. 'Percival was not a very good preacher, I'm afraid. Do you not agree?' she added in Mr Hinder's direction as he came back in with the tray.

'I beg pardon, ma'am?' he replied, as he set the tray down.

'I was telling Miss Warburton that Percival's sermons were not good.'

'Yes, they were complete nonsense from beginning to end,' the young man agreed with cheerful disregard for the reputation of the deceased clergyman. 'Are we all having brandy?'

Jessie saw that he had put enough glasses on the tray for all of them. She made no objection when he poured brandy into three glasses. She did not normally consume strong drink, but today she felt in need of it.

'How did you come to write your husband's sermons?' Jessie asked curiously.

Mrs Machin took her glass and leaned back comfortably in her chair. It occurred to Jessie that almost for the first time, this lady seemed to be at ease in her presence. 'It began soon after we were married,' she said, smiling reminiscently. 'Until our marriage, I had never heard him preach, you see. My father was a clergyman and always spoke very well, so I was used to a high standard. Then I married Percival.' She paused. 'The shock to my system was severe. I knew that if I had to sit listening to him for the rest of our married life, I would either strangle him or expire from boredom.'

'So what happened?' asked Jessie, fascinated.

'When we were first married, he used to spend hours and hours in his study writing his sermons. It always astonished me that so much time and energy could be applied to so little effect. Then, a few weeks after our wedding, he became ill, and although he made a good recovery, he had very little energy. In order to help him, I offered to write his sermons. He was very surprised to discover how quickly I could accomplish what had often taken him half a day at least. When he was fully recovered, I encouraged him to use his time in ways that yielded positive fruit and benefited his health, such as fishing and gardening, and with his willing acquiescence I continued to write the sermons myself. They were very well received, if I do say so.'

'How remarkable,' commented Jessie. 'Did no one ever suspect?'

'Never. Well, Hector discovered the truth, quite by accident.'

'I come from the same village, you see,' Hector interrupted eagerly. 'And we had already found that we enjoyed the same kinds of books. One day I visited the vicarage unexpectedly in order to borrow some poetry and found her in the throes of composition.'

'The problem came when Percival died,' Henrietta went on. 'I no longer had an outlet for my creative talents, you see.'

'Was that when you started writing tracts?' Jessie asked.

'Yes; but I got so bored with them,' complained the other lady with a sigh. 'I blame it on Henry. He is for ever sending me ideas for new ones. It seems to me that he only has to think of something that is pleasant, and he instantly has to be disapproving of it. Really, he must be a terribly depressing person to live with.'

It did not seem to occur to her that she was commenting on Jessie's future. Jessie had no desire to embarrass her by reminding her, so she said quickly, 'Did I understand Mr Hinder to say that he is writing tracts as well?'

'Not "as well", but "instead",' put in Mr Hinder. 'That's why I took lodgings in this very street as soon as any became available.'

'We work together, you see,' said Mrs Machin.

'Are you just writing a novel, then?' Jessie asked her hostess.

'My second,' answered the lady, unable to keep a note of pride out of her voice.

'Your second novel?' echoed Jessie, amazed.

'Sshh!' exclaimed Mrs Machin urgently. 'No one must know. Henry would be so disapproving, and I do not want to upset him, for with all his faults I do love him dearly. He is my brother after all.'

'If you are writing a second, what happened to the first?' Jessie asked curiously.

'It was published and was something of a success,' answered Mrs Machin proudly. 'At least, all the copies of it were sold, so that they had to print some more.'

'What was it about?'

'It was about a corrupt clergyman who used his position in his parish in a most unscrupulous way,' confided Mrs Machin. 'If you would like to read it, I can lend you a copy. It is called *A Scoundrel in the Church.*'

'You cannot have used your own name, surely,' Jessie exclaimed.

'No indeed. The author is simply stated to be *A Gentleman.* It was printed by a man in Paternoster Row.'

'And what of the new one? How much have

you written?'

'I have written five chapters,' answered Mrs Machin. The same printer is prepared to publish it, if it is up to the standard of the previous one. It is by no means easy to write a novel, you know.'

'I am sure that it cannot be,' Jessie assured her. 'I have to say that I am all admiration for anyone who can succeed in writing a book. Does your new novel have a title yet?'

'It is called *Lady Meredith, or, the Female Rake,*' answered Mrs Machin. 'I have made a perfectly splendid start. My heroine has been cruelly rejected by her betrothed, and she has now decided to remove to London. There, she will punish him, and her family, who promoted the engagement, by dragging her name through the mud.'

'How intriguing,' murmured Jessie, reflecting that now Mrs Machin's secret was out, she could hardly stop talking about it. 'I can quite see, though, that Henry would not approve.'

'No indeed,' agreed Mr Hinder fervently. 'That is why it is vital that it must be kept a secret from him—for everybody's sake.' His face wore an anxious expression. Jessie could imagine what must be going through his mind. His own reputation, whatever his chosen career might be, would almost certainly suffer if it were known that he was associated with the writer of a scandalous novel.

'You may be sure that I will not tell anyone,'

Jessie promised them. 'How exciting it must be to create characters and situations for oneself.'

'It has been very exciting so far,' Mrs Machin agreed, 'but now I have reached something of a standstill. My heroine has reached London, and is about to begin raking. The thing is, I have no knowledge of how she might go about it, or where, and no idea of how to find the information, either.' She paused. 'That is, I had no idea until this morning.'

Jessie stared at her aghast. 'You are surely not thinking of asking Lord Ashbourne how he goes about raking?' she asked in failing accents.

Mrs Machin had the grace to blush. 'It seems to me that a man of his reputation is probably rather proud of his . . . his misdeeds,' she replied, trying to sound innocent. 'He is bound to have the entrée to all kinds of events that are denied to humbler persons. For instance, the Prince of Wales is to be married this very week. It strikes me that Lord Ashbourne is exactly the kind of man with whom the Prince would be intimate. What if his lordship were to be a guest at the ceremony? Think of what descriptions he could give me! I was hoping that I might have the chance to ask him about such matters. After all, he is an old friend of yours.'

'It is true that I have known him for a long time,' Jessie agreed. 'However, I would never dream of questioning him about his morals. You are right in saying that he is a man of doubtful reputation.' She hesitated, feeling disloyal, then reflected that she was not saying anything that Ashbourne's own sister had not said. 'In sum, he is a gambler, a drinker and a libertine. He is certainly not the sort of man who should be encouraged into decent female company.'

'Is that not exactly what I have been saying?' Mrs Machin insisted. 'Still, I can understand your reluctance to question him. It would look intolerably inquisitive, after all.'

'I don't suppose Mr Lusty would be very pleased to hear that you had been in his company either,' Mr Hinder pointed out.

'No, that is true,' agreed Mrs Machin, with some regret. 'And however much one resolves to be discreet, these things always come out. We will just have to do our own investigations, that is all.'

'Our own investigations into what?' asked Jessie cautiously.

'Our investigations into where a lady rake might go and what she might do,' Mrs Machin explained patiently. 'Now where do you think we ought to start?'

CHAPTER EIGHT

Several days later, Jessie was still congratulating herself on her quick thinking. Upon Mrs Machin's enquiry as to where to go to conduct her research, she had immediately suggested that they should procure a daily newspaper.

'An excellent suggestion!' her hostess had declared. Straight away, she had gone about ordering a copy of *The Morning Chronicle*, which now arrived regularly at the little house in Sloane Street.

From now on, Jessie and her hostess called one another by their Christian names, (although Jessie did not confess what her full name really was). This was not the only way in which life became more comfortable. Now that Mrs Machin's secret occupation was revealed, Jessie was no longer banned from the book-room. On the contrary, her presence was welcome, as long as she did not disturb her hostess's creative flow. She would often sit reading the paper, sewing, or writing letters, whilst Mrs Machin's pen moved like lightning across the page, with the author occasionally pausing to ask for a spelling, or the exact reference to a quotation from Shakespeare, or consulting her companion concerning the felicity of her choice of some word or phrase.

Thankfully, there was no longer any pretence that Mrs Machin was rising to study in her room, for that lady freely admitted that she did not like early rising and often stayed abed until ten. If Henrietta reached a point in her writing where she felt that a change would be beneficial, then the two ladies would often walk into town, sometimes accompanied by Mr Hinder.

About a week after the secret was out, Henrietta announced that she needed some information. 'I have decided that Lady Meredith could be rather daring and take snuff,' she said, 'but I have no idea what sort she might take. I think that I need to obtain a book about it.'

'Mr Long in Piccadilly was very helpful to me,' Jessie remarked. She had read the books which Raff had purchased for her, and had found them very interesting. She had also recalled that she had not offered to pay for them. This had caused her a twinge of guilt, but she knew that it would be quite improper for her to seek him out in order to pay him.

'Then let us go at once,' said Henrietta. A message was sent to Mr Hinder, who appeared with eager alacrity, so much so that Jessie almost expected him to be carrying a lead in his mouth.

'I could always tell you something about snuff, you know,' said Hinder, as they walked along Sloane Street. 'I don't take it myself, but

111

m'father does.'

'That is very good of you, but I have one or two ideas about how I might use this snuff-taking habit in another way and I want to see if it is possible.'

'How do you think you might do that?' asked Jessie curiously.

'I cannot tell you, I'm afraid,' Henrietta answered mysteriously. 'I do not know why it may be, but I find that if I tell too much about what I intend to write, then I lose all desire to set it down on paper.' Both Jessie and Hinder agreed that this would never do, and began a new topic of conversation.

As they entered Piccadilly, Jessie remembered how she had met Ashbourne there, and felt her heart beat a little faster at the memory. Immediately she told herself sternly to have more sense. London was a large place. They were very unlikely to encounter him, and even if they did, what was that to her?

'Shall we do a little shopping after we have been to the bookshop?' suggested Mrs Machin. Mr Hinder groaned audibly. She turned to him, looking severe. 'Hector, you must be used to shopping with a mama and five sisters!'

'Exactly!' he replied with feeling. Both the ladies laughed. Their faces were still alight with amusement as they entered Long's bookshop. Two gentlemen customers were looking at the plates in a book held for them by Mr Long. They turned as the shop bell rang, and it was with very mixed feelings that Jessie saw that one of them was Ashbourne. He was, as always, immaculately dressed in matching dove grey coat and breeches, with a violet and silver striped waistcoat. His companion looked a little older, and was dressed more colourfully, in shades of green and pink, but with less style. He wore a wig rather than his own hair, but the colour of his brows and lashes was sandy. He was much the same height as Raff, perhaps a little shorter, but with a fuller figure.

Jessie saw Raff put up his chin, and lift his quizzing glass, the cynical expression upon his face unchanged. Instinctively, she knew that he would not acknowledge her in front of another for the sake of her reputation.

He had reckoned without Henrietta Machin. For a woman who had lived in London for a number of years, her *naïveté* was astonishing, for she stepped forward exclaiming, 'Lord Ashbourne! How delightful to meet you! You have not called again, as you said you would. Jessie and I are quite disappointed, are we not, Jessie?'

Raff's cynical expression was replaced by one of rueful amusement, as he swept them an elegant bow. 'Ladies,' he declared, 'this is an unexpected pleasure. May I present to you Sir Wallace Weary?'

113

'Good day, ladies,' responded Sir Wallace in a measured nasal tone.

'Mrs Machin resides in London,' Ashbourne continued, 'but Miss Warburton usually resides with my sister. She is here on a visit'

'And a very welcome visitor she is, too,' said Mrs Machin warmly.

'I have no doubt,' murmured Sir Wallace, eyeing Jessie in a decidedly predatory way.

'You have chosen a pleasant day for your expedition,' said Ashbourne, after Hinder had been introduced. 'Are you looking for anything in particular? What may I desire Long to find for you?'

'You are very good, my lord,' responded Mrs Machin, smiling at his lordship as if he were a long lost relative. 'I am looking for a book about snuff.'

'That is an unusual choice for a lady,' said Sir Wallace, smirking in a way that Jessie did not like, although she could not have explained exactly why.

There was, of course, no need for Mrs Machin to feel obliged to offer the baronet any explanation. Instead of simply murmuring *perhaps,* or *yes, isn't it*, she became flustered. 'Oh! Yes, well it is not exactly for me.' There was a brief silence, after which she went on, 'It is for . . . for . . .'

'It is for my father,' said Mr Hinder hastily, coming to the rescue.

'Indeed,' replied Sir Wallace, his brows

going up, but failing to recreate the elegant shape produced by the same features on Raff's face. 'How singular.'

'I am very much in favour of sons bestowing gifts upon their fathers,' Raff contributed in a rather bored tone. 'Unfortunately, my son does not seem very inclined to do so.'

Seeing in this a skilful ploy to divert Sir Wallace away from Henrietta's clumsiness, Jessie added 'You forget, my lord, that your son has recently presented you with a charming new daughter-in-law.'

'I stand corrected, Miss Warburton,' Raff answered with a slight bow. By mutual unspoken consent, they had adopted a more formal mode of address in this company. 'However, you forget that that gift almost inevitably means that some day soon I shall have the doubtful pleasure of being called *Grandpapa*.'

Weary laughed. 'How you will dislike that to be sure,' he sneered. 'But back to Mrs Machin's purchase. Long, you old rogue, do you have anything that will suit the lady?'

Mr Long soon produced several volumes from which Henrietta could make her choice. 'Lord Ashbourne, you must come and advise me,' she said gaily. As the book was supposedly for Mr Hinder's father, he was already looking at some of the volumes that the shopkeeper had produced.

'I should be charmed,' replied the earl.

'Weary, do you care to assist?'

'And leave Miss Warburton to entertain herself? By no means!'

Jessie was not sure of the wisdom of going apart with Sir Wallace. By the predatory look in his eye, as much as by the company he kept, she judged that he was probably a rake. There was a limit to the number of people who could crowd around the books that Long was offering, however, so she allowed him to lead her away from the group. After all, there was very little that he could do to harm her in broad daylight inside a shop with four other people present.

'I take it that you reside in London, sir,' she began, choosing what she thought was an innocuous topic.

'I do. Now why the devil have I not seen a little beauty like you here before?' He had dropped his voice so that the others could not hear. His expression made her feel rather hot.

'As his lordship has already told you, I am his sister's companion,' she replied repressively, trying to inject some of Lady Agatha's haughtiness into her tone.

'Really? I thought perhaps he had made that up. You're far too pretty to be anyone's companion—unless of course you'd like to be mine.'

'Sir!' exclaimed Jessie. 'I am an engaged woman.'

'Engaged are you? Who's the lucky fellow?'

'He is a clergyman,' Jessie answered.

Sir Wallace pulled an expression of distaste. 'Dull fellows, all of them,' he said dismissively. 'Still, plenty of advantages with the married state, what? More freedom, for instance.'

Jessie felt her temper rising. 'Sir Wallace, if you are implying—'

He raised his hands in a gesture of surrender. 'I'm not implying anything; just suggesting. You can't blame a man for making a suggestion.'

At this moment, the discussion over Mrs Machin's book was concluded, and Lord Ashbourne wandered over to join Jessie and Sir Wallace. She was never more glad to see anyone in her life, for she had found the conversation with the baronet confusing and insulting. 'Well, Miss Warburton?' said Raff. 'Has Weary entertained you well?' The usual polite society expression was on his face, but in his eyes there was a certain stillness, and Jessie made an astonishing discovery. Raff was clearly well aware of what manner of man had been talking to her. He was inviting her to tell him if she had been insulted. If she told him that she had, then he would be obliged to demand an apology of the other man, and insist upon satisfaction if no apology was forthcoming.

She *had* been insulted, but she could not ask that of Raff. Instead of saying how she really felt, therefore, she forced herself to lower her eyes and say, 'Sir Wallace has been very amusing, my lord.' With her averted gaze, she was unable to see Ashbourne's expression harden. She was also unaware that the baronet was now looking at her in a decidedly speculative way.

*   *   *

The paper delivered to Mrs Machin's house often provided fresh inspiration, and the reports dealing with the royal wedding were particularly interesting to the two ladies. 'This is just the sort of event that Lady Meredith ought to be attending,' sighed Mrs Machin one morning, as she was reading about that occasion. 'The report here says that the Princess is a handsome woman with a fine head of hair. Oh *how* I should like to see her.'

'If the Prince of Wales is as good-looking as people say, they should make an attractive couple,' Jessie observed.

'Have you never seen him, then?'

Jessie laughed. 'Remember that I have never been to London before,' she answered. 'Where would I have seen him? I don't think he's been to Illingham.'

Henrietta looked at her speculatively. 'Might the Prince not have gone to Ashbourne?'

'I don't think so,' Jessie answered, determined to put a halt to this line of enquiry.

'Lord Ashbourne is ten years the Prince's senior, remember. He has also spent a good deal of time abroad.'

'I suppose so,' agreed Henrietta reluctantly. 'You know, Jessie, reading these reports makes me long to attend some of these glittering occasions myself.' She paused hopefully.

'Henrietta, neither of us is well enough connected to gain the entrée to any of the social functions listed in the paper. And before you say anything, Lord Ashbourne's recommendation would not do either of us any good, and you know it.'

Mrs Machin sighed again and turned back to the paper, leaving Jessie to get on with her letter.

For a long time, Jessie sat with her pen in her hand and her thoughts elsewhere. She had to smile. She had never supposed that this visit would be anything other than a quiet opportunity to get to know her new sister-in-law. If Henrietta had her way, the visit would be anything but quiet. Jessie only wished that there was something more that she could do to assist her.

Her birth might entitle her to enter London society without any eyebrows being raised, but her circumstances were not affluent enough to enable her to take such a step. The only person of any rank known to her was Lord Ashbourne and she would not ask him for help. She was engaged to Henry Lusty, and to her Ashbourne must only be a family friend and kept at arm's length for the sake of her peace of mind.

The following morning, as Jessie was preparing to come downstairs, she was startled to hear a scream. Hurrying out of her room, she looked around and seeing no one, listened for hurrying feet in order to discover whether anyone might have been hurt. Instead, Mrs Machin came out of her room in such haste that one might have almost supposed that she had been propelled by some unseen force. Her hair was awry, her cap missing, and clutched in her hand was something that looked like a letter.

'Jessie!' she cried. 'You will never guess our good fortune! This might be the start!'

'Never say that it is an invitation to dine at Carlton House with the Prince and Princess of Wales!' exclaimed Jessie, teasingly.

'No; but who knows what may come of it! Some cousins of Mr Hinder are out of town and unable to use their box at the Theatre Royal in Drury Lane. They have offered it to him, and he has invited us. He says so in this note. What do you say to that?'

'The theatre!' exclaimed Jessie; and for all that she did not scream, she was now starting to feel almost as excited as her hostess. For a moment the two ladies stared at one another, then, as with one voice, they said together, 'What shall we wear?'

120

CHAPTER NINE

Because she had spent some weeks staying with the elegant Lady Hope, Jessie had several gowns that she knew were very becoming. They might not be in the first stare of fashion, modes changing more quickly in London than in the provinces, but she knew that she would not look like a dowd. Mrs Machin's wardrobe was more limited. Her circumstances were modest and her opportunities for going out socially were few, so she tended to wear a small selection of gowns, mainly in black or grey.

'I must visit a modiste,' she said anxiously. 'Where to go, though? I do not want to spend a large sum of money and get very little for it.'

'Why not ask your maid?' Jessie suggested. 'She may sometimes need to purchase fabrics and may know where good stuff can be had for a reasonable sum.'

'An excellent idea,' exclaimed Henrietta enthusiastically. 'Let us summon her immediately.'

Dilly did indeed know of a very reasonably priced silk mercer's in Covent Garden, and the three of them set off that very afternoon to buy some material. Mrs Machin, who had confined herself to half mourning for several years, became almost like a skittish child when confronted with the wide selection of fabrics and colours available to her, and Jessie and Dilly had to be quite firm with her in order to prevent her from running amok.

Eventually, her choice was made, and she came away with a length of dark-blue silk, together with some trimming. As a reward for being so helpful, Dilly was permitted to choose material for a new petticoat, and she left the shop with a length of pale-green fabric wrapped in paper and tightly clasped in her hands. The next problem, that of making up the fabric, was soon solved. 'There's a woman lives a few doors down who is glad of a bit of work,' said Dilly, still smiling with pleasure at her acquisition. 'I'll ask her if you like.'

'We'll all go,' said Mrs Machin firmly. 'If someone is making me the first new gown I've had in five years, I want to meet her personally.'

It was as Dilly was procuring a hackney carriage for them that disaster struck. She had succeeded in attracting the attention of one driver, but before Henrietta and Jessie could join her, two noisy young men, who were rather the worse for drink, elbowed her out of the way and took the carriage for themselves. As they did so, she was caught off balance, and dropped her precious parcel. Before she had time to retrieve it, the carriage had set off and dragged the parcel under its wheels, tearing it open and ruining the contents.

Jessie and Henrietta both hurried forward to comfort Dilly, whose eyes had filled with tears. 'Perhaps something might be salvaged,' said Jessie doubtfully, bending to pick up what was left of the parcel.

Dilly caught hold of her arm. 'No miss,' she said bravely. 'Ain't no call to ruin your gloves as well. Just leave it.'

'It hardly seems fair,' said Henrietta sympathetically. 'We'll come back and get you some more another day, Dilly.'

'Yes, of course, ma'am,' said Dilly, trying to smile. 'I'll get us another carriage now, shall I?'

'I rather think that that ought to be my task,' said Lord Ashbourne's voice from behind them.

'Oh, would you?' said Henrietta thankfully. 'Poor Dilly, here, found us a carriage, but some young men seized it from her and she lost her parcel in the process.'

The earl glanced down at the ruined material on the ground. 'That's very unfortunate,' he murmured. 'I trust they did not hurt you, Dilly.'

'Oh no, my lord,' Dilly stammered, clearly overcome at being addressed by a peer in the open street.

In no time, a hackney was summoned, and the ladies were helped in, followed by Dilly. 'Thank you, Raff,' said Jessie.

'My pleasure,' the earl replied.

'May we drop you anywhere, my lord?' Henrietta asked him. 'Thank you, no, I have some business to transact. Good day to you.'

Miss Simms was a pretty, worn-looking woman in her early twenties, who stood up to greet her visitors when they were announced by a stolid looking housemaid. Jessie noticed that there was a large pile of sewing on the table in the window, and guessed that this was how she earned her living. The faint sound of a child crying seemed to be coming from somewhere in the house.

Miss Simms was delighted when the ladies explained their errand, and even more pleased when she heard the sum that Mrs Machin was prepared to offer for the work. 'It's no distance at all to travel for fittings,' Henrietta explained, 'but I do need it made for a week from today.'

Jessie was impressed by the fact that Miss Simms looked businesslike rather than alarmed. 'In that case,' said the seamstress, 'I must insist that we start as soon as possible. When may I take your measurements, ma'am?'

Henrietta looked round at Jessie then at Dilly. 'This moment, if you wish,' she declared, standing so that Dilly could help her out of her outdoor garments.

Dilly had remained very quiet during the journey home, and Jessie suspected that she was thinking about her loss. It must have been very hard to have something new for so short a time, only to have it snatched away, she concluded. Unfortunately, Henrietta did not have a large amount of money to spare, and would not be able to purchase more material for Dilly for another quarter at least.

On their arrival at home, Henrietta and Jessie went upstairs to take off their outdoor garments. As Jessie came down the stairs, Dilly was standing in the hall with a package in her hands. 'It's just come, miss,' said Dilly, who by now had recovered her composure. 'It must be for Mrs Machin, I should think.'

Jessie took the package from her. 'No, Dilly, it's for you, care of Mrs Machin,' Jessie replied, reading the superscription.

'For me, miss?'

By this time, Henrietta was coming down the stairs. 'A parcel has been delivered for Dilly,' said Jessie. 'It's just come.'

'I ain't never had a parcel delivered before,' said Dilly in awestruck accents.

'Bring it into the drawing-room and open it there,' said Henrietta.

Once in the drawing-room, they went over to the table in the window, and Jessie and Henrietta stood watching whilst Dilly opened the parcel with trembling fingers. As she lifted the paper, a length of material in the finest pale-green silk came spilling out over her hands. 'Oh, my goodness,' she cried, her hands going to her cheeks, whilst Henrietta caught hold of the fabric so that it did not fall to the floor.

'Jessie, this is beautiful stuff,' she said admiringly. 'It's far better quality than we purchased originally, and there's a lot more of it —enough for a gown, at least. Where can it have come from?'

Jessie did not need to read the note that had fluttered to the floor in order to discover who had sent the stuff.

To replace what was spoiled.
Ashbourne

'Oh, how kind,' exclaimed Dilly, crying all over again. 'How very, very kind!'

'You must thank him in person when next he comes, Dilly,' said Henrietta. 'Would you like me to write him a note for you?'

Jessie smiled, but like Dilly, she was moved by the earl's kindness and could feel tears prickling at the back of her eyes. She was remembering her figurine.

*   *   *

The next week was punctuated with fittings and also additional outings to purchase stockings and gloves, for it would not do, both the ladies agreed, to go finely dressed with grimy or darned accessories. Jessie was a capable needlewoman, and when she saw how

126

much there was to be done, she willingly offered to help Miss Simms by doing the more pedestrian chores such as tacking pieces together, or stitching up hems. 'You will still receive the same sum,' she assured the seamstress. 'It is just that I enjoy sewing, and I am glad to help. What is more, I have seen that waists are higher in London than in the provinces, and I am hoping that if I help you to finish, you in your turn will help me to alter my gown.'

'With pleasure,' smiled Miss Simms. Colour came into her cheeks making her look quite pretty. After that, Jessie spent nearly every morning sitting in the window of Miss Simms's house, where they could get the benefit of the morning sun as they both stitched busily. They talked a little, mostly about their work. Jessie told the other woman something about her life in Illingham, and the simple country pursuits that took up her time as Lady Agatha's companion. For her part, Miss Simms told Jessie about her youth spent in a small market town; but she did not name the town in which she had lived, and she was very reticent about her reasons for coming to London.

On the third day, Jessie began to get an inkling of what might have happened. She had heard a child's voice on one or two occasions, and if she had thought about the matter at all, had supposed the sound to come from the garden belonging to the house next door, where a solicitor lived with his wife and three children. On the day in question, the ladies had paused in their work, and Miss Simms asked the maid to bring them a cup of tea and some biscuits. The woman had just brought the tray in and set it down, when a small child aged about three came tottering in. It was not possible to tell the sex of the child, for it was in skirts, as was usual with any child of that age.

On seeing Miss Simms, the infant gurgled 'Mama! Mama!' and made straight for her, its arms raised.

With a heightened complexion and a look that was half embarrassment, half defiance, Miss Simms bent down, and saying, 'Come to Mama, then,' scooped the child on to her lap, where it sat, thumb in mouth, staring gravely at the visitor. 'This is my daughter Bryony,' said Miss Simms. 'As you are aware, I am not married. I suppose you will want to take your sewing elsewhere, now.'

Jessie smiled at the little girl. 'Hello, Bryony,' she said. In response, the child immediately hid her face in her mother's shoulder. 'I can think of no reason why I would want to take the sewing elsewhere,' she went on. 'Unless, of course, you have discovered that with a child to care for, you do not have sufficient time to do the work.'

The young woman's expression seemed to relax a little. 'I have time enough, with good Bess, here, to help me.'

The rather stolid looking middle-aged maid put out her hand to the child. 'Come on with Bess, then. I've something for you in the kitchen.'

The child scrambled down and went with Bess willingly enough. 'What beautiful hair,' Jessie said involuntarily as she observed the child's copper-coloured locks.

'Yes. She has her father's colouring,' said Miss Simms in the same defiant tone as before. Then after a brief silence, she said, 'I might as well tell you as much as I'm prepared to say. I was a governess for a family in London. A man came to the house, and made me the object of his attentions. I believed his protestations. I was a fool. By great good fortune, just as I was being dismissed from employment, I inherited this house from a great aunt. I supplement the tiny income she left me by taking in sewing.'

'Does Bryony's father ever see her?' asked Jessie.

'No never. He is unaware of her existence, and that is the way that I would like things to remain,' replied Miss Simms. 'That's all I'm willing to say. Shall we get on with our sewing now? I want to have these sleeves ready for Mrs Machin to try on this afternoon.'

Jessie did not say anything to Mrs Machin about Miss Simms's past. This was not because she feared that Henrietta would withdraw her custom; on the contrary, with the vicar's widow's desire to write a scandalous novel, Jessie's fear was that she might want to interview Miss Simms more closely in order to get more ideas for her book, a thing that she did not think the seamstress would take to very kindly.

Miss Simms proved to be a quick worker, and on the evening when they were due to go to the theatre, both ladies were able to get ready in the knowledge that they would not look out of place among the *ton.*

Mr Hinder arrived wearing a green brocade coat with knee breeches and a dull gold square cut waistcoat. He did not look anything like a man who was considering a career in the church. Jessie told him that he looked splendid and his cheeks glowed with boyish pleasure. With his cheerful enthusiasm for almost any project, he always made an entertaining companion.

They dined together at four o'clock, for the evening's performance began at six. 'I know that it is fashionable to be late for everything, but I cannot bear to miss a single minute,' confessed Mrs Machin.

For her part, Jessie was in agreement. She could not imagine anyone booking a seat in a theatre and then arriving late. Although she was thirty years old, her experience of the theatre so far had been limited to an occasional small provisional performance. The theatre at Drury Lane seated over 3000 people. She had never been in such a big crowd in all her life. What would it be like?

Mr Hinder had ensured that a hackney would be ready for them at the door, and after their repast was finished and their outdoor garments donned, they climbed into the waiting carriage. Miss Simms came to her own front door and wished them a very pleasant evening.

'I'll come and tell you all about it tomorrow,' Jessie promised, before they drove off. For a short time as they travelled, Jessie could almost imagine herself to be back in Illingham, so quiet were the streets. It was not long, however, before they entered a more populous area, and as the evenings were now drawing out, she could see that the streets were busy. Mrs Machin was eagerly looking out of one window then the other, obviously storing up information for use in her book. Would any of the people whom they saw on the streets of London figure as characters in the pages of her novel, Jessie wondered?

The Theatre Royal itself positively defied the imagination. 'Oh, my goodness,' breathed Mrs Machin, as she took in the huge building, so tall that it even threatened to dwarf all but the tallest churches.

'Have you not even seen this building before then, ma'am?' asked Jessie curiously.

'No, for it was only built recently.'

'Last year,' Mr Hinder added, clarifying

matters. 'It is the third theatre to be built on this site.'

The inside was every bit as overwhelming as the façade. The entrance lobby was very spacious, with an elegant green carpet, and plenty of chairs designed to accommodate those who might be waiting for their carriages. It might not be fashionable to be in good time for an evening at the theatre, but Mrs Machin and her party were glad to see that quite a number of people had already arrived, and were chatting in an animated fashion.

Fortunately, since no attendant seemed to be available, Mr Hinder had been in his cousin's theatre box before, and was able to show them where to go. The ladies were very thankful for it as some lively young men, who clearly intended to sit in the pit, were becoming rather excitable, and seemed inclined to comment upon the appearance of any female present.

If the well-lit lobby with its elegant appointments had excited their admiration, the appearance of the auditorium itself almost took their breath away. There were five tiers of boxes which were arranged in a semi-circle. The colour scheme of these boxes was chiefly one of blue and white, with cameo paintings on the fronts. As if that were not enough, the pit was enormous, looking as if it must almost seat as many as a thousand people. The stage seemed to them to be positively cavernous.

'I do believe the whole parish church at Illingham would fit on to that stage,' Jessie told Henrietta. Meanwhile, Mr Hinder sat back with a pleased smile. Being the only one of the party who had visited the theatre before, he was conscious of an agreeable feeling of superiority.

The orchestra was already playing when they arrived, and Jessie, who seldom had the opportunity to hear an orchestra, was surprised and not a little annoyed that people chattered as loudly as if nothing was happening. Because the whole experience was new to her, however, she was almost as intrigued by the spectacle taking place around her as by what was happening on the stage. Observing the fashions of those arriving, she was glad that she had taken the time to alter her gown. Waistlines were clearly being worn much higher. She resolved to take the rest of her gowns to Miss Simms for alteration as soon as possible.

The play began soon after their arrival, but to Jessie's surprise, although the chatter lessened, it certainly did not cease. Obviously, many people attended the theatre not so much to watch the play as to meet their friends and show off their fashions.

Before she could become really irritated, however, Mrs Siddons made her appearance, and with that, the crowd fell silent, giving that great actress the respect that her performance fully deserved. This was just as well, for the size of the theatre meant that even when the audience was completely quiet, it was not always easy to hear what the actors were saying. Many people in the theatre found the play very affecting, and as Jessie wiped away a tear at the end, she turned to see that Mrs Machin was doing the same.

The evening's entertainment comprised the play which they had just seen followed by a farce. In between the plays, and during the intervals, the orchestra played, and, at times, singers or dancers performed. Jessie felt particularly sorry for the singer who came on after the play had ended, for her entrance appeared to be the signal for half the audience to get up and go out, some to appear moments later in other people's boxes, and others to go for refreshments, or to take a turn about the spacious corridors.

Part of Jessie would have liked to stay and give the poor singer some support, but she was very thirsty, so when Mr Hinder suggested that they should go in search of a drink, she readily concurred. They found their way to a very handsome semi-circular saloon, where refreshments were available.

'I'll just find you somewhere to sit, then I'll bring you something to drink,' said Mr Hinder. This former intention was easier to say than to do, however, for those experienced habitués of the theatre had already claimed all the available seats and there were no more to be had.

'Don't worry about looking for chairs for us,' said Mrs Machin. 'For my part, I have had quite enough of sitting down for the time being and would be glad to stand for a little.'

Jessie readily agreed, so Mr Hinder went off in search of refreshment whilst the ladies promised to remain in the same place so that he could find them easily. The room was warm, because of the large number of people present, and there was a constant buzz of chatter. Most people seemed to be gathered in larger groups than their small party, and nowhere else did Jessie see two ladies standing alone.

'I hope that Mr Hinder will soon return,' she said to Mrs Machin in a low tone. 'I feel that we are a little conspicuous.'

'Do you?' replied Mrs Machin, looking about her. 'I had not noticed. To be truthful, I was taking careful note of our surroundings. I think that Lady Meredith ought to come to the theatre, do not you? I must get my description right. It would never do for people to read my book and find fault with my inaccuracies.'

'No indeed,' agreed Jessie, stepping to one side in order to catch Mr Hinder's eye, because a group of people was now standing in between themselves and the direction in which he had gone.

After they had drunk the glass of wine and

eaten the sweet biscuits that he brought them on a tray, they made their way back to the box so as not to miss any of the farce.

'Now what should happen to her when she is here?' mused Mrs Machin, once they were sitting down again.

'To whom?' Jessie asked. Looking down at the stage, she could see that six dancers in rather short costumes were executing some complicated steps to lively music, cheered on by a noisy group of young men who were sitting in the pit.

'To Lady Meredith, of course,' answered Mrs Machin, in tones that seemed to imply that Jessie was being particularly dense. 'I suppose in a place like this she could encounter almost anyone. She could meet a rake here. Someone really wicked, like . . . Lord Ashbourne!'

'There is no denying that Lord Ashbourne is a shocking rake,' Jessie agreed.

'No, my dear!' replied her companion insistently. 'Over there!'

A box which was on the same level as their own and which had previously been empty was now occupied. At the centre of the laughing group was a dazzlingly beautiful woman in a shimmering low-cut gown, with a mass of guinea-gold hair piled on top of her head. She was accompanied by another lady who looked to be a little older than herself, and who was wearing a gown of a darker shade, with a rather more modest neckline. If she was there to act as a chaperon, then she was not doing a very good job. Both ladies were in animated conversation with the other occupants of the box, all four of whom were men. Lord Ashbourne was leaning over the back of the blonde beauty's chair, addressing some remark to her. As Jessie watched, the earl moved his hand from the back of the chair to the lady's shoulder. At this, the lady struck his hand with her fan and laughed in what Jessie thought was a quite unnecessarily flirtatious way.

Ashbourne also laughed, spoke to the other lady, stepped back, and then engaged one of the other men in a conversation which seemed to demand that they both take out their quizzing glasses and examine the dancers on the stage. Jessie now realized that the man to whom the earl was speaking was Sir Wallace Weary.

'So *that* is how rakes go on,' said Mrs Machin in an interested tone.

'How? What? Where?' exclaimed Mr Hinder, craning his neck in just the kind of way that would make their box conspicuous.

'Oh, for goodness' sake look away,' said Jessie crossly. 'They are only behaving badly so that people will look at them.'

'Who?' Mr Hinder asked again, this time leaning forward with his hand on the back of Jessie's chair.

'Sit *down*,' she insisted, striking him on the

137

hand with her fan, and thus providing a rather amusing caricature of the piece of flirtation that had been going on in the nearby box. Unfortunately, however, her handling of the fan was not as delicate as that of the lady with Ashbourne, for on receiving a rather sharp blow on the knuckles, Mr Hinder responded with a cry of pain that drew the attention of those near to their box in just the kind of way that Jessie wanted to avoid.

She knew the very moment when Ashbourne became aware of them. His figure stilled briefly before he turned his handsome head and saw her. She could not read his expression. Then, as if the whole situation could not possibly get worse, Mrs Machin lifted her hand and waggled her fingers at him! Jessie looked at her two companions in despair. For two pins, she could have ducked down beneath the front of the box and out of view. That would have made them look more ridiculous than ever, so she could only sit and wait to see what he would do.

After a moment, his features relaxed into a polite smile, and he bowed slightly, his hand on his heart. Sir Wallace Weary, who had noticed Mrs Machin's gesture, also bowed.

'They have acknowledged us!' exclaimed Mrs Machin. 'Oh do you suppose that they may come round to our box?'

'I don't know and I don't care,' replied Jessie, determined to avoid attracting further notice. 'Look the farce is beginning. Can we *please* conduct ourselves so that we do not look as if we are on intimate terms with every rake and scoundrel in London?'

Thankfully, this piece of firmness appeared to bring the others to their senses. They settled down to watch the farce, a rather thin tale which involved a lot of running in and out for which Jessie never did discover the reason. By the time they were ready to leave, the box in which Lord Ashbourne had been sitting was empty once again. Jessie told herself firmly that it was a very good thing, too.

*   *   *

'Who were those people, Raff?' asked Lady Winterson, laying her hand on Lord Ashbourne's arm as their party left the theatre. They had made their exit shortly before the end of the farce in order to avoid the crush on the stairs.

'Which people, my dear?' asked Ashbourne at his most suave. 'You must know that in your presence, I only have eyes for you.'

'Fiddle,' replied the blonde beauty tranquilly. 'Your glass became virtually glued to your eye from the moment that the dancers came on stage.'

'Only for purposes of comparison,' the earl assured her. 'Entirely in your favour, of course.'

139

Lady Winterson allowed her gaze to survey him from beneath long sweeping lashes. He really looked extraordinarily handsome this evening. Eschewing the extravagances of some of the other men present, he was in a coat of darkest purple, with matching breeches, and a silver waistcoat with self-coloured embroidery.

The two of them had been everything to one another some years before and, after their parting, they had remained upon good terms. Since then, she had consoled herself very satisfactorily, and she had no doubt that he had done the same. Nevertheless, she would have no objection to renewing intimate ties with an exceedingly accomplished lover.

'So kind,' she murmured, as he handed her into her carriage. 'But you still have not answered my question.'

'Have I not?' he replied, climbing in after her. 'I must confess that your beauty has entirely driven it out of my mind. Was it very important?'

'Not at all,' she answered, swaying closer to him in the darkness.

*   *   *

An hour later, he let himself out of Lady Winterson's house and wandered in the direction of St James's Street. He had shared a glass of brandy with her, and indulged her with a desperate flirtation, but had then made his farewells. His liaison with her had been very agreeable, but he had always made it a rule never to retrace his steps. Furthermore, he had a suspicion that the glamorous widow was now in search of a new husband, and he had long since determined not to marry again. His first marriage had not been such a roaring success that he was anxious to repeat the experience.

His mind went back to his son's wedding. Were they still happy? He had no way of knowing. Thanks to his early youthful anxiety to distance himself from the pain of the past, he had allowed his son to grow to maturity without knowing him. He would have to rely upon other sources to inform him if Ilam looked likely to produce an heir. Judging by the way in which the viscount and his bride had difficulties keeping their hands off each other, the time would not be long.

What would it be like, he wondered, to have a wife who adored him? He thought immediately of Jez Warburton. Had he wanted that, he could have married her years ago. He was well aware that she had been besotted with him for half her life, although he had tried never to encourage her.

He had been acting the rake for the past twenty years and more. By many, he was simply known as Rake Ashbourne. Others, remembering the fact that the males of his family were always given the names of angels, called him the Fallen Angel.

Jez Warburton deserved better than that. She had looked an elegant lady that evening in her golden gown, cut fashionably low, although not as low as some, notably that of Lady Winterson. She deserved a happy marriage to a man who would appreciate her. He only hoped that Henry Lusty knew how lucky he was. He, Raphael, had no intention of making her unhappy himself; but he would not stand by and let some other man make her unhappy either, if he could help it.

He had not expected to see Mrs Machin and her party at the theatre that evening; but then he had not expected to see them in any fashionable place. Mr Lusty's sister's house was in an unfashionable part of town and, from what he had seen on his brief visit, she lived in a very quiet, modest way. He was glad that Jez had had the opportunity to enjoy such a treat, but he had been horrified at the way in which Mrs Machin and her buffoon of an escort had managed to draw attention to their acquaintance with himself. What was more, they had also drawn the attention of Sir Wallace Weary. The baronet had noticed Jez at almost the same time as he himself had seen her.

'There's that dashed pretty wench from the bookshop,' he had murmured. 'Damned if I wouldn't like to make her better acquaintance.' Fortunately at that point one of the other men had invited him to go on to another function and the moment had passed. But the danger was still there. They were two women, living alone without the protection of a man. Mrs Machin was more naïve than a widow of her age had any right to be. Jez had no idea of how to go on in London; and there was Weary, a man whom he barely tolerated at best, starting to think that they were both prime articles because of Mrs Machin's silliness. What on earth could he do to protect them?

'Raff! Raff, I say! Windmills in your head?'

Roused from his abstraction by Toby Wayland's hearty voice, the earl realized that he had arrived at the corner of St James's Street. He responded to the greeting and putting aside his anxieties he accompanied his friend up the steps and into Brooks's, ready to enjoy a night's gaming.

CHAPTER TEN

Now that Mrs Machin had abandoned the fiction of copying and ordering her husband's writings, and composing moral tracts, the two ladies generally breakfasted together. On the morning after their visit to the theatre, when they sat at table, Mrs Machin said, 'My mind is positively buzzing with ideas for my novel. Will you excuse me, my dear, if I disappear into the book-room to work? There is so much that I must write down whilst it is fresh in my mind.'

'Of course,' Jessie replied readily. 'Shall we perhaps have a walk later?'

'Yes, perhaps,' agreed Henrietta. Jessie could see from her expression that she was already back amidst the sights and sounds of the theatre. It seemed as though her sense of obligation as hostess had not entirely deserted her, however, for she was three parts out of the door when she turned and said, 'How will you occupy your time? Do you have something to do, or would you'—she swallowed—'prefer me to entertain you in some way?'

'By no means,' laughed Jessie. 'Pray do not tear yourself away if the muse is upon you. Only tell me if there are any charitable institutions nearby where I may make myself useful for an hour or two.'

Mrs Machin looked thoughtful. 'The parish of St George has a poor house,' she said after a brief consideration. 'I don't know what they do there by way of education. I know they do some teaching at the Foundling hospital but that is rather a long way to walk.'

'I will go to St George's, then,' Jessie answered, 'and see if I can help with anything.' After a short pause, she added, 'Is St George's church really the nearest?'

'I haven't the slightest idea,' said Henrietta frankly, 'but it's by far the most fashionable. See if Mr Hinder wants to go with you. His

144

presence might be valuable to you.'

Seeing the sense of this, Jessie went to Mr Hinder's house and found him in the very act of preparing to go out.

'I'm going to Paternoster Row,' he answered in response to her enquiry. 'I want to talk to a bookseller there. I'll gladly take you to where you want to go first.'

The journey initially followed the same path as their route to St George's, Hanover Square. Jessie was beginning to get used to this walk as she had now visited the church on more than one occasion. It was, however, the first time that she had been alone with Mr Hinder, so she took the opportunity to ask him something about his family and background.

'I know that you have five sisters,' she said. 'That must have been a busy household.'

'There wasn't much to go round, so Papa reckoned I would be best off entering the church,' he disclosed, a piece of information that did not surprise her.

'Do you think that you might do so in the end?' she asked him curiously.

'I don't think so,' he answered. 'I have no calling, you see. I would like to make my living by writing.'

'Like Mrs Machin,' Jessie remarked.

As they arrived outside the poor house, Mr Hinder declared himself to be very happy to wait for Miss Warburton, and escort her home again. Jessie knew that he had an errand of his

145

own, so she told him not to trouble. 'I shall ask the matron to send for a hackney for me,' she promised.

The quality of the lady visitor was quickly understood by the servant who admitted her, and the matron, a stout dame in a starched apron and cap, soon came down to greet her, and took great pleasure in showing her round the whole premises.

'It's been enlarged three times that I know about, miss,' said the woman. She explained that people who came into the workhouse were separated according to sex and age. Furthermore, the children were taught to read and write and say their Catechism. When the matron heard that Jessie would like to help in this work, she was overjoyed. 'We do what we can, miss, but it's very hard to educate them, what with so many other things to do.'

Jessie smiled. 'My hostess is often occupied in the mornings, so I would be very pleased to help you while I am in London.'

After enjoying a cup of tea in the matron's sitting-room, Jessie made her farewells, promising to call again soon. She was very well pleased at her morning's work. It was an activity that she could report upon in her next letter to her fiancé, unlike the visit to the theatre, which she had decided that she would not mention for the time being. Perhaps later, she thought blushingly, she might drop the visit into the conversation, giving the impression that it was a concert of sacred music. Whatever happened, she would certainly not mention how Mr Lusty's own sister had waggled her fingers at Rake Ashbourne!

It was only after the poor house door had closed behind her that Jessie remembered that she had intended to ask the matron to summon a hackney. She had no idea how to do such a thing, and was reluctant to make herself look foolish by knocking on the door again. She would just have to walk, she decided. It was a fair walk, but well within her capabilities. Then, as luck would have it, it suddenly came on to rain heavily.

She was just contemplating the possibility of arriving back in Sloane Street looking like a drowned rat when a carriage drew up beside her, the door was flung open, and a familiar voice drawled, 'Climb in, Jez.' She only hesitated briefly before doing as she was bid. After all, she told herself, it was an emergency.

She watched Ashbourne as he gave the direction to the coachman, then settled back in his place. The contrast between them was almost painful. To visit the poor house, Jessie had worn one of her older gowns, a brown silk with a cream fichu modestly tucked in the neckline. Her cream shawl and her bonnet had fared badly from the sudden onset of the rain, and she felt distinctly shabby as well as damp and rather grubby. Lord Ashbourne, by way of contrast, lounged very much at his ease in the far corner of the carriage, one immaculate buff pantaloon-clad leg crossed negligently over the other. He stared at her quizzically before taking out his snuff box and helping himself to a pinch.

'Where is your escort?' he asked her.

'I am only a stone's throw from home,' she told him.

'That does not answer my question,' he replied.

'A lady surely does not need an escort when about charitable business,' she declared, reminding herself that she was thirty years of age, and not answerable to him or to anyone else for her actions.

'A lady walking in London needs an escort whatever business she might be about, as I believe I told you before,' he answered. 'You appear not to have heeded my warning. Where have you been, anyway?'

'I went to St George's poor house.' Jessie told him. 'You see, it really was no distance at all, and besides, Mr Hinder walked with me from Sloane Street. I was only walking home on my own.'

'That, of course, makes it perfectly acceptable,' replied Ashbourne sarcastically. 'Rakes such as myself never molest women on their way home, only as they are setting out'

'Oh, for goodness' sake!' exclaimed Jessie, exasperated. Then, in tones of real alarm, she added, 'Raff! What are you doing?'

He had leaned towards her and with one swift movement, whisked her fichu from the neckline of her gown, thereby exposing rather more of her bosom than she had originally intended. He then leaned back in his place, taking up his former position, waving the fichu negligently in front of him like a handkerchief.

'Give it back at once!' she demanded, colouring. She half sat forward as if intending to try to take back her property.

Ashbourne uncrossed his legs again, and leaned towards her. 'Oh, please try to wrest it from me,' he purred. 'I would enjoy it so much.' He glanced down at her neckline. 'That's a very attractive view, by the way.'

Immediately, she sat back in her seat, placing as much distance between them as possible. 'You really are a libertine,' she declared, her colour still high, her heart beating rather fast. 'I don't believe you have any proper feeling.'

'No I haven't,' he agreed. 'I'm a rake. All proper feeling is drummed out of us at rakes' training academy.' She had to laugh, albeit reluctantly, for she was still angry with him. 'Didn't you believe it before?' he asked, raising his brows. 'Well, next time you obey the dictates of modesty by covering up your excellent shape, remember who uncovered you and take more care in the future. I'm not the only rake in town, but I'm by far the most

149

friendly, at least as far as you are concerned. What would you have done had you met with Wallace Weary rather than with myself?'

'How can you say such a thing?' she demanded. 'It was you who introduced him to us.'

'Given your friend's eagerness to claim me as an acquaintance, I had very little choice. Anyway, if we are talking of our encounter in the bookshop, you did not seem at all averse to going aside with him.'

Jessie remembered how offensive the other man had been, and how she had said nothing of it so as not to cause trouble between the two men. Swallowing anything she might have said about the baronet's behaviour, therefore, she merely replied, 'He was very amusing.'

'In that case, I'm surprised you did not wiggle your fingers at him in the theatre in emulation of your friend's example,' he answered unsmilingly, and with less of his customary suavity than usual.

'I would not dream of doing anything so'— she was about to say vulgar, then she recalled that it would be disloyal to Henrietta—'silly,' she concluded.

He laughed. 'Egad, I believe you wouldn't,' he answered. 'Has the green silk made up well?'

Jessie smiled. 'It has, and you should have seen Dilly's expression. That was very kind of you, Raff.'

He waved a hand dismissively. 'It was nothing,' he replied. He laughed derisively. 'To tell the truth, I couldn't bear the thought of the wench's tear-stained face.'

'Plenty of men would not have bothered,' she answered, 'but I know how kind you are.'

'Pray keep it to yourself, my dear,' he drawled. 'Here is your destination.'

As the carriage drew up, Jessie made ready to alight. Fortunately, the rain had now eased. 'Thank you,' she said simply. 'You have saved me from a wetting.'

'The pleasure was mine,' he responded. 'And do tell your friend not to wave at me in public. It will tend to give people the wrong impression.'

Seeing at last an opportunity to get her own back, Jessie said, 'I'll tell her, but I doubt it would make any difference. No doubt you will find her wiggling her fingers at you everywhere you go. She wants to observe you, you see.'

'To observe me?' he echoed, drawing his elegantly shaped brows together.

'She is writing a book about a rake,' Jessie replied. 'I will tell her that you are a perfect specimen. Good day, Raff.'

His brows shot up. Before he could reply, she had gone indoors, feeling satisfied that in the end, it was *she* who had caught *him* unawares. It was only after she was inside that she remembered he had not given back her fichu.

151

*   *   *

Two days later, Jessie visited St George's poor house again to read with some of the children. This time, she made arrangements with Mr Hinder to take her on his way to transact some business, then collect her on his way back. It was not that she felt the slightest need to obey Lord Ashbourne, she told herself; it was simply that the wretched man was sure to appear if she went abroad alone, contrary to his instructions.

On their arrival back at the house, Jessie invited Mr Hinder to come inside, an invitation which Mrs Machin, putting her head round the door of the book-room, endorsed. 'I have had a perfectly splendid idea for my next chapter,' she said, 'and I want you to help me to carry it out. Hector, you may stay for something to eat if you wish.'

Mr Hinder gratefully accepted—the provisions in his lodging not being of the best—and soon they were sitting down in Henrietta's dining-room enjoying some bread and cheese followed by fruit whilst she told them about her plan. 'It has occurred to me,' she said, as she carefully peeled an apple then cut it into quarters, 'that if Lady Meredith is a woman of the world then she really ought to visit Vauxhall Gardens. They have just reopened in preparation for the season and I wondered whether we might go one evening. Would you like to go, Jessie?'

Jessie had heard of Vauxhall Gardens, but she had never, ever thought that she might go. She was very curious to see the famous pleasure gardens but had one very strong reservation. 'What of Henry?' she asked. 'Do you think he would approve?'

Henrietta straightened her spine. 'His Royal Highness the Prince of Wales has been,' she said with great dignity. 'How can Henry possibly take exception to anything that his prince might do?'

Thinking that there were a good many things that the prince was said to have done, to which Henry might take great exception, Jessie contented herself with merely looking thoughtful.

'Anyway,' Henrietta went on, 'are you not aware that there is a statue of *Handel* in the gardens? What could be more proper than Handel, pray? And if there is a statue of him, they will surely perform music that he has composed. You cannot tell me that Henry would disapprove of a concert of sacred music.' After a brief pause, she completely spoiled the virtuous effect that she had created by saying, 'He need not know that we are to attend, after all, and what he does not know will not hurt him.'

Soon after this Mr Hinder, who seemed to enter into all of Henrietta's plans with great enthusiasm, took his leave, promising to find out about the cost of entering the gardens and the best method of travelling to them.

'Oh, this is such fun,' said Mrs Machin, her eyes gleaming. 'I had never thought that I would enjoy myself so much.'

Jessie eyed her curiously. 'Surely though, ma'am, you must have had many opportunities for visiting Vauxhall Gardens. After all, you have lived in London for some years, now.'

Mrs Machin nodded solemnly. 'Yes, that is very true,' she agreed. 'But you do not really understand my situation. My husband was a clergyman, as you know. His parish was in the country, to the south of London. He had no private means, and I had only a small inheritance from my father, not enough to live on, given that there was no property to go with it. After Percival died, the new vicar who came to take my husband's place had several children and needed someone to look after them, so I stayed on as a sort of governess.'

'In what had been your old home?' asked Jessie incredulously. 'How awful for you.'

'They were very kind, but it was not the life that I would have chosen,' Henrietta admitted. 'That was when I began to write, as an escape.'

'For how long did you live there?' Jessie asked her.

'For two tedious years. Then the miracle happened. Our old nurse left me this house. There was no income to go with it, but I felt

154

sure that with what my father had left me, I would just be able to manage. I was also hoping that eventually I would be able to make some money by writing. The one difficulty was that I did not have enough money to employ a companion. Dear Henry, who has never, ever said a grudging word about my inheritance, found one for me, the widow of a clergyman who had been helpful to him when he was a raw curate.'

'Would that be Mrs Smales?' asked Jessie.

'Exactly. Mrs Smales, though a very good person in her way, keeps up a regular correspondence with Henry, telling him of all my doings—after all, it is he who employs her—so I have had to be very careful to keep her ignorant of any of my activities of which she might disapprove. I had to be cautious when you arrived as well, which is why I was so unwelcoming to you to start with; for which I must ask your forgiveness, my dear Jessie.' She leaned over and caught hold of one of Jessie's hands.

'Not at all,' smiled Jessie, returning her grip. 'I am only glad that you decided I was to be trusted after all.'

'I knew it at once, when I found that you were friendly with Lord Ashbourne,' Henrietta explained. 'Henry would never approve of such a friendship. It therefore followed that you would either have to omit all mention of him in your letters, or say so little that Henry would barely notice it. If you can keep that secret, then you can certainly keep mine.'

'In any case, you gave yourself away,' Jessie pointed out. 'You couldn't decide whether to make Ashbourne welcome or reprimand me for knowing him.'

'Yes I did, didn't I?' her hostess agreed ruefully. 'I have to say, I think it a great pity that—'

'Forgive me, Henrietta, but you don't know what you are talking about,' said Jessie bluntly. 'The less we see of Lord Ashbourne, the better for all of our reputations.'

While she was speaking, the door bell rang, and moments later, a very flustered-looking Dilly appeared. 'Please, ma'am, it's Lord Ashbourne,' she said. Her tone could not have been more reverent had she been announcing the Archbishop of Canterbury.

Raphael strolled into the room and greeted them with his customary elegant bow. 'Ladies,' he said. 'I trust I find you well.' He was dressed in a lilac wool coat with an embroidered waistcoat and charcoal grey pantaloons with exquisitely shiny black boots. His tall-crowned hat and cane he carried in his left hand, as he took hold of his hostess's hand in his right. 'You must forgive me for not calling upon you earlier.'

'It's quite all right, Raff,' said Jessie calmly. 'We know that you are a man of many affairs.'

He turned his head and looked at her for a

long moment. 'Just so, my dear Jez,' he replied. 'You have always understood me so well.' Before she could guess what he was about, he moved closer to her, took her hand, then leaning across, kissed her on the cheek. While Jessie was still recovering from the shock—for he had never done such a thing before—he turned to Mrs Machin. 'No doubt Jez has told you that we are old friends,' he said easily. 'We have known one another for nearly twenty years.'

Jessie blushed at his effrontery, but to her relief Mrs Machin did not appear to think his behaviour at all out of the ordinary, for after she had begged him to be seated, she simply remarked how agreeable it must be for Jessie to have a friend in town. 'May I offer you some refreshment, my lord?' she asked him. 'Wine? Coffee? Tea?'

'A glass of wine would be very welcome,' Ashbourne replied, with one of his most charming smiles.

'It is very good of you to call upon us in this way,' said Mrs Machin.

'Not at all,' he responded. 'I have it on very good authority that you would like to observe me, ma'am.'

'Observe you?' Mrs Machin asked.

'While I am a-raking—for your book,' he explained kindly.

Jessie turned fiery red for she had not told Henrietta about her encounter with

Ashbourne in the rain, or about what she had said to him. She now feared that Henrietta would resent the fact that she had mentioned her hostess's writing without her permission. Mrs Machin did not seem to take it amiss, however; quite the reverse, for she clapped her hands delightedly. 'I *knew* you would help me,' she exclaimed. 'I wonder, would you like to go with us to Vauxhall?'

At that moment, Dilly came in with the wine and set it down on a table next to the earl, smiling shyly at him as she did so. Whilst he was setting the glasses out and pouring, Jessie pulled Henrietta to one side. 'You can't ask him to go with us just like that,' she hissed.

'Why not?' Henrietta whispered back. 'I thought from the first that it would be better to have a second gentleman.'

'Precisely,' whispered Jessie. 'A gentleman! Ashbourne is a rake. You heard what he said; and if you want to take him along to Vauxhall then watch him whilst he misbehaves, I, for one, do not.'

'Would you like me to leave the room?' Ashbourne asked amiably, as he carried two glasses over to them. 'You clearly have matters that you wish to discuss.'

'Yes,' Jessie said, whilst at the same time, Mrs Machin said, 'No:

'Shall I stand in the doorway, then?' he asked innocently. His lips twitched, and Jessie could not help laughing. 'Now what were you

158

saying about Vauxhall?'

'We had decided that we would go,' replied Henrietta. 'I am indeed writing a book, which is to be set in London, and I would like my characters to visit Vauxhall. Yet how am I to make the scenes there realistic if I have never been myself?'

'You are very right,' Ashbourne agreed, his tone as serious as if they had been discussing some point of law. 'Who will believe your tale if you make simple mistakes that even a child could spot? I do trust that you were not intending to go alone. I feel that I should warn you for Jez, I fear, is inclined to be somewhat intrepid.'

Jessie, who had been on the point of sipping her wine, choked, and while Ashbourne took her glass from her, Henrietta kindly provided her with a handkerchief. 'Oh dear, you have splashed wine on your fichu. Perhaps you had better change it.'

'If you can find another one,' murmured Ashbourne.

Jessie turned a fulminating glance upon him before leaving to go to her room. Once there, she removed the fichu, put it into the basin on the cupboard in the window, and added water from the ewer. She would ask Dilly to wash it later after the visitor had gone. She was about to open her drawer in order to get another square of linen to tuck into her neckline, when she caught sight of her own reflection and paused to look more carefully into the mirror. Today, she was wearing a dull gold gown with thin brown stripes. The neckline was low, but not immodest. After a moment's thought, she put on a golden chain and locket which had been given to her one birthday by Lady Agatha. Then she went back downstairs.

The two occupants of the room were chatting as she came in. On seeing her, Ashbourne took up his quizzing glass, which hung on a ribbon around his neck. 'Charming,' he murmured, as he examined her.

Feeling oddly breathless at his scrutiny, Jessie reclaimed her wine, and said, 'Have you made any decisions about Vauxhall?'

'Why, certainly,' Henrietta replied. 'Lord Ashbourne has had such a good idea.'

'Please, call me Raff,' said the earl.

'So kind,' said Henrietta, her eyes glowing.

'Just don't let Henry hear you doing so,' put in Jessie in rather a waspish tone.

'Oh no,' answered her hostess. She looked regretfully at Ashbourne. 'It seems so unfair, doesn't it?'

He shrugged. 'I've made my bed. Anyway, Jez, my suggestion is that we should go to Vauxhall on a masquerade night. That way, we may go masked and nobody will be able to recognize any of us.'

Not long afterwards, he rose to take his leave. He gave Mrs Machin his card. 'Tell Hinder to contact me here,' he said. 'I'll talk to him about the arrangements.'

Before he left, Jessie found the opportunity to speak to him without her hostess hearing. 'I warn you, Raff, Henrietta may want to watch you playing the rake, but if you do so in front of me, I shall come home immediately, escort or no.'

Ashbourne inclined his handsome head. 'Rest assured, my dear Jez, that with you present, I shall save my raking for another occasion.'

CHAPTER ELEVEN

It was very agreeable to have gentlemen to make arrangements for one, Jessie decided, as she returned from visiting the poor house two days later, accompanied by Dilly. This was a luxury that had not come her way very much. As the companion of Lady Agatha, she normally found that arrangements for holidays, visits or parties were her responsibility.

For the visit to Vauxhall, matters had been taken completely out of her hands. Raff had made it his business to discover the date of the next masquerade. He had passed on the information to Mr Hinder, who had told them that it would be the following week. Raff would make all the travel arrangements and, in addition, he would book a box and bespeak a supper. All they had to do was to organize their clothes and get themselves ready on time. He would do himself the honour of calling for them at seven o'clock. For a woman who had never been anywhere or done anything, it was heady stuff and would be something to remember when she was a sedate clergyman's wife. She could not help giving a little skip as she arrived back at the house and opened the door. 'Hettie, I'm home,' she called.

'Jessie, my dear, such a delightful occurrence,' said Henrietta, meeting her in the hall, with an expression on her face which was one of warning rather than delight. Behind her stood Henry Lusty.

'Henry,' she declared after only a moment's hesitation. 'This is a charming surprise. Are you able to stay for long?' She was guiltily aware that her mind had leaped immediately to the question of whether he would be gone before the Vauxhall masquerade.

'Jessica, my dear,' he said, stepping forward and taking her hand. 'Henrietta tells me that you have been out attending to the needs of the poor. That is very seemly; very seemly indeed. I am glad you took a maid with you. These London streets are not safe for a lone female.'

'No, so I believe,' she replied, thinking that on that one subject, if on nothing else, he and Lord Ashbourne would certainly agree.

'Well, shall we all have a cup of tea?' suggested Henrietta.

'That would be a rather unnecessary luxury, I would have thought, when it cannot be long until dinner,' answered Henry, putting an end to that particular conversation.

Jessie handed her outdoor clothes to Dilly, then went into the drawing-room. Once inside with the door closed, Henry said, 'I will greet you properly now, if I may,' and leaned forward to kiss her on the cheek. Jessie was stabbed by guilt as she recalled how a similar salute from Raff had caused shivers to run up and down her spine, whereas Henry's embrace left her completely cold. Then her feelings of guilt were increased as he looked down at her hand and said, 'Where is your ring, Jessica?'

'I never wear it to go to the poor house,' replied Jessie honestly. She did not add that she frequently forgot to put it on at other times as well. Then, she added less truthfully, 'I do not like to . . . to flaunt jewellery when I go there.'

Henry's puzzled look cleared. 'You do very right, my dear. I see, too, that you have returned to your customary modest garb, which pleases me.' The gown that she was wearing was old, and reserved only for visits to the poor house, but naturally she kept that piece of information to herself.

'For how long are we to have the pleasure of your company?' asked Henrietta brightly. 'I do

163

hope that it will be for a good long time.'
Jessie struggled to hide a smile. She knew that
Mrs Machin was also thinking about Vauxhall.

He shook his head. 'My stay can only be
brief, I fear. I have a matter of business to deal
with tomorrow morning. I will be with you
over the weekend, of course, as I will not be
travelling on a Sunday, but I must go back on
Monday.' Both ladies tried not to sigh with
relief.

Shortly after that, they all went upstairs to
change. Jessie looked carefully amongst her
clothes and, with some reluctance, took out an
evening gown that she had not worn for some
time. It was cut rather high in the neck, and
the waistline was lower than had become
fashionable. It was also in a very sober shade
of brown. Thinking ruefully how very different
she looked from when she had gone to the
theatre, she went downstairs for dinner
confident that she could be commended for
her sobriety. She almost left her room without
her ring on, but remembered to don it at the
last moment. It felt very strange on her finger.
Guiltily, she was aware of how seldom she
wore it.

Henrietta was already downstairs when she
arrived, and Jessie suspected that her hostess
had been busily hiding away any evidence of
her novel writing. She found herself marvelling
at the fact that both the clergy widows with
whom she was acquainted appeared to be

mistresses of deceit. Lady Agatha, with whom she had resided for several years, thought nothing of manipulating all kinds of people to get her way. Mrs Machin had constructed a whole other occupation for herself so that she could write scandalous novels in secret. Now she, Jessie, engaged to be married to a clergyman, was already deceiving him in an underhand fashion. Would she be doing the same as those two other ladies in twenty years' time?

*   *   *

In the event, the evening passed pleasantly enough. Henry had one or two mildly amusing tales to tell concerning church business, and some messages from Lady Agatha, whom he had made it his business to visit before he had set off for London. He also had rather a momentous piece of news. 'The bishop favours me to be the next incumbent at Illingham,' he said, beaming at Jessie. 'It looks as though you will be able to stay in your own home after all, my dear.'

Jessie stared at him, not knowing what to say. Fortunately, her lack of response was more than adequately covered by Mrs Machin's exclamations of delight. 'My dear brother, your own parish! The very thing you have always wanted! How thankful you must be!'

'Yes indeed,' Jessie added, her temporary silence overcome. 'Congratulations.'

'My position as vicar of Illingham is not yet confirmed,' he said, a little tight-lipped. 'There is some question about a signature from Lord Ashbourne which he has not yet been inclined to give. As soon as he and the bishop have signed the document, then it will all be settled.'

Jessie was a little anxious that Mrs Machin, who had seemed to have had quite a preference for Raff, might react in an indignant manner. To her relief, the lady's obvious powers of invention did not desert her now, and she merely smiled and turned her attention to her floating island pudding. 'That must be very vexing for you, dear. I'm sure that Lord Ashbourne is not doing it on purpose, however.'

After a moment's pause, Mr Lusty agreed, 'Of course not,' and then went on to talk about other things.

That night, Jessie thought about the news that Mr Lusty had brought. She had always known that he had his eye upon the parish of Illingham, but foolishly enough had never imagined herself living there as his wife. If she had ever pictured married life with him, it had been in some fictitious place, far from those she knew. Now, the idea of returning there after her marriage seemed unsettling, and although she could not put her finger on why, the notion kept her awake long after others in the house had gone to sleep.

The following morning, coincidentally, both ladies were up betimes, but not so early as Henry, who had spent an hour in the book-room before they arrived downstairs for breakfast. On learning this, Mrs Machin darted an anxious glance at Jessie, and Jessie could guess that she was thinking how glad she was that she had put all her novel writing things away out of sight.

As soon as breakfast was over, Mr Lusty declared his intention of walking into the City in order to transact his business. 'I will be back later and perhaps this afternoon we might visit the poor house,' he suggested. Jessie was thankful that she had been truthful in her descriptions of her work there. At least in introducing Henry to the matron she would have nothing to blush for. Indeed, he seemed so pleased and proud at her efforts that, as she took his arm to walk home, she felt as contented about her forthcoming marriage as she had ever done, and quite guilty about deceiving him. Her behaviour seemed doubly wrong when she reflected that he was only snatching a day or two's leisure, whilst she was enjoying herself in the capital. For two pins she could have told him about the Vauxhall scheme. She remembered in time that it was not just her secret to disclose.

On Sunday, Mr Lusty, Mrs Machin, and Jessie all set out to attend St George's for the morning service. The day was fine, and the walk promised to be agreeable. Mr Hinder appeared and asked for permission to join them.

'There are one or two questions of philosophy that have been on my mind, and I would be glad to have your thoughts upon them, sir,' he said to the clergyman.

'Certainly,' replied Mr Lusty, smiling benevolently. 'In what way may I assist you?'

'I was wondering whether you had any views on the writings of Rousseau?'

Mr Lusty's face went rigid with disapproval. 'That is very shocking material you are reading,' he said. 'I am persuaded that it will not do you any good.'

'Do you really say so?' asked Mr Hinder.

'Come, Jessie, let us walk ahead,' said Mrs Machin, seizing her opportunity. 'The gentlemen have much to discuss, I can see.' As soon as they were out of ear-shot, she said, 'I cannot tell you how relieved I was when Henry said that he is leaving tomorrow. What on earth would we have done about Vauxhall had he stayed?'

'I expect we would just not have gone,' Jessie replied.

'Yes, but think,' Henrietta insisted. 'We

would have had to send word to Raff telling him not to come. Can you imagine the scene had he turned up at the door cloaked and masked, with Henry in residence?'

'Oh heavens!' Jessie exclaimed. She could picture the situation all too vividly.

'We really ought warn him, ought we not?' said Henrietta thoughtfully. 'It would never do if he were to send us some message about our outing, and Henry were to receive it.'

'Hettie, do you think we ought to confess to Henry what we are planning?' Jessie asked, after they had walked in silence for a short time.

'Good heavens, no,' Henrietta exclaimed, much alarmed. 'How can you even suggest such a thing?'

'I have a guilty conscience,' Jessie confessed in a small voice.

'I cannot imagine why,' said Henrietta candidly. 'Jessie, we have not done anything wrong, nor are we planning to do so. Attending Vauxhall is not a crime, is it?'

'Well no, but—'

'Henry would not approve,' Henrietta interrupted, finishing her thought. 'I dare say he would not. That is why we are not telling him. We are indulging in a little harmless amusement, not intending to steal the crown jewels!'

They reached the doors of St George's without realizing how far the gentlemen had

169

fallen behind. 'Goodness,' chuckled Henrietta, 'And they say that ladies like to talk! Had we better go in, do you think? We do not want to miss the beginning of the service.'

'Do you find yourselves without an escort, ladies?' said a familiar voice. 'May I assist?' They both turned in astonishment to see Lord Ashbourne clearly preparing to enter the church. Like Henry, he was dressed in black, but somehow, on him the sombre shade looked decadent rather than sober and puritanical. As always, his garments fitted him to perfection. The linen at his wrists and throat was dazzling white, as were his stockings, which were decorated with gold clocks.

'Raff!' exclaimed Jessie. 'You are not intending to go into church!'

He grinned wickedly. 'Strangely enough it is permitted. I do not dissolve into a pile of ash on crossing the hallowed threshold, either.' Henrietta looked round. 'My brother should be with us,' she said, frowning a little.

Ashbourne raised his brows. 'He would seem to be late,' he murmured in disapproving tones. 'Well? Shall we go in?'

As there was no sign of Mr Lusty or Mr Hinder—who had, in fact, become so involved in a heated debate in which the former propounded the doctrine of original sin, whilst the latter just as vigorously defended the essential goodness of human nature, that they

170

had stopped to argue on the corner of Mount Street—the ladies consented to go inside with Ashbourne, where he found them all places to sit.

It was immediately obvious that his presence caused something of a stir. Jessie heard his title mentioned under several people's breath, and a number of worshippers, notably ladies, turned to look at him. All of this attention he ignored effortlessly, and Jessie could not help thinking that he must be very used to it. She told herself firmly that it would surely be exceedingly annoying to be married to the owner of so much male charm and beauty.

There was still no sign of Mr Lusty and Mr Hinder when the service began, but the church was so full that it would not be difficult to miss them. They rose to sing the first hymn, 'All people that on earth do dwell,' and Jessie was rather surprised to hear Raff, who was standing next to her, striking up with enthusiastic vigour. He certainly did not conduct himself as one who only attended church if he had to.

At the close of the service, the earl escorted them out of the building, where they found Mr Lusty and Mr Hinder waiting. The clergyman did not look very pleased, and his expression of displeasure was doubled when he caught sight of who was escorting his womenfolk.

'My lord,' he said, with a stiff bow. He

171

turned to his sister and Jessie. 'I am sorry that you did not wait for us. It was most unfortunate that we were not able to sit together.'

'We did not want to disturb your debate,' Henrietta replied. 'Shall we return home, now? R . . .' Just in time, she recollected that her brother would hardly approve of her addressing one of London's libertines by his Christian name, let alone his nickname. 'Lord Ashbourne,' she went on, 'would you care to join us for a little light refreshment?'

Ashbourne bowed, his hand over his heart. 'I'm honoured, ma'am,' he replied, the twinkle in his eye revealing that he had guessed how she had almost slipped up.

'I am sure that Lord Ashbourne has many other calls upon his time,' said Lusty repressively.

'Not on a Sunday,' Ashbourne replied virtuously. 'I should be delighted to join you and your party, Mrs Machin.'

Lusty was all for setting off immediately, but their departure was not to be effected so quickly. Last time they had visited St George's, they had been beneath the notice of the fashionable. Today, because they were with Ashbourne, they at once became objects of curiosity, and by the time they managed to get away, almost being dragged down the steps by Mr Lusty, Jessie had been introduced to a duchess, two countesses, a marquis and at least half-a-dozen fashionable matrons, all of whom appeared to know Raff exceedingly well, more than one promising to call once Jessie's connection with Lady Agatha had been explained.

By the time they were at last able to begin their journey home, the rigid cast of Henry Lusty's countenance would have assured any but the most obtuse person that he was in a bad temper. Not wishing to make his mood worse, Jessie took the arm that he offered her, and allowed him to walk with her a little ahead of the others, leaving Mrs Machin the pleasure of being escorted by two gentlemen. She had no doubt that Henrietta would make the most of the opportunity to warn Raff not to mention Vauxhall. Jessie felt another pang of guilt. Bad enough that they should be deceiving Henry themselves; they were drawing Raff and even Hector Hinder into conspiring in the deceit as well.

'Shocking!' exclaimed the clergyman under his breath, as they set off down the road. Jessie almost gasped audibly. For one dreadful moment, it seemed as if he had guessed her thoughts and passed judgement upon her. It was with quite a sense of relief that she heard him continue, 'I do not know when I have been more embarrassed.'

'I should not allow the matter to disturb you,' said Jessie, not immediately understanding what he was talking about. 'I am sure that most people did not notice that you were late for the service.'

'I was not late for the service,' he answered, speaking rather more sharply than he was wont to do when addressing her. 'You misunderstand me. I was talking about being obliged to associate with that man.'

This time, Jessie understood immediately to whom he was referring, but she could feel her temper rising and decided to make him spell it out. 'I thought you liked Mr Hinder,' she said innocently. 'If he made you late, then I am sure that he did not do so on purpose.'

'I was not late and I was not speaking about Mr Hinder,' Mr Lusty insisted, his tone definitely impatient now. 'I was talking about that . . . that degenerate!'

'I beg your pardon?' said Jessie, looking straight up at him. He had the grace to blush.

'I am only telling the truth,' he said, in a more moderate tone. 'Ashbourne is a libertine, and all of London knows it.'

Jessie was conscious of a sudden longing to defend Raff, but she bit her lip. The fact of the matter was that Henry spoke the truth. She could not allow his comment to pass unchallenged however, so in a neutral tone, she merely said, 'I would have thought that you would have been wise to keep your thoughts about his morals to yourself, at least until he has signed the document confirming your appointment to the parish of Illingham.'

He looked down on her in surprise, as if such a notion had not occurred to him. Her words clearly had some effect, however, for on their arrival in Sloane Street, he was perfectly courteous, if not affable, towards their noble visitor. For his part, Raff refrained from saying or doing anything calculated to shock or annoy the clergyman. The only time that Henry appeared tight-lipped was when the subject turned to his appointment.

It was Mrs Machin who, taking pity on Henry, asked Lord Ashbourne whether he had been approached by the bishop. The earl shook his head. 'He has not addressed one word to me, either in person or in writing.'

'I know that such is not the case, my lord,' Lusty protested, his chin up. 'The bishop has told me himself that he is waiting for your signature.'

'Then the bishop is either very forgetful or a liar,' replied Ashbourne blandly. 'I have heard nothing of the matter.'

'I would never imagine *the bishop* to be a liar,' said Lusty daringly.

Ashbourne stared at him for a long moment, those famous eyebrows of his soaring. The clergyman flushed. Then, breaking the tension, the earl turned to Jessie. 'I must certainly do something about it for your sake, my dear Jez,' he said smoothly. 'You will enjoy living in a place that has been home to you for so many years, I imagine.'

This was the issue that had kept her awake the night before last. At the time, she had not been able to think why it was so disturbing. Now, all at once a number of images flashed through her mind. She had certainly been happy living in the rectory with Lady Agatha, but how would it feel to be there with Henry Lusty instead? How would she feel to be so close to the town of Ashbourne, knowing that Raff might turn up at any time? She thought of being able to see more of Lady Ilam, which she would enjoy; but being near to Lady Ilam would mean being close to Illingham Hall, where a certain portrait of Raff, which had caused her heartache in the past, was hung. Instead of saying something polite and meaningless, she simply stared blankly at Raff, and he stared back at her, a puzzled expression on his face.

Fortunately, Henry had been distracted by another matter. 'From where does that nickname "Jez" come?' he asked disdainfully.

'You would prefer that I used her full name?' the earl enquired lazily, the long shapely fingers of his right hand turning the stem of his wine glass. He was aware of Jessie's eyes fixed upon him, willing him not to give away her secret. He grinned ruefully.

Mr Lusty would have preferred it infinitely if Lord Ashbourne never came closer to his fiancée than shouting distance over perhaps two fields. Naturally he did not say so. 'I think that Jessica is a charming name,' he said. 'I regard all abbreviations of names as a vulgarity.'

Ashbourne inclined his head. 'I must remember to tell the Prince of Wales so next time he calls me Raff,' he remarked. 'As for your fiancée, you must excuse me. I have known her for more than half her life and during all that time I have called her Jez. I am a creature of habit. You really cannot expect me to change now.'

Mr Lusty looked as if he might challenge this, but fortunately Mr Hinder asked the clergyman about another point of philosophy, and the difficult moment passed.

'If I might but borrow your copy of Rousseau, my dear Mrs Machin, I could make my point with more authority,' said Mr Hinder, his enthusiasm making him forget the need for discretion.

Lusty turned a shocked face towards his sister, but before he could make any comment she said smoothly, 'You are mistaken, Mr Hinder. I do not possess a copy of that book. You must be confusing me with another acquaintance.'

Hinder blushed. 'Yes, of course,' he agreed. 'Then, sir, pray come to my lodgings, so that I might show you what I was talking about earlier.'

While the clergyman hesitated, Lord Ashbourne said easily, 'In that case, Lusty, I will say goodbye, as I am on the point of leaving myself.'

The fear of leaving his sister and his betrothed in the company of a rake disposed of, the clergyman left, eager to pursue an argument which had not by any means been finished as they walked to church.

After Lusty and Hinder had gone, Ashbourne sat back down in his chair, crossed his legs and leaned back with the air of a man intent upon taking his ease.

'Another glass of wine?' Henrietta asked him, indicating the bottle. 'Don't worry. They'll be ages yet.'

'Thank you,' answered Ashbourne with a grin. 'If I were you, though, I'd hide that copy of Rousseau, at least until your brother's gone. Do you have anywhere to put all your other suspect reading matter? Would you like me to procure a hackney, or maybe two, and take it all away?'

Henrietta laughed. 'You are teasing me, Raff. All dangerous works are safely in my bedroom.'

Jessie sat up rather straight. When Mr Lusty had criticized Raff, she had wanted to defend the earl. Now, oddly enough, she felt obliged to speak a word for the clergyman. 'It does not become you, my lord, to criticize a man when he is not here to defend himself,' she said.

'I'm not criticizing him,' he replied reasonably. 'I'm just suggesting that Henrietta should take steps to make sure that her reading matter doesn't offend him.'

'You have no need to tell me that,' Henrietta replied frankly. 'I love my brother dearly, and have the greatest respect for him, but it is not necessary or desirable for him to know about everything that I do:

'Hence your decision not to tell him about our visit to Vauxhall, I assume.'

'Exactly so,' replied Mrs Machin, beaming at his understanding. Ashbourne looked quizzically at Jessie. 'Am I right in thinking that you disapprove?' he asked her.

She looked directly at him. 'Yes, I do,' she replied frankly.

'But not sufficiently to say that you will not go,' he observed. 'Is that not just a little hypocritical?'

She coloured. 'Yes, you are right,' she admitted. 'You may add that to all my other sins.'

Henrietta came to her rescue. 'She wanted to confess to Henry,' she said, 'but I would not let her.'

Ashbourne leaned across and took Jessie's hand. 'Sins!' he exclaimed. 'You don't know the meaning of the word. You must be one of the best people I know, Jez. Come to Vauxhall and don't belabour your conscience about it either. You may tell Henry about it when you have been married a few years. It will be one of the adventures of your youth.'

She smiled at him, and the sweetness of her expression tugged at his heartstrings.

CHAPTER TWELVE

Mr Lusty came back from Mr Hinder's lodgings a little later looking very well pleased with himself. 'The fellow does not understand what he is talking about,' he said. 'I suppose one must make allowances for the inexperience of youth, but I would be glad, my dear Henrietta, if you would try to see as little of him as possible. I do not think that the tone of his mind is suitable for the company of females.'

'That would make life a little difficult for us,' his sister protested. 'It is not proper for ladies to go about the town without a male escort. When we went to the theatre—'

'The theatre!' exclaimed Mr Lusty. Two spots of colour appeared on his cheeks. 'You have been to the theatre!'

Mrs Machin made a swift recovery. 'Certainly we have been to the theatre,' she answered, her head held high. 'It is a perfectly rational and respectable occupation. Really, Henry, anyone would think that we had been consorting with the actresses!'

Jessie was astonished to hear Henrietta squaring up to her brother so vigorously. She

180

was just as surprised when he accepted her reproof. 'I beg your pardon,' he answered. 'Of course, it must have been some improving work. No doubt, too, you left before the farce.'

'We saw Mrs Siddons,' Jessie contributed, ignoring the last part of his speech. 'Her performance was elevating in the extreme.'

'No doubt, no doubt,' agreed Lusty. 'The chief danger of the theatre, I am bound to say, is in the company in which one finds oneself rather than in the performance. It is there, I fear, that one finds oneself forced to rub shoulders with such degenerates as Lord Ashbourne.' His expression changed to one of grave disapproval. 'I do trust, Sister, that you are not encouraging him to run tame in your house. His company is unsuitable for respectable ladies.'

At this criticism, Jessie felt her hackles rising and she found herself speaking before she had had time to consider whether her words were wise. 'May I remind you, sir, that the gentleman whom you are criticizing attended church with us today? What is more, he actually managed to arrive in time to sit with us for the service. In my opinion, it ill behoves a clergyman to speak against a fellow-worshipper in this way.'

Mr Lusty stared at her, entirely bereft of speech. Henrietta spoke into the silence, saying placatingly, 'Indeed, Henry, he certainly seemed to be well acquainted with the responses, and he has an excellent singing voice for the hymns.'

Her intervention did not have the desired effect. Lusty's expression turned from baffled to furious. 'Oh, it's well known that the Devil can pipe a good tune,' he said savagely.

Jessie's backbone stiffened. 'That is enough,' she said coldly. 'If you cannot express yourself with more moderation, I have no further desire to converse with you, and I will bid you good day.' She swept from the room.

'Jessica!' exclaimed Mr Lusty. 'Come back at once!' She did not do so. He turned to look at his sister, an expression of consternation on his face.

'She will come back presently,' said Mrs Machin soothingly. 'Really, Henry, you were a little unwise, you know.'

'Unwise?'

'Why yes,' she agreed, rather enjoying the novel sensation of being the one who was offering advice rather than having to listen to it. 'Remember that she has lived with Lord Ashbourne's sister for eight years. It would indeed be a shocking thing for her to listen to her patroness's brother being maligned without saying anything.'

'Yes, but—'

'Remember, too, that your living cannot be confirmed without the earl's signature. Doubtless Jessie was thinking about safeguarding your future—yours, and hers.'

'Yes, but . . . ' Mr Lusty said again, but stopped, this time of his own accord. 'All that may be as you say, but I cannot like his being here,' he went on eventually.

'There cannot be any harm in his being here in *your* company, surely,' said Henrietta soothingly.

The clergyman's expression lightened. 'Well, if you say that he has only been here today, it is a different matter,' he said in a relieved tone.

'He might even have wanted to become a little acquainted with you,' his sister suggested, not deeming it wise to contradict his misunderstanding over the number of times that the rakish earl had visited them. 'To make sure that you are a suitable incumbent for the parish, perhaps.'

No one who knew Lord Ashbourne even very slightly could possibly indulge such a bizarre notion. Fortunately, Mr Lusty was not one of those people. 'Yes, that may be so,' agreed Lusty. His face took on an arrested expression. 'I do hope that I did not say anything to vex him.'

Mrs Machin could remember very clearly one or two infelicitous remarks that her brother had made, but she did not think that now was the moment to remind him of them. Instead she said, 'I think that you might have been a little severe in your manner, but I have often found that severity is commended in a

183

clergyman. In any case, I do not think that Lord Ashbourne would find a fawning manner at all pleasing.'

'You are very right,' he agreed in a relieved tone. 'I must remember that when I meet him again.'

He did not have the opportunity of renewing his lordship's acquaintance before his departure the following day. He did, however, make a point of seeking out his betrothed and mending matters between them.

A younger son of a minor country squire, Henry Lusty had a very small private income, but had always known that he would need to make his way in the world. A fortunate family acquaintance with the Bishop of Sheffield had meant that when the vacancy of bishop's chaplain had occurred, he had been the first choice to fill it. It had been in connection with his duties carried out for the bishop that he had first met Jessie, whilst she was companion to Lady Agatha Rayner.

Lady Agatha, the widow of the last incumbent of the parish of Illingham, had employed all kinds of methods, some of them of very dubious morality, to try to avoid vacating the vicarage. It had been Henry Lusty's unenviable task to keep calling upon her to try to carry out the bishop's wishes.

During these visits, Lusty had met Jessie. Of pleasing appearance, although not so extravagantly pretty to attract undue attention, she had impressed him both by her modest demeanour, and by her calmness in the midst of all her employer's schemes. He had always intended to marry, but knew that it would be wise to wait until a parish became available to him. The bishop had made it plain that if he managed to achieve Lady Agatha's eviction smoothly, then the living of Ilingham was as good as his. He could not doubt that to continue to live in the house that had been her home for the past eight years would be pleasing to Jessie. He would even—and here he swallowed convulsively—be prepared to have Lady Agatha to live with them if necessary, like a sort of adopted mother-in-law. He had forgotten that his marriage to Jessie would, of necessity, bring him into a closer relationship with Lord Ashbourne.

He was not well acquainted with the notorious earl, having met him for the first time shortly before Lord Ilam's wedding. He had known of Ashbourne's reputation and had been very disapproving of it. He did not expect to like the earl, but then he never expected to have to meet him. He knew, from popular rumour, that his lordship spent a large part of his time raising hell all over Europe. He had always thought that the earl would take no interest in the choice of vicar, and would leave the matter to his sister or possibly his son.

Once Ashbourne had come back to England, Lusty well understood the necessity for being courteous to him. He had simply not thought that their paths would cross. It had certainly never occurred to him that he would find his lordship escorting his sister and betrothed to church, sitting next to them—he ground his teeth—and joining them for refreshments. He found it very irksome indeed that Henrietta and Jessie should seem to be so much at ease with a man whose company he found it hard to stomach. He found it even more irksome that the moment he had ventured to make some perfectly justifiable criticism of the rakish earl, Jessie should have stalked out, for all the world as if *she* had some right to be offended. However, he told himself that he must bear in mind the close association between her and Lady Agatha. No doubt, as his sister had said, Jessie was also concerned that he should not speak intemperately and lose the chance of his first parish.

Fortunately Jessie, too, was anxious to make amends, and when he sought her out the following morning—having been unable to see her later on the Sunday because he had a dinner with some other clergymen to attend— they were both determined to forgive and forget.

'I spoke intemperately of one related to your employer, and you were right to reprove me,' he said, taking her hand. 'I must beg your pardon.'

'Your concerns were understandable,' Jessie

replied in a neutral tone. 'Indeed, Ashbourne's reputation is very bad; I cannot deny it.'

'As a clergyman, I should have remembered that there is good in everyone.'

'He has been very kind to me. I must always be grateful to him for that.'

'When was this?' asked Lusty suspiciously.

'When I was a little girl.'

'Oh. Well, I dare say we shall have nothing much to do with him when we are married. He is often abroad, is he not?'

'Yes; often. At what time does your coach go, Henry?' They said no more about the matter.

Later that evening, after the ladies had said goodbye to him in the hall, they wandered back into the drawing-room. 'You will . . . be kind to him, won't you?' Henrietta ventured after she had rung for some tea.

'Kind?' echoed Jessie, frankly puzzled.

'I know he can be very annoying at times, but he is my brother after all. I should hate to see him hurt.'

'I have no intention of hurting him,' Jessie replied, her colour rising. 'I do not know why you should suppose it.'

'I know you would never do so intentionally,' Henrietta assured her soothingly. 'Your long acquaintance with Lord Ashbourne might make him feel vulnerable, though.'

'Henrietta, I have no desire to cast stones

but really, you were the one who insisted upon inviting Raff into this house in the first place. I have to tell you that although I have known him for more than half my life, I have only ever—' she stopped abruptly. She had been about to say 'worshipped him from afar', but that would never do. Eventually she contented herself by simply adding 'met him occasionally.' That part of her life was now over. Her only feeling for Raff must be one of friendship.

Dilly brought in the tea at this point, and Mrs Machin did not speak of the subject again that evening.

CHAPTER THIRTEEN

There was something about wearing a mask, Jessie concluded, that made one feel rather strange and daring. It seemed to impart a certain glamour to the wearer. She had been conscious of that even when she had first tried hers on with her ordinary clothes. Now, as she stood in front of the glass in her room and surveyed her reflection, her mask in place, her gown—the golden one again—covered by a russet-coloured domino with a cream lining, she looked like an alluring stranger. The domino had been made for her by Miss Simms, who had recently been commissioned to do some work for a merchant's wife. The customer had purchased too much material and had carelessly told the dressmaker that she might keep what was left over. Miss Simms had therefore been able to make dominos for both Jessie and Henrietta far more inexpensively than they could have expected, had they gone to a Bond Street dressmaker.

For all she tried to tell herself that she was thirty years old, and only going out for the evening, for goodness' sake, she could not help feeling a flutter of excitement. Because of the circumstances of her upbringing, she had never had the opportunity to enjoy the kinds of treats that other girls of her station took for granted. Tonight, for instance, was the very first time that she had ever gone masked. There would have been no point in wearing masks at the kind of entertainment that she was used to attending in Illingham where she lived with Lady Agatha. Everybody there knew everybody else. This evening, they would be shoulder to shoulder with complete strangers. If there was dancing, then masquerade etiquette permitted those attending to dance without the benefit of an introduction. Needless to say, in such circumstances, mature, sensible ladies careful of their reputation would only dance with gentlemen of their own party. This strategy would only work, however, if the gentlemen of the party were of good character, and whilst one of the two matched that description, the other most decidedly did not. In that case, would the mature, sensible lady only dance with the respectable man of her party? Unfortunately, Jessie was conscious of no particular desire to dance with Mr Hinder, and she certainly ought not to want to dance with Raff.

Decidedly, Henry would not approve of this outing, Jessie thought guiltily, as she began to descend the stairs. She consoled herself with the thought that her presence was needed so that Mrs Machin could be properly chaperoned, but she knew that this was only a sop to her conscience. After all, a single woman of thirty needed a chaperon far more than did a widow of forty. I am only half single because I am engaged, she told herself. Then she felt guilty all over again because, not for the first time, she realized that she had forgotten to put on her engagement ring. She was about to go back upstairs when the door-bell rang. At first she thought that it must be Mr Hinder, then she saw that he and Mrs Machin were both waiting in the hall, looking rather unlike themselves in their masks and dominos.

As Jessie paused on the stairs, Dilly went to answer the door and Lord Ashbourne was admitted. Then, indeed, Jessie forgot all about her engagement ring and even about the engagement itself and her heart started beating rather fast. He was in a black domino, the sides of it thrown back over his shoulders to reveal a rose-pink lining. His breeches and coat were black, and his waistcoat was of white silk with pink satin stripes, to match the lining of his domino. His black hair was caught behind his head in a bow, and the silver wings at his temples gleamed in the candlelight. Unlike the two already present in the hall, he had not donned his mask, but carried it carelessly dangling from his fingers. No man has the right to be as handsome as that, she thought to herself, as she reached the hall.

Lord Ashbourne executed an elegant bow, then said, as he straightened, 'Good evening, fellow masqueraders. My carriage awaits us. Shall we go?' The carriage into which they climbed was the same one that Ashbourne had been using on the day when Jessie had been caught in the rain, and she coloured as she remembered how he had snatched away her fichu. What had he done with it, she wondered? Involuntarily, she pulled the edges of her domino closer across the neckline of her gown.

They were to go in the carriage as far as Ranelagh, and from there travel by boat to Vauxhall. 'It's possible to go all the way by carriage these days, but I thought that you would enjoy the trip on the river instead,' Ashbourne remarked.

They all made approving noises concerning the arrangements that he had made. 'I've never travelled by water before,' Jessie added, intending to sound merely informative, but finding that the effect was to make her appear rather pathetic.

'Not at all?' asked Mrs Machin incredulously. 'Not even out on a lake, or down a stream?'

'No, never,' Jessie answered. 'I have lived a very dull life, I fear.'

'Well, not this evening,' declared Henrietta.

'No, definitely not this evening,' Jessie agreed.

Lord Ashbourne had evidently taken some trouble to make sure that events ran smoothly, for when they arrived at Ranelagh, the carriage was taken away and a boat procured without his speaking a word.

Jessie was enchanted with the whole experience, and had to restrain herself from constantly moving from one side of the boat to the other, in order to see more. Ashbourne watched her with growing interest. His usual choice of female company came from the ranks of the mature and worldly wise. The inexperienced debutantes, who tried to look bored with everything, did not interest him, and were usually kept well out of his orbit by watchful mamas. Jessie was certainly of the same kind of age as those ladies with whom he usually associated. Yet her unaffected enjoyment of what, for him, was not an unusual treat, he found strangely touching. It seemed to him that it made her look younger. Life had made her age too quickly, he decided. She might be fated to live a sensible, respectable life as a parson's wife. For now, he would make sure that occasions such as this one were as enjoyable as possible.

For her own part, Jessie had made much the same kind of decision. She had the rest of her life to be sensible. Henry might not approve, but there was no need for him to learn about what was, after all, only an evening out with friends. Doubtless when they married, these kinds of entertainments would be a thing of the past, but at least she would have her memories. Before this reflection could make her melancholy, they drew near to the landing stage at Vauxhall.

The scene appeared to be chaotic in the extreme. Many sorts of craft were jostling to take their places at the side, people were shouting all kinds of remarks to one another, some good-humoured, and others less so. At one point it seemed quite likely that a nearby boatful of rather drunken bucks might end up overturned in the water. Jessie held on to her seat rather tightly, and looked to see how her companions might be affected. Mrs Machin was drinking it all in, and Jessie wondered whether this incident would figure in a future chapter. Mr Hinder was looking rather longingly at the young men in the next boat, as if he would like to be engaged with such a party. Ashbourne lounged at his ease and, as Jessie watched him, he raised one hand briefly in the direction of the landing. At once, a group of strong-looking men came striding into the water, and hauled them ashore.

Lord Ashbourne stepped out first, and turned back to help Mrs Machin, who laid a hand on his arm. 'By your leave, ma'am,' he said, and instead picked her up and carried her well on to dry land. Jessie could have burst out laughing when she saw the expression of astonishment on Mr Hinder's face. She did laugh in good and earnest when he turned back towards her, this time his expression one of utter consternation, for he was a slim, willowy young man.

'It's quite all right,' she told him. 'I would far rather get damp feet than be deposited on the ground.'

Before she could do more than take Mr Hinder's hand, however, Ashbourne came striding back. 'I'll take her,' he said to Hinder. 'You look to Mrs Machin.' After the young man had done as he was bid, the earl turned to Jessie and grinned. 'Do you trust me, Jez?' he asked her.

'Not at all,' she replied calmly, as he picked her up, causing her heart to give a little lurch. Clearly, his exquisitely cut coats must conceal some formidable muscles. She knew that at times, he had teased Ilam for having coal-heaver's shoulders. Obviously the viscount was not the only strong member of the family.

As they approached the entrance to the gardens, Jessie could see that the earl had indeed arranged everything very thoroughly, for a servant, who had been sent on ahead, gave them their tickets, and exchanged a few words with Ashbourne in a low voice.

On entering the gardens, Jessie could barely repress a gasp of delight, for at one moment they were walking down a dark passage, and at the next, they were in a magical world, illuminated with the blaze of what seemed to be hundreds of lights. A delightful vista opened up before them, with trees planted to form walks, temples, colonnades, and a grove with a pavilion in the centre, from which drifted the sounds of the orchestra. This area was populated by a good many people, chattering and laughing, all dressed in their best and masked.

'Oh Raff, it's wonderful,' Jessie breathed, squeezing his arm a little in her excitement. He looked down at her and smiled. He had been to Vauxhall more times than he could remember, and it had long ago ceased to be a place of wonder for him. As he heard the delight in her voice, he could almost see it with new eyes.

'Jessie, my dear, this is wonderful,' said Mrs Machin, echoing Jessie's own words. 'My mind is positively buzzing with ideas already.'

Mr Hinder, who had never been to Vauxhall

either, found much to take in. 'Mrs Machin, Miss Warburton, look at this!' he exclaimed.

Ashbourne, a man known throughout London as one careless of his own reputation, found himself fighting a desire to say 'sh!' like some prim governess. Instead, he contented himself with drawling, 'There is very little point in going masked if you intend to announce your identities to all and sundry. May I suggest that we use Christian names only, for the sake of discretion?'

Mr Hinder blushed at his gaffe. 'Beg pardon, my lord,' he mumbled.

'Raff,' Ashbourne reminded him. 'Now, shall we walk about a little and see the sights? We can have supper later.'

There was, indeed, plenty to see, beginning with the variety of persons present. Vauxhall was a very egalitarian place, for anyone who had two shillings to spare could enter. Fashions on display, therefore, ranged from the flamboyant to the discreet, from the wickedly expensive to the threadbare, from the up-to-the-minute to the twenty years old.

They strolled down the Grand Walk, looking their fill at all the many people who, like those at Drury Lane, seemed to be there as much to be seen as to take part in any amusement. For a time, Jessie was so entranced with the whole spectacle that she could not take anything else in. Then, gradually, she became aware of something rather curious. She had always known that he was the kind of man who attracted admiring glances from women wherever he went. Now it occurred to her that although Raff had insisted that they should go masked, plenty of people, women in particular, seemed to be aware of who he was. Whilst they were standing for a moment to look at the obelisk at the far end of the walk, for instance, two women paused briefly quite close to them.

'That's the Fallen Angel, I do believe,' one murmured. 'I suppose that must be his latest ladybird.'

'Lucky for her,' answered the other one enviously.

Their remarks were a shock to Jessie. She had known that the masks were necessary to conceal their identities. It had, of course, been almost inevitable that some would recognize Raff because he was well known. It had simply not occurred to her that anyone would mistake her for a woman of the streets because she was with him. The idea made her feel slightly grubby. She did not think that anyone else had heard, but when they began to walk again, this time turning into the Grand Cross Walk so that they might admire the statue of Handel, Ashbourne murmured, 'Come on—ladybird.'

'How dare you; I'm nothing of the sort,' she retorted under her breath, as she removed her hand abruptly from his arm.

'Better that people should think that you

are, rather than enquire about the identity of the lady I'm accompanying here,' he reminded her, taking hold of her hand once more, raising it to his lips, and kissing it lingeringly, never taking his eyes from her face whilst doing so. How good he is at playing this part, she thought to herself. No doubt it was a role he had taken on many other occasions. Briefly, this reflection took the edge off her enjoyment, until once again she was diverted by the many different sights and sounds.

After they had had their fill of strolling, and viewed the cascade, a wonderful optical illusion which created the effect of a waterfall, they made their way to the box which Lord Ashbourne had reserved and prepared to enjoy their supper.

'Good gracious look at this ham!' declared Mrs Machin when it arrived. 'One might almost see one's face through it.'

'Vauxhall is noted for the thinness of its ham,' Ashbourne told her.

'And the smallness of its chickens, no doubt,' put in Mr Hinder, who then blushed and attempted to stammer that he had not intended to criticize the generosity of his host's provision.

Ashbourne laughed. 'Pray do not give it another thought,' he said. 'The chickens are also famous for their smallness. They've even been described as being no bigger than a sparrow, so much so that one can count the amount they cost in mouthfuls.'

Mr Hinder laughed. 'You relieve me greatly, Raff,' he said.

A lady coming past the box at that moment stopped, looked at their party and narrowed her eyes. 'Good Lord, Raff, it *is* you,' she exclaimed. She was a full-figured woman of about Jessie's own age, in a very low-cut gown of crimson silk, and a black mask trimmed with crimson. 'How the deuce is it that you're in London and haven't called upon me?'

'Oh, you know how it is,' Raff murmured, lounging back in his chair and at the same time putting a proprietary arm around Jessie's shoulders. 'One gets—caught up.'

Mindful of Raff's earlier warning, Jessie made no protest at his familiarity.

'So that's the way of it,' said the woman, eyeing Jessie up and down. 'I wouldn't have thought she was your style. Let me know when you're free again.'

'If I ever am,' Raff answered, using his other hand to reach up and stroke Jessie's cheek.

As the woman left, a small party of people walked past the box. They looked very out of place, because they were unmasked, and dressed much less elaborately than everyone else. One of the party was a clergyman and, as he looked at Jessie, his face wore an expression of contempt. She had already become aware of what onlookers must think of her. Suddenly she thought of Henry. She had managed to convince herself that a visit to Vauxhall was an innocent outing. Now, the whole affair took on the guise of an underhand activity, filled with low intrigue.

'Release me at once,' she said under her breath in tones of suppressed fury.

'Of course,' he answered, smiling blandly. 'I thought that you wanted to know how a rake behaved.'

'That was Henrietta,' Jessie reminded him in the same low tone. 'I have absolutely no desire to witness your sordid activities, and even less to take part in them myself. Find some other less fastidious female to paw.'

Raff let go of her as she asked. His smile had disappeared. 'As you please,' he said indifferently. Then he added, 'Excuse me, I see someone that I must speak to.'

As he vaulted lightly over the front of the box, Mrs Machin said, 'This is wonderful. Jessie, my dear, you are playing your part splendidly!'

Jessie said nothing in response. She simply stared at Raff as he strolled with his usual grace, approaching two gentlemen accompanied by three ladies. Was that how rakes behaved, kissing and caressing one moment, and then moving on to another female? She could hardly complain if he did. She had told him to do exactly that. Deliberately she looked away from him, and found herself subjected to a searching gaze by a heavily built man in mask and domino. She looked away hurriedly, but was aware of the man approaching the box.

'I thought I couldn't be mistaken when I saw you were with Raff,' said the man in the accents of Sir Wallace Weary. 'How delightful to find you at Vauxhall.'

Jessie was on the point of telling him that he was in error when Mrs Machin said, 'Sir Wallace! Yes indeed, we are having a delightful time, as you see. Are you with a party, or are you alone, perhaps?'

Jessie was so vexed that she could have hit her. She was exceedingly vexed with Raff, but as far as their reputations were concerned, she knew that he could be trusted. She did not feel anything like the same certainty about Sir Wallace, and she could not forget how insolent he had been in the bookshop.

'I am sure that Sir Wallace must be engaged,' she said coldly. 'We must not keep him from his friends.'

Belatedly, Henrietta realized that she had been indiscreet. 'Yes . . . yes, of course, we must not keep you, sir.'

'But I cannot think of anything that I would rather be doing than conversing with you— especially when your escort has so ungallantly deserted you.' Mr Hinder cleared his throat, but beyond offering him a curt nod, Weary paid him no attention.

His reference to Raff's desertion made

Jessie look in the earl's direction. At that moment, he was whispering something in the ear of one of the three women, and making her laugh in what Jessie felt was quite an unnecessarily excessive manner.

She looked back at the baronet and smiled. 'Indeed, he is not very gallant,' she answered.

Weary's smile widened. He had, Jessie noticed, one or two discoloured teeth. 'I am thinking that it would serve him right if he were to come back and find that you were dancing with . . . somebody else.' He put out his hand.

Jessie glanced again at Raff. He was still talking to his friends, but he was now looking in the direction of the box. She stood up. 'You are very right,' she said. 'Let us go.'

She regretted it almost as soon as she had put her hand in his for his grip was hot and rather damp, and the expression in his eyes, glittering through the slits of his mask, made her feel much more lightly clad than she knew was the case. However, the deed was done, and she did have the satisfaction of seeing that Raff was no longer paying any attention to his conversation, but was watching her instead and looking rather annoyed.

Sir Wallace laughed softly. 'Well, my pretty, if you wanted to make him jealous, then you've succeeded, I think.'

Jessie did not comment upon this. She knew that Raff was not jealous, for there could not be jealousy when there was no love. He was simply irritated that his conversation with his lady friends had been interrupted. Instead, she said, 'Why are you so pleased at annoying him? I thought that you were friends.'

He laughed unpleasantly. 'Friends? In society one tolerates certain people, but friends with the Fallen Angel? Good God, no. By the way, where's that clergyman fiancé of yours?'

'He is in the country, about his duties.'

'Long may he stay there, I say.'

His mention of Henry gave her pause, and she suddenly wondered what she was doing agreeing to dance with a man whom she did not like, just because she wanted to give Raff something to think about. But it was too late to go back, for by now, they were taking their places on the floor, and soon the dance began. Although Jessie usually enjoyed dancing, treading a measure with Sir Wallace gave her no pleasure. His grip was too tight, he touched her whenever he could, whether or not the movements of the dance called for it, and some of his flirtatious remarks were much warmer than she liked. She was very glad when the dance ended, but somewhat alarmed when he appeared to want to lead her away from the floor in the opposite direction to her box. She had no doubt that his actions were quite deliberate. She did not know where the Dark Walk was to be found, but she very much

203

doubted whether Sir Wallace was similarly ignorant. It seemed to her to be just the sort of place where he would want to take her. Most fortunately, however, a group of noisy bucks pushed past them, breaking Sir Wallace's grip, and without any hesitation, she hurried off towards their box, not wasting any time looking to see if she was being pursued.

In the meantime, Raff, having said farewell to his acquaintances, was watching with some annoyance the spectacle of Jessie dancing with Sir Wallace Weary. It did not improve his temper to remember that it was through him that Jessie had actually met the baronet. Unlike Raff, Weary had absolutely no scruples about whom he despoiled. In pursuit of his own pleasures, there were very few lengths to which he would not go. To watch Jessie partnering him was, in Raff's opinion, rather like observing a gazelle at the mercy of a slavering wolf. This evening of pleasure had taken a turn that Raff really did not care for.

He was anxious to be on hand at the end of the dance, so that Weary might not take her off somewhere else; but before he could find a pillar to lounge against, he became conscious of a presence at his elbow. Turning, he saw the woman in crimson silk who had addressed him earlier.

'Raff,' she said, her tone much more hesitant than when she had addressed him before in the box.

'Katie?' answered Raff, looking at her quizzically. 'All on your own?'

When Raff had met Katie Duncomb, she had been the mistress of a youthful acquaintance of his. Recently, the young man's engagement had been announced, and Raff wondered how this had affected her.

'Yes, all on my own,' she acknowledged ruefully. 'In fact, Brook's thrown me out.'

'When?'

'Today. Well, it was really his father. He said Brook had cost him enough, and that now he was to be married, he would only continue to pay his allowance if he let me go, so guess what?' Her tone was airy, but Raff could see the desperation in her eyes.

'I trust he was suitably generous with his parting gift,' Raff responded.

'Sad how trust can so often be misplaced,' she responded. Again, she attempted an airy tone, without much success.

'Do you have somewhere to go?' he asked her quietly.

She shrugged. 'I was hoping to meet someone tonight, but I've had no success. You're obviously spoken for.'

He took out his purse and extracted several coins. 'Here,' he said, 'this should tide you over.'

'Bless you, Raff,' she replied. 'Does that ladybird of yours know how lucky she is?'

'I doubt it,' he answered as she melted away.

At the same moment, he looked up to see Jessie standing watching him from about six feet away.

He strolled across to her side, took her hand and tucked it in his arm. With one part of her mind, Jessie noticed that his grip was very different to that of Sir Wallace, cool and firm, rather than tight. With the other, she was thinking about the scene that she had just witnessed, in which Raff had given money to the woman who had made eyes at him earlier. Was this for services rendered, or in anticipation of pleasures to come?

'Let go of me,' she said angrily, attempting to pull away from him.

'Why so violent?' he asked her.

'I wish to return to Henrietta,' she said, still pulling, but with no avail, for he was holding her hand firmly, whilst keeping it tucked within his arm.

Presently,' he replied. 'First of all, you and I are going to have a little talk.'

CHAPTER FOURTEEN

Jessie looked up at him. 'A talk?' she said, uncertainly.

'If you please,' he said with exaggerated courtesy. She looked into his eyes and suddenly became aware that he was furiously

206

angry. She remembered how incensed he had looked when she had got up from the box to go with Sir Wallace. She toyed briefly with the idea of trying to pull away from him, but she had no desire to indulge in an unseemly struggle in public. Besides, as she looked round at those present she very much doubted if anyone would take any notice. They were all bent upon their own amusement, and a few were engaged in half-hearted struggles of their own. She had no desire to add to their number.

'Very wise,' Raff murmured, as if he could read her mind. 'No one would believe that you really wanted to get away from me, you know.'

She took a moment or two to take this in. 'Your conceit knows no bounds,' she exclaimed incredulously. 'Do you really think that you are irresistible to women?'

'My opinion has nothing to do with it,' he replied. 'What we are talking about is the judgement of others.'

'Meaning those women of the town with whom you were consorting, I suppose,' she said, tossing her head.

'Those among others.' He stopped and turned to face her. She looked around and saw that they had left the crowds behind and were now in a dark, tree-lined avenue. Now, you'll tell me what the deuce you were doing wandering off with Weary,' he said, his easy, good-humoured tone completely gone.

207

'I see no reason why I should,' Jessie replied, straightening her shoulders.

'You'll tell me because you're my guest and under my protection this evening,' he replied.

'When it suits you,' she added.

'And what the devil is that supposed to mean?'

'Only that your idea of protection is to paw me at will, then go off entertaining yourself with other rakes and their women.'

'For your information, they are acquaintances of mine.' Jessie laughed derisively. He caught hold of her by the arms and shook her. 'I could see them coming towards our box, and I wanted to avoid another scene like the one that had just taken place. I couldn't depend on you or the other two to refrain from blurting out each other's names in public.'

'Oh, very noble of you,' said Jessie sarcastically. 'Perhaps I should point out to you that if you were not acquainted with these women of the town, then such problems would not occur.'

'Were I not acquainted with them, I doubt whether Henrietta would have invited me to Vauxhall. Perhaps *I* should point out to *you* that it is not currently my conduct that is in question but yours.'

'Oh, is it? Then tell me what exactly I was supposed to do when Weary came wandering over to the box, and Henrietta greeted him like a long lost relation.'

He closed his eyes briefly. 'I might have guessed,' he sighed. 'If that woman has even a modicum of sense, I have yet to discover it.'

'At least her intentions are good,' she flashed.

'No doubt. Weary's, however, are anything but.'

'Which is why you should have been there,' she said in an exasperated tone.

'If I left the box to fend them off, then you only have yourself to blame. You forbade me from fending them off in another way.'

'What other way?' she asked, frankly puzzled.

'By demonstrating that I was already occupied.'

Jessie coloured, but said firmly, 'I will *not* be blamed for this. I am not the libertine here.'

'I am not the only libertine,' he reminded her. 'I seem to recall that Weary's intentions did not trouble you when you were making cow's eyes at him.'

'I was doing no such thing. I think he is a perfectly dreadful man. But then, you must know what manner of man he is. You're obviously two of a kind.'

'Don't blame me,' he replied. 'It was you who wanted to come into my milieu.'

'I didn't,' she said, struggling against his grip. 'I only wanted to go out for the evening with a party of friends. I never had any idea of involving myself with your decadent way of life. I certainly had no desire to watch you purchasing services from a woman of the streets.'

'Purchasing services?' he echoed, frowning.

'Raff, I saw you,' she responded in an exasperated tone. 'You gave her money. What else am I supposed to think?'

'Think what you please,' he answered. 'You obviously will anyway.'

'Your arrogance knows no bounds,' she declared scornfully. 'Take me back at once. When I think that you've just touched me after touching those . . . those women, it makes me want to be sick.'

'Oh, does it,' he answered grimly. 'Then let's see if I can't make you feel a little worse.' He pulled her off the Dark Walk, and there held her in the shadows with her back against a tree, her hands pinioned firmly above her head with one of his, whilst with the other he caught hold of her chin. 'You've pulled the tiger's tail with a vengeance, my dear,' he said softly. 'Now, you must face the consequences.' Then his mouth was on hers, unrelenting and hard at first, as if to punish, then coaxing and seductive.

Jessie, who had been hot with anger up until the very moment when he kissed her, now began to feel consumed with flames of quite another kind. His desertion, his accusations were all forgotten. He released her hands and

210

pulled her into his embrace. Instinctively, she struggled at first, then all the fight went out of her as his kiss demanded a response from her. From pushing at his shoulders, her hands crept around the back of his neck and returned his embrace as she allowed him to pull her closer to him. She was quite unable to resist the power of his touch; unable to stop herself from opening her mouth at the pressure of his lips and allowing him to deepen the kiss.

Eventually, he broke off. 'Jez . . . ?' he said. For a moment or two, she stared at him, until the sound of a man's low laughter nearby broke the spell. Suddenly she came to her senses. What on earth was she doing? She was engaged to Henry, but had allowed the Fallen Angel to kiss her in the Dark Walk, like any common woman of the streets. Had Raff kissed the woman in the crimson gown at Vauxhall, she wondered? Would he be kissing her again later, in exchange for the money that he had given her?

'Let go of me if you please,' she said, her voice only trembling a little.

He released her, and for a moment she felt very cold. 'Jez,' he said again.

'If you have quite finished mauling me, I would like to go back to Henrietta,' she went on as if he had not spoken. 'We will be missed.'

He caught hold of her shoulders again. 'Mauling?' he echoed incredulously. 'You cannot pretend that you did not return my

211

kiss.'

'But I would prefer to forget that it ever happened,' she told him. 'I am as disgusted at myself as I am at you.'

'I see. Then come, madam.' He offered her his arm and they returned to the box.

Henrietta was pleased to see them, but did not appear to be unduly anxious. 'I saw Lord Ashbourne waiting for you beside the dance floor, so I knew that all would be well,' she said serenely.

If only you knew, Jessie thought to herself. Oh Henrietta, I could write a whole chapter for you if it were something that I could share.

Their party stayed for a little longer. Lord Ashbourne exerted himself to please and if Jessie was a little quieter than usual, Henrietta's good spirits more than made up for it. Jessie went for a dance with Mr Hinder, and took pains to make sure that Raff—with whom she certainly did *not* want to dance— could see how much she was enjoying herself.

They did not see Sir Wallace again until they were on the point of departure. They were just walking towards the boats when a shout of laughter drew their attention. Glancing in the direction from which the laughter came, Jessie saw Sir Wallace exchanging banter with two other men. He had his arm round the waist of a young woman. So much for his interest in *my* charms, she thought to herself.

As they reached the shore, one of the boatmen came to pick Henrietta up, but Raff waved another fellow away and lifted Jessie in his arms. She looked into his face, remembering how he had kissed her, and saw that the same thoughts were going through his mind. She turned her face away, and at the same moment, caught sight of Sir Wallace and the young woman. At that moment Raff turned his head and saw the baronet.

'You see, he's found consolation already,' said Ashbourne.

'As will you, no doubt,' she retorted.

'How well you know me, dear Jez,' he replied with an unpleasant smile. They were the last words that they exchanged that evening, apart from the brief word of thanks that she offered to him as they arrived at Sloane Street.

It was a long time before Jessie was able to get to sleep that night. Why on earth had Henry's sister chanced to be living in London? she asked herself. Had she but made her home in Bath, or Harrogate or anywhere else in the world, she might have been safe from encountering Raff. She had been aware that in coming to the capital, she would risk meeting him, but she had told herself that it was a big place, in which his social activities would never coincide with those of Henrietta Machin. Perhaps they would not have done had Henrietta been the sedate clergyman's widow

213

that her brother believed her to be. Instead, once having discovered her guest's connection to the notorious rake, Henrietta had done her best to seek him out, at the expense of Jessie's peace of mind.

Jessie had always known that she would have to master her infatuation if she was to marry Henry. Since she could not do this by not seeing Raff, she had to find some other method of conquering her feelings. In trying to do this, she had veered wildly between telling herself that she could regard him just as a family friend, and vowing that she could only despise a man who was, by his own admission, a libertine.

The incidents that had taken place that evening had done nothing to dispel her confusion. Tonight was the first time that Raff had ever kissed her, apart from an occasional friendly peck on the cheek. Now that he had done so, she wondered how she would ever be able to kiss Henry without thinking of Raff. She could not even pretend that he had forced her. Her cheeks burned again as she remembered how she had wrapped her arms around his neck, and opened her mouth under his kiss so that his tongue could gain an entrance.

She could not deceive herself. Despite that kiss, Raff was no more within her reach than he had ever been. She had once overheard his sister, Lady Agatha, say that she was not the kind of pretty slut who attracted him. That evening at Vauxhall, she had had the chance to view one such pretty slut at close quarters. It was not so much that she had been pretty, more that her charms had been well on display. 'He disgusts me,' she told herself fiercely. 'Henry is worth ten of him.'

She had done wrong, but it could have been far worse. She was not yet married, after all. Perhaps it was a good thing that it had happened, for she now knew how dangerous it was for her to go anywhere near Raff. From now on she must avoid him as much as possible, for the sake of her sanity. Eventually, realizing that sleep would prove impossible for the time being, she got out of bed, put on her wrapper, lit some candles and took them over to the table in the window. Then, after mending a pen and taking out a sheet of paper she began to make a list.

Things to be done
Write a letter to Henry, confessing about going to Vauxhall
Wear my engagement ring
Go to read at the poor house
Make Henry the best wife possible

Those first few were easy. She was particularly pleased with the last one. After all, many people married for reasons other than love. She knew that Henry himself was not in

215

love with her, and at least she respected him. After she had written them down, she sat chewing the end of her pen for a long time. There were all kinds of other things that she could put down like writing to Lady Hope and Lady Agatha, darning the hole in the toe of her stockings, and calling to see Miss Simms to thank her for the work done on her gown, but she knew that she was only avoiding the real issue. In the end, after a sigh, she put pen to paper once more.

Never, ever see Raff again

She stared at this last item briefly before drawing a line through it. Then, underneath, she wrote again.

Refuse to see Raff again before my wedding

No, that would not do either. Again, she crossed out what she had written, thinking before having another try.

Not allow Raff to kiss me again

That was better, she thought decisively. After all, how could she possibly decide not to see Raff when he was Lady Agatha's brother and when Mrs Machin showed a distressing tendency to welcome him like a long lost relative? But deciding not to allow him to kiss her was a wise decision. He probably would not want to kiss her again, anyway, and she certainly did not want more kisses from such a depraved rake. He had only done it because he was annoyed with her. She could still feel his mouth on hers, firm, demanding . . . Shaking off these dangerous thoughts, she took up her list again. After another long pause, eventually she wrote down her final item.

Keep out of the way of Sir Wallace Weary

This was also a wise decision. Having exhausted the possibilities for her list, Jessie put down her pen and taking up her candles, went to sit next to the empty fireplace in order to read the book that Lady Ilam had given her. She opened the copy of *A Vindication of the Rights of Woman* and smiled bitterly as she read these words:

Till women are led to exercise their understandings, they should not be satirized for their attachment to rakes; nor even for being rakes at heart, when it appears to be the inevitable consequence of their education. They who live to please—must find their enjoyments, their happiness, in pleasure!

Jessie sighed. At least, it seemed, Miss

217

Wollstonecraft would not blame her for having had a weakness for a rake; but she would have to take issue with the rest of the sentence. Her life had certainly been one of attempting to please others and when she had attempted to take pleasure for herself, she had only ended up feeling guilty.

Eventually, she did drop off to sleep after reading a few more pages. She was glad that Mrs Machin did not insist upon early rising, for the sun was well up before she stirred, and even then, when she got downstairs, she found that the other lady was still abed. Her meal concluded, she went upstairs again to examine her list in the clear light of day.

The first resolution she discounted immediately. There would be absolutely no purpose served in making such a confession. It would only make Henry angry over something that he could not do anything about. As for the second, it was all very well to resolve to wear her ring. The problem was, there were some places where it would not be suitable to risk its loss—at the poor house, for example. How shocking it would be if she mislaid it. Then she would indeed have something to confess!

The third item on the list—visiting the poor house—she would do that very day. It would serve as an act of penance. The items on the list that concerned Raff, and the one concerning Wallace Weary, she would look at another time. For the present, she would occupy the rest of the morning with writing to Henry. That would be a good preparation for her fourth resolution. Then, after luncheon, she would go to the poor house, unless Mrs Machin wanted her company for a walk, or to go shopping.

When Henrietta did eventually emerge, however, it seemed that going out was the last thing she wanted to do. Her mind was positively seething with ideas after the previous night's experience and she desired nothing more than an afternoon's solitude in which to write down all her impressions.

'Do you mind if I take Dilly with me?' Jessie asked. 'I think Mr Hinder said that he would be from home this afternoon.'

'Take her by all means,' replied Mrs Machin, in rather abstracted tones. 'And now, I must get on with my work.'

For going to the poor house, Jessie went upstairs to change into one of her plainest gowns. She was coming down the stairs tying the strings of her bonnet when the door-bell rang, and Dilly came into the hall and opened the door to admit Raff. He was in a dark-blue coat with buff breeches and waistcoat and shiny black boots, and all at once he made Jessie feel quite shabby.

'Good afternoon, Jez,' he said, executing an elegant bow. 'I've come to call on you, but I see you are going out.'

'I am,' Jessie agreed, 'and I do not advise

219

your interrupting Mrs Machin at the moment. She is wrestling with her muse.'

'Then I will leave her in peace. Where are you going? You shouldn't go out alone, as I've told you before. London is full of unsavoury characters.'

'Yes, so I have discovered,' she answered staring pointedly at him, which gaze he returned with a bland expression. 'Dilly is going with me, so I am not going alone,' she continued, annoyed with herself for blushing. 'I am going to the poor house.'

'Thrown out already?' he said in sympathetic tones. 'Shall I plead with Henrietta on your behalf?'

She had to smile at this, even though her feelings towards him were in turmoil. 'No, I am going to read with the children,' she replied.

'Then let us go,' he responded. 'Leave Dilly at home. I will be your escort instead.' She stared at him for a moment or two. 'Any objections?' he asked, his brows soaring.

'You are always telling me that I shouldn't be seen with you,' Jessie pointed out.

'Yes, but I need to talk to you.'

'All right,' she said after a moment or two. 'It will at any rate give you the opportunity to apologize.'

'Apologize?' he asked, raising his brows again.

Then, a moment or two later, he added, 'As

a matter of fact, I *was* going to apologize, but I don't like being told to do so. Are you quite ready? Shall we go?'

They set off walking along Sloane Street in the direction of Knightsbridge. Ashbourne offered his arm, and after a moment or two's hesitation, Jessie took it. 'It's all right,' he told her. 'I don't bite.'

'Don't you?' she replied dubiously.

'Very well, I apologize,' he said wearily. 'Will that do?'

'I don't know,' she answered him candidly. 'I'm not at all sure what you are apologizing for, you see.'

They both halted, and for a moment, they locked gazes as he looked down at her and she looked up at him. 'Neither am I,' he said, both his tone and his expression utterly serious. As she looked into his eyes, it was if she was transported back to Vauxhall, to that moment in the Dark Walk when he had kissed her. She remembered the feel of his mouth covering hers and she knew that her face was flaming. They walked on for some time in silence.

Then, in a different tone he went on, 'With regard to Wallace Weary—'

She cut him off. 'Shall we consider the matter closed?' she said. 'You made it quite clear last night that you are not prepared to hear my criticisms of your life. You therefore have no right to tell me what I should do in mine.'

221

'The two cases are not the same,' he replied. 'You are a complete innocent. You have no idea of what the likes of Wallace Weary are capable; whereas I—'

'Whereas you know all too well, since there is very little to choose between you,' she interrupted. 'May I remind you that it was you who walked off and left me completely at his mercy?'

Two red spots of colour appeared on his cheekbones. 'I had not realized that your entire party would be so utterly lacking in sense,' he responded. 'Conducting a party from Bedlam would have been easier. Would to God I'd never agreed to take you there.'

'In case you had forgotten, it was not my choice, was it? It was Henrietta's idea to invite you.'

'I suppose you would have preferred it, then, if you had had Wallace Weary's escort instead.'

'Infinitely,' she answered with vigour, if not with complete truth. 'At least he did not drag me in amongst the bushes and force his embraces upon me.'

He laughed shortly. 'Force? Is that how you remember it? I seem to recall that you were a willing participant.'

'How dare you!' she exclaimed, all the more angry because she knew that he was right.

'The truth hurts, does it? Well here's another fact. The only reason that Weary did not drag you into the bushes was lack of opportunity. No doubt you would have been quite happy to receive such attentions at his hands. How would you have responded to his kisses, my lovely Jezebel?'

She stared at him. 'You're disgusting,' she said. 'A rake, a libertine, who pays women to ... to ...'

'At least I'm not engaged to a clergyman who is conveniently away in Derbyshire,' he retorted.

The fact that she had been belabouring her conscience with this very matter did not improve her temper. 'How can you bring Henry into this?' she demanded. 'Henry is worth ten of you—twenty!'

'Of course he is,' Ashbourne answered. 'What is that to the purpose?'

'Why nothing,' she answered, trying to think of the most hurtful thing that she could say. 'I suppose what I mean is that although being with a well-known rake is diverting in a way, a woman looks for someone of greater substance in the man she marries.' She paused. 'I've outgrown you, Raff. Pray do not put yourself out any further on my account. I would much prefer it if you stayed away from me completely. I will give your excuses to Henrietta. Doubtless she will understand that infidelity in any kind of relationship is one of the hallmarks of a rake.'

They had just reached the entrance of the

poor house. Ashbourne bowed, with his usual elegance. His face was chalk white. 'Very well, ma'am. It shall be as you say,' he responded. 'Don't be afraid that I will trouble you any further.' He touched his hat and walked away. She stood and watched him until he went out of sight.

CHAPTER FIFTEEN

Jessie had not thought that the day could possibly get any worse, but she was proved to be wrong when she returned home in a hackney, procured for her by the matron, to be told by Dilly that a gentleman had come to visit them. Jessie's first thought was that it might be Raff, come to make up their differences, and her heart gave a little skip. Then she recalled that Dilly knew Raff, and would hardly refer to him just as a gentleman. It could not possibly be Henry or Mr Hinder for the same reason.

'Has he been here long?' Jessie asked, when she had established that Dilly had no idea of the gentleman's name.

'Only just come, miss,' Dilly replied.

Jessie went upstairs, took off her outside garments and smoothed her hair, then came back to join Henrietta in the drawing-room.

'So you see, that is why we were at Vauxhall;

so that I might conduct further research,' said Hettie's voice.

'My dear ma'am, I understand completely. How very ingenious of you.' Jessie was conscious of a slow, creeping sensation of dread as she heard the rather nasal accents of Sir Wallace Weary. What was more, it sounded as though Mrs Machin had been so indiscreet as to confide in the baronet with regard to her novel writing. She took a deep breath and opened the door.

Sir Wallace looked up at her entrance, and got to his feet, a wide smile spreading across his features. 'Miss Warburton, how delightful to see you,' he said. 'Mrs Machin told me that you had gone out, so I did not dare hope for this pleasure.'

'Indeed,' Jessie replied in frosty accents. 'Henrietta, is the tea fresh, or shall I ring for more?'

'Please do ring,' Mrs Machin replied. 'Sir Wallace, you will stay for another cup?'

'I should be glad to do so, but I fear that my presence is not welcome to Miss Warburton.'

If he had decided on a direct approach, thought Jessie, then she too could be similarly frank. 'I cannot imagine how you could ever suppose that it would be, sir, after your insinuations of the other night.'

'Insinuations!' exclaimed Henrietta. Jessie was not sure whether she was on the point of asking him to leave, or of demanding that he repeat his remarks so that she could use them for her book.

Sir Wallace looked abashed. 'I fear that I rather over-indulged in arrack punch,' he confessed. 'I am glad of the opportunity to admit that I did not act like a gentleman and to apologize for it.'

'Had you also over-indulged in arrack punch when we met you in the bookshop?' Jessie asked, opening her eyes wide.

'No,' he admitted, 'but I was with Ashbourne. He always brings out the worst in me, I fear. I would be very grateful, ladies, if you would forget my past misdemeanours, and allow me to make a new start.'

Despite her quarrel with Ashbourne, Jessie immediately found her hackles rising at this implied criticism. Henrietta did not seem to be similarly affected, however, and she said immediately, 'I am sure that we would be less than Christian if we did anything else.'

Sir Wallace stayed for half an hour and during that time, took another cup of tea and exerted himself to please. Jessie did not completely let her guard down, but his cheerful good humour made a welcome change to her recent angry exchanges with Raff.

Before he left, he invited them to go with him for a drive in Hyde Park. 'Such an outing will be an opportunity for me to make up for my past sins,' he told them.

'I am afraid that our arrangements are a little uncertain,' said Jessie, still not convinced of the man's sincerity.

Henrietta appeared to have no such doubts. 'My friend is thinking of evening outings,' she said. 'During the day, however, we can easily make arrangements to join you.'

'Splendid,' declared Sir Wallace. 'Shall we say tomorrow, if it is fine?' The ladies agreed, one with enthusiasm, the other with barely concealed reluctance, and soon afterwards he took his leave.

The moment the front door had closed behind him, Jessie exclaimed, 'Hettie! That dreadful man! What upon earth can have possessed you?'

'Do you think he is so very dreadful?' Henrietta asked, wrinkling her brow. 'He has always seemed perfectly civil to me.'

'Well he has not been to me,' Jessie replied frankly. 'In fact, at Vauxhall he was vulgar and insinuating.'

'But he has explained that, dear. He had too much to drink. I have never had a relative inclined to that sort of habit, but I am told that it can have a shocking effect upon the most proper person.'

'It certainly can,' agreed Jessie with feeling, thinking not just about Sir Wallace but about Squire Warburton.

'There you are then,' replied Henrietta. 'Anyway, we are only going out with him for a drive. What could be more harmless than that? He will not have had a chance to get drunk then, surely?'

'No, perhaps not. But you are forgetting that he was just as bad when we met him in the bookshop. I don't trust him, Hettie.'

'Well, of course, I do not trust him either. You must not think me completely naïve. I intend to make very good use of him.'

'For your book?'

'For my book. He will be another rake to observe, besides Raff.'

Jessie remembered rather guiltily that she had told Raff not to come again, and thus had cut off one of Henrietta's sources of information. 'I suppose a drive in Hyde Park would not do any real harm,' she said slowly.

'Exactly what I have been saying all along,' Hettie pointed out.

'You must be very discreet about what you disclose to him, though,' Jessie warned her. 'I would give something to find out how he discovered our address, for instance.'

'Perhaps through the bookshop,' Hettie suggested. 'Anyway, let us leave that subject, for there is another matter that I want you to help me with.'

'Something else to do with your book?'

Hettie nodded. 'I have decided that I need to find out about brothels.'

Jessie was glad that she had finished her cup of tea, or she would certainly have choked.

'Brothels?' she exclaimed.

'My heroine is to visit one in search of a gentleman who has wronged her,' Henrietta answered. 'So I have decided that we ought to go to one in disguise.'

'Surely you do not intend us to go inside?' said Jessie, much shocked.

'Certainly not,' Henrietta replied. 'All we need do is to sit outside in a closed carriage and watch as people go in and out. It will give me an idea of how many people attend, what the women look like, at what times they are busy, and so on. If we are lucky, someone might even leave the door open for long enough for us to see inside.'

'What if we are spotted?' Jessie asked. 'Not that I have agreed to go, you understand.'

'We will go heavily veiled. We may even wear masks if you wish. Of course,' she mused in a thoughtful tone, 'One could always slip inside if one were masked, for just a little minute. Oh do, please, say you will go, Jessie. It would mean such a lot to me.'

'I will think about it,' said Jessie. 'But you may dismiss that idea about ever setting foot in such a place immediately. What's more, you must promise me that you will not mention the matter to anyone else and certainly not to Sir Wallace. Heaven knows what he would make of that.'

'Of course, dear,' replied Hettie, her eyes on her sewing.

Jessie awoke the following morning having had second thoughts about their outing with Sir Wallace. So uneasy did she feel that she decided to say that she would not go. She felt a little guilty because this would mean that Henrietta would not be able to go either. She would no doubt be disappointed, but it could not be helped.

Having made this decision, Jessie went downstairs for breakfast and steeled herself to give her friend the bad news. As is often the case when such a decision has been made she found that she had to wait to disclose it because Mrs Machin had not yet come downstairs. Jessie was very much afraid that she might be taking special trouble with her appearance. When that lady did appear, however, she looked as disturbed as her guest.

As soon as Dilly had left them alone, Henrietta said, 'Jessie, my dear I have been thinking about what you said yesterday and I have come to the conclusion that perhaps we ought not to go out with Sir Wallace.' Much relieved, Jessie was about to agree when the other lady held her hand up. 'You may say that I am imagining things, but I am convinced that Raff did not approve of him. I do not think we ought to associate with a man of whom Raff does not approve.'

'Really?' said Jessie, remembering the conversation that she had had with Raff in the street the day before. 'And when did Raff become the arbiter of our decisions?'

'Well, I . . . ' murmured Mrs Machin.

'Sir Wallace is no more a rake than Raff; probably less so,' said Jessie forthrightly. 'In fact, if Raff does not approve of something, then that probably means that it is perfectly all right.'

Mrs Machin opened her mouth to speak, but before she could say anything, Dilly came in with the post. Among other items, there was a letter for Jessie from Henry.

Since returning home, I have been thinking about the conversation that we had before I left. I am not sure that I made it clear to you exactly where I stand upon various issues.

Naturally, I would not dream of expecting you to renounce old friends and acquaintances completely. That would be discourteous, and I cannot imagine you being anything other than the model of courtesy. As your promised husband, however, I must advise you to put some distance between yourself and Lord Ashbourne. He is a man of bad reputation and contact with him and his associates cannot help but damage your own good name as the fiancée of a clergyman and, by

231

association, must damage my own reputation too.

For this reason, I think I must advise against further outings to the theatre, or, indeed, to any other place of public entertainment until I should be available to accompany you. The company is too mixed at such places for me to be easy about your attendance.

She stared at the letter, completely non-plussed. She was thirty years of age, and Lusty really could not expect to dictate to her where she should go or with whom she could and could not associate.

'Is Henry well, dear?' asked Henrietta, looking up from her own correspondence.

'He doesn't say. He seems far more concerned with what I may be doing,' answered Jessie, throwing her letter down. 'Really, if people stopped trying to treat me like a silly chit of seventeen, I should be a good deal happier.'

Mrs Machin laid down her own letter with a small sigh. 'Oh dear, I suppose we had better not go out with Sir Wallace Weary, then.'

Jessie stared at her for a few moments. 'I see no reason why we should not do so,' she replied assertively. 'We talked about it yesterday. There is no danger in driving with a man in public in the middle of the day.'

'No, of course not,' Henrietta replied in a

more confident tone. 'We will go, then, as arranged.'

After all their heart searching, the outing itself was something of an anti-climax. Sir Wallace arrived punctually, and was dressed in buckskin breeches and a green cloth coat with an embroidered waistcoat. His clothes might not fit as well as did Raff's, but he looked like a gentleman, and his behaviour matched his appearance. He greeted them politely, and helped them up into his phaeton without making any attempt to employ such stratagems as holding hands for longer than necessary or surreptitiously attempting to fondle any other part of their anatomy.

Jessie found herself in the middle, which meant that she was pressed up against Henrietta on one side and the baronet on the other. It was not the place that she would have chosen, but Sir Wallace, although he must have been just as aware of their proximity as was she, showed no tendency to take advantage of the situation.

They encountered a number of different people in the park, some of whom, remembering meeting Jessie and Henrietta at church, were good enough to acknowledge them. The only person of whom Jessie was conscious, however, was Raff. He was mounted on the back of a magnificent bay stallion, and the moment that she saw him, it was as if there was no one else in the park.

233

Then seconds later, she realized that he was accompanying Lady Gilchrist, who was riding a dainty grey mare. Deciding that the earl should be left in no doubt that she was enjoying herself, Jessie started to pay closer attention to her own escort. She was not jealous, she told herself. She just did not want Raff to think that the presence of Lady Gilchrist bothered her.

'Your cavalier from the other night has deserted you,' commented Sir Wallace.

'He has been acquainted with Lady Gilchrist for some time,' Jessie answered in a matter-of-fact tone.

'Yes, their relationship goes back for many years,' Weary agreed. 'Of course he and Sir Philip enjoyed a friendship in which they shared many interests.'

'Indeed,' replied Henrietta interestedly. Jessie could not think what to say. The implications of the baronet's words were shocking indeed, but taken on the surface, they could have been taken to refer simply to Sir Philip and Lord Ashbourne's enthusiasm for items of antiquity.

'Oh certainly,' answered Sir Wallace. 'In view of their intimate relationship, I would not be at all surprised if in due course of time, the Angel and Penelope made a match of it. He does not need to worry about fathering an heir after all.'

Henrietta made some response, and Sir

Wallace gave her words half his attention, whilst he kept an eye on Jessie, a faint smile on his face. For her part, Jessie tried to look around the park as if she did not have a care in the world. Lady Agatha had often referred to her brother in derogatory terms and Jessie, in order to protect herself, had perfected the art of hiding her feelings. In fact, she had suffered something of a shock, for it was the first time that she had ever considered that others might be expecting Ashbourne to marry Lady Gilchrist.

This was only the first of several outings that they enjoyed with Sir Wallace Weary. Very much on her guard at first, Jessie soon found that the baronet was capable of impeccable behaviour. In his company they drove in Hyde Park more than once, visited the Tower of London, and viewed an exhibition of paintings. He never attempted to separate her from Mrs Machin, and confined his conversation to subjects that would be pleasing to ladies. Despite her suspicions, Jessie eventually came to believe his original explanation; that he had been affected by drink and had not been fully in control of himself. Taking everything into account, however, she did not really care for the man.

They had heard nothing from Raff, and Jessie found that she missed him. Now that her anger had waned, she could only think of their angry parting with regret. She would have liked to mend matters, but could not think how. Sending for him was out of the question. After all, she had her pride, and besides, not to see him really was far better for her peace of mind.

Raff had been acutely aware of Sir Wallace bowling along in Hyde Park with Mrs Machin and Jessie sitting beside him in his phaeton. They had appeared to be a little squashed, but none of them seemed to mind. Sir Wallace, who had been sitting next to Jessie, had looked very pleased with the whole state of affairs.

'Should we not pay our respects?' Lady Gilchrist had asked him. He had made a habit of taking her about regularly since their return to London, and had had the satisfaction of seeing her spirits slowly improve.

'I think not,' he answered with a sneer. 'They look to be very well entertained. I should hate to spoil sport.' In reality, he could not endure the idea of Jessie staring at him coldly after giving all her smiles to Weary. Soon after this, he escorted Penelope home, returned his horse to his stables, and went for a walk to clear his head.

He walked for some time before finally wandering into a coffee shop where he was not well known. He found a secluded seat at the back of the premises where he could order refreshment and think for a time undisturbed.

He frowned in puzzlement. Why was he so bothered? What did it matter if Jez had a little

236

fling with Sir Wallace Weary? Her reputation was not really any of his concern. Yet if he did not concern himself, who would? Henry was away dancing attention on the bishop, when he should have been by her side. Mrs Machin's overactive imagination drove her to leave caution to the winds when she was in pursuit of a story. Hinder was too young and immature to be aware of the dangers of city life. It had been left to him, one of London's notorious rakes, to make sure that Jessie did not ruin herself. What a mull he had made of that!

He thought about the evening when they had attended Vauxhall. Jez's eyes had glittered through the slits of her mask, the movement of her head and her posture speaking of her delight and wonderment in the whole spectacle. The understated elegance of her gold gown with the russet domino, her only jewellery a golden locket containing a picture of her mother, had thrown the over-trimmed appearance of some of the other females present into sharp relief. He recalled how he had impressed upon his party the need for discretion; then, in order to maintain this, he had behaved towards Jez as though she was his latest flirt. She hadn't liked it; he could see it in her eyes. That had surprised him a little. After he had stroked her cheek, for instance, she had looked at him as if she were really disgusted with him, and that had taken him aback. They had exchanged angry words and rather than argue with her, he had left their box. When he had turned round from a conversation with the former mistress of an acquaintance and two of her friends, he had seen her getting up to dance with Sir Wallace Weary.

His temper had been aroused at that. He had waited for them by the dance floor and, as he had watched them, he had worked out exactly what kind of conversation must be taking place. Jez was uncomfortable and embarrassed, and Weary was leering over her like some lecherous satyr from an old tale of the gods. Then before he had been able to rescue her from that situation, she had escaped on her own, and spotted him giving money to Katie. Of course, she had misinterpreted the situation, and he had been too proud to explain. What he should have done then, was to take her straight back to their box. That was what any decent gentleman would have done. Instead, he had marched her in the opposite direction, picked a quarrel, and forced his attentions on her.

In a flash of self-knowledge it occurred to him that he was no better than the other man. How would he have felt if it had been Jez who had been struggling in Sir Wallace's embrace? His hand curved into a fist. Now, thanks to his loss of temper, he had thrown her into Sir Wallace's way, and he only had himself to blame.

CHAPTER SIXTEEN

After Henrietta and Jessie had been on several outings with Sir Wallace, he suggested taking them to the Cumberland tea gardens. 'It's a pretty enough place, and we can stroll about in the fresh air before enjoying a cup of tea,' he told them. When the baronet arrived that afternoon to collect them in his barouche, they were both looking their best. Henrietta was in a new walking gown of a warm brown shade which Miss Simms had made for her. Jessie was in a gown of leaf green with a bonnet with matching ribbons, and Sir Wallace widened his eyes appreciatively.

The gardens were only about an acre and a half in extent, and were situated on the south bank of the Thames, not very far from Vauxhall. 'People sometimes combine a visit to the two,' said Sir Wallace, 'often adjourning here for refreshments when they have tired of the larger garden.'

'This is delightful,' said Mrs Machin as she allowed Sir Wallace to help her down. 'Thank you so much for bringing us.' She stood looking around whilst their escort helped Jessie to alight.

'The pleasure is all mine,' replied the

baronet, his eyes on Jessie's face. She looked up at him, startled, for it seemed to her that for a moment, she had glimpsed that same lascivious expression that had been in his eyes when he had danced with her at Vauxhall. In an instant, it was replaced by one of polite deference as he released her hand, then offered an arm to each lady. 'Shall we walk about a little before we go for tea?' he asked them. Both ladies concurred, and Jessie began to wonder whether she had imagined what she had seen.

*   *   *

'How very kind you have been to me,' said Lady Gilchrist, as Ashbourne helped her down from his curricle.

As Sir Wallace had done, the earl said, 'The pleasure is all mine.'

'I feel so foolish,' said her ladyship, who was still dressed correctly and very becomingly in black. 'I felt sure that I would have started to feel better now, but silly little things upset me. I was able to supervise all the clearing of Philip's things without a qualm, but when cook served his favourite pudding at dinner two nights ago, I found myself in tears.'

'That's quite usual, I believe,' answered Ashbourne, patting the hand that was tucked into his arm. 'By the way, that bowl which you gave me from Philip's collection looks

240

outstanding in the library in Berkeley Square. You must come and see it.'

'I would be glad to,' she replied, smiling up at him. Her expression and the answering smile he bestowed upon her were purely signs of the deep friendship that loss and a shared task had nourished between them.

Jessie saw the couple before either of them saw her. She witnessed the moment that the earl patted her ladyship's hand, and noticed the exchange of smiles. She remembered how Sir Wallace had said that they might soon marry. Suddenly, she began to pay more attention to the baronet, listening to a mildly amusing story that he was telling about a recent London function that had been spoiled by rain. When he came to a conclusion, she laughed a little more enthusiastically than the story warranted, and he smiled down at her. It was at this moment that Ashbourne and Lady Gilchrist drew close to the other group.

The only two people who did not know each other were Lady Gilchrist and Mrs Machin, and once this introduction had been performed, everyone professed themselves delighted at this unexpected meeting. Probably Mrs Machin was the only one who was sincere in this profession.

'We have a fine day for our outing,' said Ashbourne. 'Why do we not all take tea together?'

'By all means,' replied Sir Wallace, 'So long

241

as you do not attempt to lure either of these charming ladies away from me, Ashbourne. I warn you, I don't intend to give either up without a fight.'

'I wouldn't dream of depriving you,' answered the earl politely. 'Nor do I mean to relinquish Penelope.'

'But for my part, I would like to walk a little way with Miss Warburton,' Lady Gilchrist put in. 'It is no use the two of you squaring up to one another like turkey cocks. We ladies can decide for ourselves, can we not, Miss Warburton?'

'We can indeed,' replied Jessie. She was not sure that she wanted to walk with the lady who she was certain had at one time been Ashbourne's mistress, and now might be on the point of getting engaged to him. On the other hand, she did not want to be regarded as Sir Wallace's property either.

'I have been wanting to thank you for your kind letter of condolence,' said her ladyship after the company had rearranged themselves with the two ladies walking ahead, and Mrs Machin bringing up the rear between the two gentlemen and looking like the cat that had got the cream.

'It was a trifle late, I fear,' Jessie replied. It was only after Lady Gilchrist had left for the Continent that she had heard the news of Sir Philip's death.

'It was a very kind gesture,' her ladyship told

242

her. 'It is at such times that one discovers one's real friends—like Raff, for instance.'

'Really,' Jessie replied politely. 'What a fine show those roses make, do they not?'

'Very fine,' Lady Gilchrist agreed. 'Miss Warburton, I have known you for some years. You have known Raff for longer than I, and, I believe, also consider him to be a friend. Do not, I beg of you, assume that you can view Wallace Weary in the same light. The world may put them in the same boat, but they are cast from a very different mould, I assure you.'

'Thank you for your views,' said Jessie tightly. 'I will bear them in mind.'

'I have annoyed you,' said Lady Gilchrist in a resigned tone. 'I feared it would be so, but I could not reconcile it with my conscience not to warn you about Sir Wallace. I know you are not experienced in London ways—'

'Yes, thank you,' Jessie interrupted. 'I may not be experienced, but I am not a complete idiot either. Tell me, are you going back to the north country soon?'

Judging that she had done her best and could not say any more, Lady Gilchrist allowed Jessie to change the subject, and by the time they all sat down for tea, the two ladies were rather stiltedly discussing contrasts between the countryside surrounding London and the Yorkshire scene.

Everyone around the tea table was on their best behaviour; but their party could not have been described as convivial, much less comfortable. Sir Wallace seemed determined to behave towards Jessie with a proprietary air, particularly when he sensed that Lord Ashbourne's attention was upon them. For his part, the earl was at his most suave, lounging at his ease, smiling his practised society smile, treating everyone at the table with distant courtesy, but reserving most of his attention for Lady Gilchrist. Mrs Machin alone was in very good spirits, talking and sharing ideas with everyone present.

The party soon broke up after they had had tea, and Lord Ashbourne escorted Lady Gilchrist back to his curricle. 'An unexpected encounter,' murmured her ladyship, after the earl had taken his place next to her. 'Why do I get the impression that it gave you no pleasure?'

'I have no idea,' he replied. 'Perhaps because the company of Weary is not to my taste.'

'Or perhaps because the way in which he was monopolizing Miss Warburton was not to your taste either.'

He smiled. 'Now how can you imagine that that would concern me when I only have eyes for you,' he said urbanely.

'You may abandon that suave manner,' said Lady Gilchrist calmly. 'I could see that you did not like the attention that he was paying her.'

'I have known her for many years,' he

answered in an even tone. 'I don't like to see her being taken in.'

'Keep telling yourself that, and you might convince yourself that that is the whole truth of the matter,' she answered conversationally.

'My dear, if you are going to become so cryptic in your pronouncements, I shall have to hire an interpreter,' he said smoothly.

'Then let me elucidate,' she answered. 'That young woman has been in love with you for as long as I can remember. It would be a tragedy if you should fail to snap her up because you are not prepared to acknowledge that *you* are falling in love with *her.*' At that, Ashbourne dropped his hands in surprise, and had to give all his attention to his horses in order to get them back under control. Her ladyship kindly asked his pardon for startling him. 'Since Philip's death I have begun saying things when the opportunity occurs, for fear I may not get another chance,' she explained.

'How many heart attacks have you caused so far?' he asked her. She laughed, and soon they were talking of other things, but it must be acknowledged that Ashbourne gave their conversation only half his attention.

Could he be falling in love with Jez? The question occupied his mind as he drove away from Lady Gilchrist's house. On one level, the question seemed utterly absurd. Of any man in London, surely he could not be the one upon whom love could creep up unsuspected!

Doubtless many who knew him would suppose that he had been in love many times. He could have enlightened them: in fact, he had only ever been in love once, and that had been with Dora Whitton, the mother of Michael, his illegitimate son.

Since first meeting Jez, he had kept a benevolent if distant eye upon her, ever since he had found her crying over her broken figurine, but he had never pursued her. If pressed to describe his feeling for her, he would probably have called it affection.

Everything had changed with her arrival in London. This had brought about a closer relationship with her than he had experienced before, whilst he sought to guard her from scandal in a world which he knew well and she did not. Despite the fact that she was thirty years old, she was still such an innocent!

He was not accustomed to worrying about another person in this kind of way. His upbringing had taught him that the best way to survive was to think of his own needs, and to use his undoubted charm and good looks to get what he wanted. There were very few people of whom he was really fond. If you didn't become attached to people, then they couldn't hurt you.

The trouble was that because of their argument, he and Jez had become estranged, she had obviously transferred her interest from himself to Wallace Weary and something deep inside him was hurting most damnably.

*   *   *

'Have you decided whether to go with me to observe a brothel?' asked Mrs Machin the following morning. 'My novel is at a crisis point, and a visit to a brothel might just fit the bill.'

'Can you not simply use your imagination?' Jessie asked.

'My imagination is for conjuring up the characters and the situations in which they find themselves,' was the reply. 'For the actual settings, I need real experience.'

After a few minutes thought, Jessie shook her head regretfully. 'I cannot agree to it,' she said. 'The very idea offends. Besides, what if Henry were to hear about it? A visit to the theatre and even an outing to Vauxhall could be explained away. An outing to a brothel would be quite another thing.'

'I will just have to think of another way round it,' said Henrietta thoughtfully. 'In the meantime, I still have plenty of other material to keep me going. I have just thought of some splendid lines to add to my Vauxhall scene. How do you think it might work if my heroine, the lady rake, meets a rakish gentleman there?'

'I would think that sparks might fly,' said Jessie honestly, remembering her own experience. 'If you are going to write, then I think that I will pay a visit to Miss Simms. I have neglected her recently.'

Miss Simms was very pleased to see Jessie, but apologetic as well. 'I have two gowns to finish, and must not delay,' she said. 'They are for the twin daughters of a wealthy merchant, and they celebrate their birthday at the weekend.'

'Then let me help you,' said Jessie at once. 'What can I do?'

In no time, the two ladies were busily at work, Jessie securing some of the hems that had already been pinned with tiny stitches. For a time, they worked in silence, then eventually Miss Simms said, 'How did your visit to Vauxhall go? Did you enjoy it?'

Jessie put some of the more disturbing memories of the night to the back of her mind. 'Yes, it was very different from anything else that I have ever experienced.'

'Who was of your party?'

'Mrs Machin and myself, of course. We were escorted by Mr Hinder and Lord Ashbourne.'

Miss Simms dropped her scissors. 'Ashbourne?' she echoed.

'He is the brother of Lady Agatha Rayner, with whom I normally reside.' After a short pause Jessie added, 'I can see that you are shocked. I expect you know that he is a rake; but truly, he has always been very kind to me.' She added this last comment a little wistfully.

It seemed a long time since she and Raff had had the chance just to talk and laugh together.

'I have nothing against Lord Ashbourne,' Miss Simms answered. 'Indeed, I do not think that I have ever met him. It is the set that he runs with that concerns me.'

After a short silence, seeking to change the subject, Jessie added, 'The music was delightful.'

'I am very fond of music but seldom have the chance to hear it,' Miss Simms admitted. 'Did you dance?'

'Yes I did; with Sir Wallace Weary.'

This time Miss Simms dropped a whole tinful of pins, and the next few minutes were spent in picking them up. As they both bent to gather up the pins, she wondered whether she dared ask the dressmaker for the reasons for her agitation. Before she needed to do such a thing, the other woman spoke. 'Do not involve yourself with Sir Wallace Weary, I implore you,' she said, her voice not quite steady.

Whether she would have gone on to say anything more was uncertain, but before the matter could be decided, the door opened, and Bryony came toddling in, followed by her nurse. Miss Simms picked up her child, and looked at Jessie, an involuntary look filled with apprehension. In that moment, Jessie guessed everything concerning the other woman's relationship with Sir Wallace Weary.

'Bess is bringing you some tea, ma'am,' said

249

the nurse, 'so I thought you might like to see young Bryony for a bit.'

'Is it that time already?' exclaimed Miss Simms in a relieved tone. 'Yes, by all means leave her with me for a little.' After the tea had arrived and they both had a cup, whilst Bryony was playing on the rug with some bright pieces of material from her mother's bit box, Miss Simms spoke again. 'I can see in your eyes what you are suspecting,' she said, 'and you are quite right. But it changes nothing.'

'Surely he ought to help—' Jessie began, looking at Bryony's down-bent copper-coloured head.

'I don't want his help,' said Miss Simms sharply. The child looked up, alarmed by her mother's change of tone. The dressmaker bent over and, smiling, showed the child a scrap of trim that she had not seen before. 'He does not know,' she went on in a more tranquil tone. 'I see no reason for him to do so. I have no desire for her to learn anything about him and his way of life.'

A short time after this, the nurse took Bryony away, and the ladies got back to their sewing. Later, Jessie went home in a very thoughtful frame of mind. She did not share what she had learned with Henrietta. She was too afraid that that lady might want to question Miss Simms in order to get more ideas for her book.

That evening, Mrs Machin received a note which puzzled her a little. 'It is from Mrs Smales,' she said. 'Apparently she has a confidential matter which she wishes to share with me, and there is nothing for it but for her to speak with me this evening. I suppose I had better go and see her.'

'Do you wish me to come with you?' Jessie asked.

Henrietta looked a little uncomfortable. 'She particularly asks that you should not come, because of your forthcoming relationship to Henry,' she answered.

'It sounds very odd to me,' said Jessie frankly.

'Well it does to me too,' Henrietta agreed. 'But I think I had better go. If she comes here, I might find it hard to get rid of her, and she might find out something to report to Henry that I don't want him to know about. I will take Dilly with me, so I shall be quite safe. Besides, if you are here alone, I shall have the perfect excuse to get away early.'

It felt very odd to be in the house without Henrietta. Jessie knew that she was not completely alone, for the cook lived in, but the man who did any rough work and the woman who did the laundry both came in once or twice a week as needed, and lived in their own homes. It was a quiet street, and Jessie was not a nervous person, but she felt that she would be very glad when Henrietta came back.

251

Only half an hour after her hostess had gone, there was a knock on the door. Jessie toyed with the idea of waiting, and just allowing the visitor to go away. The knocking became more insistent, however, and it occurred to Jessie that perhaps Henrietta had sent for her after all. With some hesitation, she answered the door and, to her great astonishment, found Sir Wallace Weary standing on the threshold.

CHAPTER SEVENTEEN

Jessie could not hold back a gasp of surprise as she looked at the baronet. 'Sir Wallace!' she exclaimed. 'This is most unexpected. I fear I must be inhospitable, however, for I cannot admit you at this hour.' She did not say that she was alone, but he appeared to be already in possession of this information.

'I would not dream of asking it, especially when I know that you are alone,' he said. 'Believe me, I would not be here if this were not an emergency. I wonder . . . ' He appeared to be struggling for words. 'Miss Warburton, forgive my indelicacy, but are you aware that Mrs Machin is writing a . . . a novel?'

'Yes, I know of it,' Jessie replied carefully.

'I was afraid you might be shocked,' he replied. 'She was good enough to confide in

252

me a short time ago about some of her plans for the next chapter.'

Jessie stared at him, puzzled. 'Sir, I am at a loss as to the reason for your visit,' she said. 'As you have guessed, Mrs Machin is from home, but if you wish to talk to her about her writing, I am sure that she will be glad to receive you tomorrow.'

'You misjudge me, ma'am,' he said seriously. 'I would never have called upon you at this late hour had I not judged the matter to be urgent. I wonder . . . ' He paused and looked as if he was weighing his words carefully. 'Has Mrs Machin spoken to you about her wish to visit a . . . a house of ill repute?'

'Oh, good God,' breathed Jessie, her hand going to her cheek.

'I see you have already guessed it,' he said heavily.

'You have encountered her this evening, then?' asked Jessie, puzzled.

He shook his head. 'No, not I,' he assured her. 'Had I done so, I would have brought her home, you may be quite certain. No, an acquaintance who met you both in my company in Hyde Park one day chanced to see her this evening in a part of London where no lady should be. He told me about the encounter, and I recalled the conversation that I had had with her and put two and two together.'

'How could she be so foolish,' Jessie exclaimed, half talking to herself. 'I thought that her visit this evening sounded rather odd. Oh dear, this is all my fault. I told her that I would not go with her, and this is the result.'

'You must not blame yourself,' he told her reassuringly.

'I should have realized that when she is in the midst of writing a novel, every bit of common sense goes out of the window,' Jessie went on. 'But tell me, are you sure, absolutely certain, that she has gone to . . . to one of those dreadful places?'

He shook his head. 'Not absolutely certain, no, but I was so uneasy that I could not reconcile it with my conscience not to come and find you, and ask you what you would have me do. I am prepared to go anywhere if you command it.'

Despite her dislike for the man, which not all his courtesy had overcome, she could not help but be touched. 'Do you have any idea where she might have gone?' she asked. 'There must be hundreds of those places in London.'

He nodded slowly. 'She was asking me about brothels a couple of days ago when we were walking in the park and you were in front with Mr Hinder,' he said. 'To my shame, I knew the names of one or two, but I refused to tell her much about them. It did not seem proper. She went very quiet, then started to talk about Mrs Smales, and how she ought to visit her quite soon. I got the impression that she was planning something.'

'When I told her that I would not go with her, she said that she would think of something,' said Jessie anxiously. 'She must have been planning this scheme even then.'

'What do you want me to do, Miss Warburton?' he asked after a short pause. 'I fear that whatever it is, we should act quickly.'

'Yes; oh yes indeed. But wait for five minutes, and I will go with you to find her, Sir Wallace.'

She ran upstairs and after a brief search, unearthed the cloak and mask that she had worn to Vauxhall. She put the mask on, and looked at herself in the mirror. With what different feelings had she donned these garments on that previous occasion! She hurried down the stairs to where Sir Wallace was still waiting by the door. 'Very well, let us go,' she said.

*   *   *

'This is very odd indeed,' said Mrs Machin, staring up at the dark windows of the house to which she had just sought, and failed, to gain an entrance. She turned to the driver who had brought them there. 'Are you sure that this is the address I gave you?'

'Certain sure,' replied the man. 'Are you stopping, or not?'

'I cannot understand it,' Henrietta replied. 'Dilly, just run down the area steps and see if you can see anything.'

'Oh ma'am, I dursn't,' Dilly replied nervously. 'It's too dark.'

'Then you had better go,' said Henrietta, turning to the driver.

'What about me horses? Anyway, missus, there's no one in. It's as plain as the nose on yer face.'

'Oh dear,' murmured Henrietta. 'There must have been some mistake. What shall we do, Dilly?'

'Best go home, ma'am,' said Dilly fervently.

The sound of footsteps in the street alerted them to the presence of a newcomer. 'Mrs Machin, your servant,' said Raff, greeting her with a bow. 'May I have the honour of serving you in some way?'

'Oh, Raff, thank goodness,' said Henrietta, curtsying. 'We were just about to go home. I had a message to come here this evening, but there is no one here. It must have been a mistake.'

'Is Jez with you?' he asked.

'No, she is at home,' Henrietta answered.

'At home? Alone?' A strange feeling of unease began to creep up the back of Raff's neck. 'Then allow me to be your escort,' he said, getting into the carriage after handing the driver a coin with the instruction to 'whip 'em up'.

When they alighted from the carriage outside Mrs Machin's house—the return journey having been accomplished much more quickly than the outward one thanks to Ashbourne's largesse—they were surprised to find the place in darkness. Before they could enter, Mr Hinder came hurrying out of his house. He had obviously been watching out for them. His relief when he saw Lord Ashbourne was quite palpable.

'Thank heaven!' he exclaimed. 'I didn't know what to do for the best!'

'Let us go inside,' said Ashbourne. 'Doubtless this is better discussed in privacy.' He made as if to pay off the driver but Hinder laid a hand on his arm.

'Tell him to wait,' he said. 'You may want to make use of him again.'

Once they were inside, Mrs Machin said, 'Dilly, bring wine for the gentlemen. And go and see if Miss Warburton is in her room, for she is clearly not downstairs.'

'She is not upstairs, either,' Hinder blurted out, obviously impatient with these niceties and, indeed, barely preventing himself from hopping from one foot to the other.

'The wine, Dilly,' said Mrs Machin firmly, when the maid stood in indecision. 'Come, gentlemen.'

'Now, Hinder,' said the earl as soon as they were in the drawing-room with the door closed, 'Tell us what you know.'

'Not long after you left, ma'am, I chanced to be looking out, as I was half expecting someone to call on me. Another carriage drew up outside this house and Sir Wallace Weary got out.'

Ashbourne tensed and swore softly under his breath. 'Go on.'

'I must say, my lord, I'm sorry if he should be a friend of yours but I've never much cared for him.'

'He isn't a friend of mine. You may speak freely.'

'Jessie—that is Miss Warburton—came to the door, and they talked for a while on the step. Then she went in and he went to speak to the coachman. A few minutes later she came out in a cloak and mask, he got in with her and they drove away.'

Ashbourne stood in silence for a moment, then took out his snuff box and helped himself to a pinch. 'There would not appear to be a problem,' he said in his most languid society drawl. 'She has clearly gone with him to a masquerade.'

'But—' began Hinder.

'I do not think you said that she was coerced in any way?' murmured the earl. Hinder shook his head. 'Very well, then. Miss Warburton is of age. It would be presumptuous of any of us were we to prevent her from enjoying an evening's . . . ah . . . romp, with the gentleman of her choice.'

'No, my lord, I am sure you are mistaken,' Mr Hinder urged.

'For what reason?'

'The message, for one thing,' said Henrietta. 'That was clearly sent to lure me away.'

'It could have been sent by Jez herself,' the earl pointed out.

'No,' Henrietta insisted. 'She would never do such a thing. Besides, it was she who had reservations about going anywhere with Sir Wallace.'

'And another thing,' said Mr Hinder, after a brief pause in the conversation whilst Dilly brought the wine. 'She was only in an ordinary gown when she came to the door. She did not have time to change when she went upstairs. Surely if she was intending to go out for such reasons as you suggest, my lord, she would have put on something more becoming. There's something else, too. As I said before, I've never cared for him, or trusted him either, so I decided to take a look outside and see what might be going on. I kept to the shadows so that no one could see me, and I saw his face clearly enough by the light of the coach lamp when he turned to speak to the coachman after she had gone upstairs. He looked pleased and triumphant, but not in a pleasant way. He said something to the coachman but I didn't hear what it was.'

'Things begin to look less straightforward

than I thought,' remarked the earl. 'Anything else?'

'Just one more thing,' Hinder told him. 'I heard Jessie speak as she got in. She said "Pray heaven we're in time to save her." Then they left.'

'"In time to save her",' repeated Ashbourne. 'With whom is she acquainted in London who might need saving?'

'There is no one, apart from myself,' said Mrs Machin. 'Why would she think I needed saving?'

'Wherever she was going, she obviously needed a disguise,' said his lordship. 'What might Weary know that he could tell Jez to make her go rushing off like that?'

Mrs Machin thought, and suddenly a look of horror crept across her face. 'He knew I was writing a book,' she said slowly. 'He knew that I wanted to find out about brothels.'

'Find out about *what?*' exclaimed Ashbourne.

Henrietta hung her head. 'I did ask Jessie to go with me to observe one, but she refused.'

'Did he know that?' the earl asked ominously, his voice dropping almost to a whisper.

'I think he may have done,' she admitted remorsefully. Ashbourne turned to Hinder. 'There is no time to lose,' he said. 'Will you come with me?'

'Of course,' replied Hinder. 'Do you know

where he has taken her?'

'I believe so. Fetch your coat and hat and meet me outside.'

'Can he have taken her to his house?' ventured Mrs Machin.

Ashbourne's lip turned over in a sneer. 'I cannot believe that Lady Weary would tolerate that, down-trodden though she is.'

Henrietta gasped. 'There is a Lady Weary?' she exclaimed.

'Obviously he did not see fit to tell you about her. He will not take Jez to his home. He does own a couple of brothels, and I suspect that he may have taken her to one of those; with what purpose I am sure you may guess.' She gasped again. 'Did he not tell you that he owns two brothels, ma'am? You appear to have been astonishingly ignorant of the man's affairs, do you not? Let us hope that Jez does not suffer for your foolishness.' He nodded curtly, and made as if to leave the room.

Henrietta hurried forward with a rustle of skirts and caught hold of his arm. 'You will bring her back safe, won't you?' she begged.

He looked at her, and for a moment his face softened. 'I'll bring her back,' he promised. It was only after he had gone that it occurred to her he had not repeated the word 'safe'.

*   *   *

261

When Jessie first got into the carriage with Sir Wallace, her mind was full of Henrietta, and how she must rescue her from the consequences of her own foolishness. It was only after they had been travelling for a little that she remembered Miss Simms's disclosures about the baronet, and she began to wonder whether she herself had been just as foolish. She looked at Sir Wallace, sitting very properly in the opposite corner of the carriage, and found that she could not see his face clearly. 'Where are we going?' she asked him.

'To the establishments which I mentioned to your friend,' he told her.

'Is it very far?'

'It's a fair drive,' he admitted. 'Why don't you relax and close your eyes? I'll wake you up when we get there.'

'I could not possibly sleep with this on my mind,' she said.

'Your concern is quite understandable,' he assured her. 'But if she has gone to the place that I have in mind, then she will come to no harm. The woman who runs it is good-hearted in her way, and will recognize a lady who has strayed into the wrong place. I am sure that she will keep Mrs Machin safely until she has time to send her home.'

'Oh, I do hope so,' breathed Jessie. What upon earth would Henry think to such an adventure, she wondered. When she married Henry, she would put all this behind her. She would return to the quiet of the countryside for good, and all her adventures would be over.

She was conscious of a quite unexpected pang of regret. Not that she wanted to spend her time rescuing her friend from the consequences of her folly. She was, as she had told Henry, a countrywoman, but she had discovered that she could enjoy town living as well. Perhaps, once they were married, they would be able to visit Mrs Machin from time to time. Of course they would not visit Vauxhall. Probably they would not attend the theatre either, and if they did, they would leave before the farce. They might occasionally catch sight of Ashbourne, squiring Lady Gilchrist, or Lady Ashbourne as she would be then. She gave a small sigh.

Eventually they drew up outside a house which, at first glance, looked very little different from any other. 'There,' said Sir Wallace. 'Madame Laura's. Shall we go in?' Jessie hesitated. 'I could go in alone, of course,' he murmured, 'but Mrs Machin would find your presence more reassuring, particularly if she has become alarmed by what is going on.'

'No, you are right, of course I will go in,' Jessie agreed, making sure her mask was in place.

He helped her down out of the carriage, and she looked at the doorway in front of her. 'It sounds like a dressmaker's establishment,' she observed. 'In fact it almost looks like one.'

'It's very discreet,' he assured her. 'Miss Warburton, in order to get in here without causing any remark, I am going to have to behave rather familiarly towards you.' Seeing her look of alarm, he went on, 'If we arouse suspicion, we may not be able to get right inside and find Mrs Machin.'

'If she is there,' Jessie pointed out. 'How do we know that this is the correct establishment?'

He looked at her with an expression that for a moment looked almost like exasperation. 'That's a thought,' he conceded. 'I'll send someone round the back to make enquiries. Servants always know what's going on.' He beckoned to the footman who had clambered down from the box in order to open the door for them. 'You know what to do,' he said. The minutes that the man took to go to the back of the house and then return seemed interminable. Eventually he reappeared, looked at his master and gave a nod.

'Come along then,' said Sir Wallace, catching hold of Jessie by dint of putting his arm around her waist. Before she had time to protest, he had swept her in through the lighted doorway.

CHAPTER EIGHTEEN

The half-open front door, by which they entered, led into a square hall with stairs leading to the next floor on the right and a passage on the left. A pair of double doors gave on to a room from which a lot of cheerful sounding noise was proceeding. A brawny woman dressed in a very low-cut gown in a vivid shade of green lounged at the foot of the stairs.

'New friend of yours?' she asked the baronet.

'We're merely in search of someone,' Weary answered.

The woman gestured up the stairs with a jerk of her head. 'Up there,' she said. 'Number five.' She held out a key in one plump hand, the bracelets jingling on her wrist as she did so.

Sir Wallace took the key and led Jessie past the insolently grinning woman and up the stairs.

'Is Henrietta up here?' she asked him.

'So it would seem,' he said, his arm still around her. At the top of the stairs, there was a corridor, with a number of doors leading off it. Various sounds proceeding from behind the doors betrayed the fact that the rooms were occupied by visitors to the brothel; doing what, Jessie did not dare speculate. Eventually, Sir

Wallace opened one of the doors, stood back for Jessie to go in first, then followed her inside and, to her alarm, locked the door and placed the key in his waistcoat pocket.

'What are you doing?' she asked him.

He did not answer her. Instead, he walked over to a side table, where there was a tray with a decanter and glasses. 'Some wine?' he asked, before pouring a glass for himself.

'No thank you,' answered Jessie absently. 'Sir Wallace, what is going on? Is someone fetching Henrietta?'

He turned round and smiled at her. It was the same lascivious expression that had been on his face at Vauxhall, and which had been almost entirely absent from his features from then until now. 'I would have thought that that was quite obvious, my dear,' he answered. 'It's a seduction. I suggest you take off your cloak and mask. You'll be much more comfortable.'

Jessie looked at her surroundings for the first time. A fire burned in the grate. There were candles on the mantelpiece, and on the table from whence the baronet had collected the wine. To her left, a large bed lay in shadow. The room was carpeted in shades of gaudy red and a brassy shade of gold, a colour scheme that was reflected in the curtains and bed hangings. The air was full of a heady scent. The whole effect was one of decadent opulence.

'Where is Henrietta?' she asked him

266

abruptly.

'No doubt trying to discover why Mrs Smales is so vigorously denying having sent any kind of message, I should think,' he answered. 'Oh don't worry. She hasn't come to any harm.'

'Then why . . .?' Her voice tailed away as she finally began to understand what he was about.

'You really have no idea how alluring you are, have you?' He finished his wine and poured another glass. 'That air of cool elegance, contrasted with your brazen behaviour at Vauxhall, not to mention your eagerness to help your companion with all kinds of research for her rather risqué novels. Just think, my dear, how helpful you will be to her now. You will be able to describe a brothel and a seduction at first hand.'

Jessie took a step back. His eyes were gleaming, his forehead glistening with tiny drops of sweat. 'You are talking rape, not seduction, sir,' she said, trying to remain angry, for if she could keep anger to the forefront of her mind, she might forget to be afraid.

He burst out laughing. 'That's rich,' he declared, 'coming from one of the Fallen Angel's paramours!'

'You hate him, then,' said Jessie, trying to look around surreptitiously to see whether there was anything to hand that she might be able to use as a weapon. 'Why is that?'

'Oh, for a number of reasons,' he replied. He took a mouthful of wine. Jessie wondered whether she could get hold of the decanter. It was one of the few things in the room that looked as if it could be used as a weapon. 'He can get any woman he wants, to start with. My wife—my own wife—only married me because she couldn't snare him. Then *his* wife had the good sense to die, leaving him with a son, whilst *mine* remains like a millstone around my neck, not even having presented me with so much as a puling daughter. Yes, I hate him.'

Jessie took a breath. 'So do I,' she answered, pleased at how steady her voice sounded. 'It appears that we are in agreement.' She took off her cloak and mask and laid them on a chair, judging that to comply with his earlier request would help to lull his suspicions. She knew that she must do that if she was to emerge from this nightmare situation intact. Then she walked over to the side table. 'May I pour myself some wine after all?'

Sir Wallace waved his hand in an assenting gesture. 'By all means, but don't try to pull the wool over my eyes. You adore him—all the women do.'

Borrowing Lady Ilam's phrase, Jessie said calmly, 'He's too pretty for me. Besides, I've known him for nearly twenty years and he's never noticed me.' This time employing Lady Agatha's terminology, she added, 'I'm not the sort of pretty slut who appeals to him, and I'm tired of being ignored.' She poured herself a glass of wine.

'You surprise me, my dear,' said Sir Wallace. 'Pray do not suppose that you will deter me from my purpose by this remarkable confession, though. I have made up my mind to have you.' He walked towards her, his back to the door. 'Do not think to use that decanter as a weapon against me, either,' he added.

Jessie looked down at the decanter which she still held in her hand. 'Weapon?' she said in a puzzled tone. 'I was merely going to offer to fill your glass, sir. Why, do you not want me to . . . minister to you?'

He grinned, holding out his own glass. 'Maybe this will be even more amusing than I thought,' he said. 'What say we go and find Raff tomorrow, and tell him what an entertaining evening we have spent?'

'Why not?' Jessie murmured.

He took a step closer to her, and put out his hand to cradle her jaw, then run a finger around the edge of her neckline. She barely repressed a shudder. 'Then, of course, there's dear Henry,' he remarked. Naturally enough, Jessie and Henrietta had spoken a little of Henry during their outings with the baronet. 'I'm afraid he isn't going to want you after I've finished with you either; but don't be afraid. I can always find a place for you here.'

As he angled his head in order to kiss her, she let her eyes wander past him towards the door. 'Oh, good God!' she exclaimed. It was not hard to sound terrified. The very idea of feeling his lips on hers made her flesh crawl, and she could not imagine how she would escape if this did not work.

'What the—?' exclaimed Weary, turning his head. In a flash, she lifted her arm and brought the decanter down on his head, wine running down her sleeve and on to her gown as she did so. To her horror, he did not fall immediately, but clutched at her gown, tearing the bodice as he fell to his knees. She hit him again, a more glancing blow because her hands were not quite steady. He fell then, but still appeared to be more stunned than unconscious. With trembling fingers that stumbled over their task, Jessie extracted the room key from the pocket of his waistcoat, unlocked the door, and sped along the corridor and down the stairs.

Perhaps the hall was now lit differently, or the arrangement of rooms was more complicated than she had thought, or maybe she was simply confused because of the experience that she had just had. Whatever the reason, instead of running straight for the front door, somehow Jessie found herself on the threshold of the lighted room, with the open double doors.

The room was lit by plenty of candles, the light being reflected by big mirrors over the fireplace and between the windows. A pianoforte was being played in the far corner of the room, and two rather dishevelled gentlemen were bellowing what seemed to be a bawdy song. A man was seated on a chair next to the fireplace, with a scantily dressed young woman on his knee. He was engaged upon unfastening her very minute bodice, egged on by her laughter and the encouragement of another couple, their arms entwined about each other. Two men were seated upon a sofa whilst the brassy-looking woman who had met Sir Wallace and Jessie in the hall lolled between them over the back of it, and another approached the group with glasses of wine. Various other persons were disporting themselves about the place.

The sudden nature of her entrance drew attention to her; and although the gown that she wore was modest and not designed to draw attention, in a brothel, its very simplicity had the opposite effect. Those already in the room were not so occupied that they failed to notice this unusual sight. The two men by the pianoforte stopped singing; the older lady who was playing rather inaccurately halted her performance a few moments later, and for a very short time, silence reigned in the room. Suddenly reminded of the damage caused to her gown, Jessie caught hold of the torn pieces of her bodice with one hand.

'It's a governess come amongst us,' exclaimed one man. 'Come on in and enjoy

271

yourself!'

Then one of those who had been singing wandered towards her unsteadily, picking up a glass from a table as he came. 'Sweetheart!' he cried, hiccoughing, which spoiled the effect a little. 'Have some wine.' He held the glass out to her, then realized that it was empty. 'Never mind,' he went on, reaching out to catch hold of her hand. 'Plenty more where that came from.'

Jessie stepped back. 'I was . . . was looking for . . .' she stammered.

'Looking for me, I daresay,' said a familiar voice from behind. An arm crept around her waist, and she looked up to see the face of Sir Wallace Weary. Evidently the blow she had struck had only been sufficient to stun him for a few moments. Behind his lascivious gaze there was anger and determination. 'Let's go back upstairs, shall we?' he said. 'We've unfinished business.' The arm about her waist felt vice-like and his fingers dug into her waist, the pressure almost causing her to cry out.

She looked at the other occupants of the room. There could be no help from them. Weary would tell them that they were playing some kind of game of chase, and they would believe him. She braced herself. He would not get her upstairs while she still had the means to resist him. Nevertheless, she knew in her heart of hearts that there could be only one result. Then, as she looked at the faces of

272

those in the room, desperately hoping that she might be able to appeal to someone's better nature, she realized that their attention had been caught by something—or someone—behind them.

'Ah, there you are, m'dear,' said Ashbourne's voice. 'I believe I warned you not to wander about in London without me to advise you. Weary, your servant.' Ashbourne was in evening dress, as immaculate as usual. In its way, his faultless appearance among all these dishevelled people, made him look as out of place as did Jessie. He was greeted good-humouredly by several people in the room. Plainly he was known by a number of those present.

The baronet turned, his grip on Jessie slackening in his surprise. Taking advantage of this, she pulled away from him and took a step towards Raff, who saw the damage to her gown for the first time. 'You appear to have met with a little misadventure, my dear,' he said softly, taking off his own cloak and putting it round her. 'Who is responsible?'

Weary grinned unpleasantly. 'You know how it is, Raff,' he said.

'Tell me.' Again, the tone was very soft; but the room was filled with an air of menace. Despite the rowdy nature of the proceedings up to this point, the rest of the room was completely silent.

'They play hard to get, but they all like it

when you're a bit rough.'

'Do they? Let's ask, shall we?' Ashbourne turned to Jessie. 'Did you find this oaf's attentions entertaining?'

She shook her head. 'He told me Henrietta was here,' she said. 'I was coming to rescue her. I never wanted—'

Watch who you're calling an oaf,' Weary interrupted, his eyes on Ashbourne's face. 'You've only that light-skirt's word for it.'

Raff turned back towards him. His movements were still graceful and unhurried, but there was a menacing light burning in his eye. 'You heard her,' he said, picking up a glass of wine from a nearby table. 'She does not find you entertaining, and neither do I.' With that, he tossed the wine into the baronet's face. 'When, and where you like,' he said. He turned to Hector Hinder, ignoring the spluttering, cursing baronet. 'Take her to the carriage and send her home; then attend me here.'

Jessie turned her white face up to his. 'Raff,' she said, putting her hand on his arm.

'Go,' he said, his face as white as hers. Without saying any more, she turned and went out with Hinder to the waiting vehicle.

*   *   *

On Jessie's arrival back at Sloane Street, Henrietta held out her arms and the two women embraced and wept a little. Mrs

Machin was horrified at the sight of Jessie's torn gown, and told her to go straight upstairs and change into her night attire. 'I will bring you some warm milk and then you will feel better,' she said.

Jessie shook her head. No, I cannot,' she said distressfully. 'I must be dressed and downstairs if Hector or . . . or Raff comes.'

'I must admit that I am surprised not to see them here now,' said Henrietta. 'How does it come about that you have returned alone?'

The most dreadful thing has occurred,' said Jessie. 'I think—but I am not sure, for I have never heard such a thing before—that Raff has challenged Sir Wallace to a duel.'

'A duel!' exclaimed Henrietta, her eyes sparkling.

Jessie stamped her foot. 'Oh, for goodness' sake, Henrietta, try to think of something other than your plots. This is real life, not a book. People get hurt, even killed in duels.'

Mrs Machin begged pardon immediately. 'I am sorry, Jessie,' she said with real remorse. 'And, oh dear, I have just realized that it was my fault that you were there in the first place.'

'It was no one's fault but Sir Wallace's,' Jessie assured her. She was torn between not wanting to move an inch from the hall just in case there should be news, and asking Dilly, quite unreasonably at this hour, to fill her a bath so that she might wash away the memory of the baronet's wandering hands.

275

'That, too, is my fault,' said Henrietta, tears returning to her eyes.

'You did not like Sir Wallace from the very beginning, but I did not listen to you.'

'I was less than honest,' Jessie confessed. 'If I had told you how badly he had behaved at Vauxhall, then you would not have given him house room.'

'I knew that he was a rake, but I wanted to talk to him—for my book, you know. I would have asked Raff, but he stopped coming to see us.'

'I was to blame for that,' Jessie admitted. 'I quarrelled with him and told him not to come. And now, despite that, he is going to put his life at risk. Oh Hettie, what can we do?'

Henrietta took hold of her trembling hands. 'We must try to keep calm,' she said. 'Whatever else you do, I think you would be happier if you changed out of that gown. Then shall we have some warm milk and wait for a little while to see if the gentlemen come? You know, we both come from clergy households. I think we might feel calmer if we said a prayer for Raff.'

Jessie agreed to all of these suggestions, but after a long tense wait, they came to the conclusion that nothing would happen that night, and reluctantly retired to their own rooms.

Jessie went through the motions of preparing for bed, actually going as far as to

276

climb in and blow out the candle, but sleep was very slow in coming. Looking at the whole affair from every angle, she could not find herself free from blame. Allowing Henrietta to encourage Raff to visit them had been her first mistake. Having done so, however, she certainly should not have gone to Vauxhall. Then, having quarrelled with Raff, like a fool she had encouraged Sir Wallace Weary, all the while guessing that he was an unsavoury customer. Tonight, she had been unconscionably foolish, as a result of which Raff was now going to put his life at risk because of her.

She sat up in bed, staring ahead of her at the dying embers of the fire. Her mind went back to the day they had met, and his kindness on that occasion, and many times since. She thought about his easy tolerance of Mrs Machin and Mr Hinder, and his thoughtfulness towards Dilly. She recalled his roguish sense of humour. No, her first mistake had not been in agreeing for Raff to visit them; it had been in accepting Henry Lusty's offer of marriage when the only man she had ever loved, could ever love, was a rake and a libertine who even now was planning an act worthy of any *preux chevalier* for her sake.

CHAPTER NINETEEN

The following day seemed to drag past interminably. Jessie was late leaving her room, having failed to get to sleep at a reasonable hour. Eventually she had dropped off just as it was turning light, only to dream of Wallace Weary covered in blood, pursuing her through Drury Lane theatre, whilst Raff and Lady Gilchrist, dressed in their wedding clothes, looked on laughing.

Once downstairs, she apologized to Henrietta, who confessed that her night's sleep had been similarly fitful. 'Do you suppose that we will hear anything today?' Mrs Machin asked anxiously.

'I don't know,' said Jessie. She suddenly looked thoughtful. 'Hector must know something!' she said in a more animated tone.

'Let us send Dilly around immediately,' suggested Mrs Machin.

'Never mind Dilly,' Jessie retorted. 'Let us go ourselves.' But the two ladies did not get any satisfaction from their visit. Mr Hinder's landlady, who knew both of his visitors by sight, could not enlighten them. Yes, the young gentleman had returned the previous night, but had gone out early. He would certainly be away for one night, perhaps more. No, she did not know where he had gone. She was sorry, but he had left no message of any kind. Yes indeed, she would let them know if there was any news.

'What now?' asked Henrietta.

'I suppose we had better go home and wait,' replied Jessie. 'That will be where any message will come.'

'I suppose we should not go to Raff's house,' said Henrietta doubtfully.

'No, we should not,' replied Jessie, barely repressing a shudder. He was already having to fight one duel on her behalf. Heaven forbid that he should have to fight more battles for her honour because she had been seen calling at Rake Ashbourne's house.

Henrietta was unable to settle to writing, so between them they turned out the loft, an area of the house into which Henrietta had not yet strayed. They found nothing of any value, but cleaned and dusted for all they were worth, in order to take their mind off things. When no news had come by the evening, they played cards against each other, staking huge imaginary sums, and even property that they did not possess, so that by the time Jessie rose from the table, she was the proud possessor of twenty thousand pounds and the London residence of the Archbishop of Canterbury. Due to her lack of sleep the night before, Jessie did manage a better night. This time, she dreamed of Raff's kisses, passionate, demanding and seductive, and she awoke with tears on her cheeks, and a feeling of bitter disappointment in her heart.

It was only a few moments after she had opened her eyes that the household was disturbed by an urgent knocking on the door. It was such an unprecedented occurrence that Jessie and Henrietta were both out of their beds and at the top of the stairs as Dilly opened to a very agitated Mr Hinder.

'Please, you must fetch Miss Warburton at once,' he said, sounding out of breath as well as anxious.

'Miss is still in her bed, so you'll have to wait,' said Dilly, pleased to be so much in command of the situation.

'I cannot wait,' declared Mr Hinder. 'In short, it is a matter of life and death. In fact,' he went on, rendered bold by the urgency of the case, 'it may simply be a matter of death if she does not come straight away!'

Jessie paused only to wrap a shawl around herself—although to be fair, the nightgown that she was wearing was cut higher in the neck than some of the gowns that she generally wore during the day—then without hesitation hurried down the stairs in her bare feet. 'What is it?' she asked. 'Has something happened to Henry—or to Lady Agatha?'

'No, no!' he cried, stepping past Dilly across the threshold. 'It is Lord Ashbourne! He is very gravely injured indeed! You must come at once!'

Jessie missed a step and almost fell. She clutched the neckline of her nightgown, her face almost as white as the fabric from which it was made. 'Gravely injured! You said it was a matter of life and death. Is he . . . dying?'

'I fear so. Will you come?'

Jessie stared at him for a moment. Then she said, 'Of course. Give me five minutes.'

'Do not take any longer,' said Hinder solemnly.

Henrietta, who had waited at the top of the stairs because the message was clearly not for her, stepped forward. 'Do you want me to come with you?'

Jessie shook her head. 'I will send for you if necessary. For now, help me so that I may get ready as quickly as possible.' She did not allow herself to think for a moment that she might be too late. Nor did she think to wonder how the earl's injuries might have been sustained until she was being helped into a carriage which displayed the Ashbourne crest.

'We are going to Ashbourne House in Berkeley Square,' said Mr Hinder, answering one of her questions. 'That is where he was taken, after the duel.'

Jessie's hand went to her mouth. 'They met this morning?'

Hinder nodded. 'I was his second. That was why I had to stay behind instead of take you home. Raff chose swords. It was a deucedly close fight. In fact, I wish that it hadn't been so

281

deadly serious, because if it hadn't been I would have enjoyed it.'

'Who won? Is Sir Wallace dead?'

'No; although he should have been. Raff could have killed him once, but stayed his hand. Given a similar opportunity, Weary didn't stay his. If his sword hadn't been deflected by something in Raff's pocket, then—' He paused, then added in a falsely hearty voice, 'But we might still be in time.'

'In time?'

'He wants to see you.'

'What of Weary?'

'He has fled the country.' After a brief silence Mr Hinder burst out, 'Would to God you had fetched me that night!'

'You cannot possibly wish that more than I do,' Jessie replied just as fervently.

They fell silent again. Jessie tried not to think of anything, fearful that to dwell on what had occurred and how culpably to blame she had been over the whole matter, would be to drive her mad. By the time they reached the front door of Ashbourne House, she had counted the plum silken squabs behind Mr Hinder over and over again until her thoughts had turned to very confused prayers to the effect that she would be prepared to do anything if only Raff might live.

They were expected. The door was flung open, they were hurried in, and up the stairs. 'The doctor is with him now,' the butler said as

282

he ushered them through the hall.

A respectably dressed man appeared on the landing. 'I'm Pointer, miss, his lordship's valet,' he said. 'I'm very glad you're here. I'm a little uneasy about the doctor.'

Jessie entered, and felt immediately as if she had walked into a battlefield. There seemed to be blood everywhere. Raff was lying on the bed, still apparently covered with it, his black hair loose and streaming across the pillow. The doctor was standing by his side, his wrist in one hand, a razor in the other, and a bowl ready beneath.

'What are you doing? Stop immediately!' she declared, horrified.

The doctor looked up from his work. 'Don't be alarmed, madam,' he said. 'It is necessary to let some blood to avoid the risk of fever. Then, in a little while, I will shave his head—for the same reason.'

'You will do neither,' said Jessie, straightening her spine. 'Believe me, if you let any of his blood, the next to be let will be yours.'

There was a very faint chuckle from the bed. 'Jez,' Ashbourne murmured.

The doctor also stood up straight, his expression affronted. 'May I ask who you are, madam, to presume to decide my patient's needs?'

'Certainly,' answered Jessie, her voice perfectly steady. 'I am his promised wife, and he is no longer your patient.'

'Very well,' said the doctor, packing up his things. 'He'll be dead before the morning. Don't say I didn't warn you.'

'Now, Pointer,' said Jessie after the doctor had gone. 'Let's make him comfortable.'

'Yes indeed, miss,' answered the valet.

'Do you know of a doctor who does not yearn to preside over a blood bath?' she asked him.

'I have heard of a man who doesn't always resort to blooding. He's had some good results.'

'Then have him sent for. Hector, can you help without fainting?'

Mr Hinder, who had turned rather white at the sight of all the blood, said, 'I think so.'

'Good, for we will need you to help Raff into his nightshirt.'

Fortunately, Raff had drifted into unconsciousness, so they padded the major wound in his chest, and cleaned other superficial wounds and dusted them with basilicum powder.

They had just finished their work, Pointer and Mr Hinder having attended to Raff's personal needs whilst Jessie tidied up the room and cleared away the bloody cloths, when the new doctor arrived. He was neither so stout nor so fashionable-looking as the previous man, but his quiet, calm manner immediately reassured Jessie, as did his examination of Raff, which was conducted in such a way as to disturb the patient as little as possible.

He commended their work, and also, to Jessie's relief, decided against letting further blood. 'He has lost enough, I feel,' he said. 'Indeed, I fear he may have lost too much. He is in good health, which is in his favour, but you must prepare yourself for the worst.'

Jessie had been trying not to think about that, and the tasks that she had been performing had helped her. Now, however, she had to face the future, however grim it might prove to be. 'Very well,' she said, as calmly as she could. 'Should his son be sent for?'

'I think it advisable.'

'It has been done,' said Hinder.

After the doctor had gone, leaving his address and some powders to be administered in case of fever and promising to return on the morrow, Jessie sat beside Raff's bed, not knowing what to do next. The announcement that she was his promised wife had come out entirely unbidden. She had taken authority over the situation, but now she felt utterly helpless. She had prayed that he might be preserved, and he had not gone yet. There was still hope. She looked down at his white, still, impossibly handsome face. This was the man she loved and no other man, however worthy, would do. She had been closing her eyes to this truth ever since Ilam's wedding. She thought of the first time that she had met Weary, and remembered how even then Raff had been ready to challenge the baronet for being insolent to her. Now, he had actually fought for her, and he had quite possibly lost his life as a result. 'It's all my fault,' she whispered, brushing away a tear.

'Don't cry, Jez.' She realized that he had woken, and was looking up at her.

'I'm all right, Raff,' she said, trying to smile.

'Should have married you . . . years ago. Why did I . . . wait till . . . deathbed?'

'It doesn't matter,' she said, her vision blurred by her tears.

He coughed. 'Where's Hinder?'

Hector came tentatively forward from the doorway, where he had been hovering. 'I'm here, my lord.'

'You have it . . . the licence?'

Hinder tapped his pocket. 'I have it.'

'Then fetch . . . priest.' Hinder hesitated briefly, then hurried from the room.

'Jez . . .'

Jessie laid her hand on his. 'Don't try to talk. Save your strength.'

He closed his eyes, and for what seemed like a long time, she stared down at him, wishing that he did not look so white. Anything, she said to herself again. I'll do anything, if he can only be spared. Eventually, he opened his eyes again. 'Katie,' he said. For one horrible moment, Jessie thought that he had mistaken her for the woman at Vauxhall. Then he spoke again. 'Her lover threw her out. Needed . . . money.'

She stared at him. How horribly she had misjudged him. 'Raff, I didn't know. I'm sorry . . . sorry for—'

'Never mind,' he interrupted. 'Jez, you will marry me, won't you?'

'Raff—'

'You'll be a rich widow. You can take Lusty a fine fortune. Buy him a smart parish.'

'Raff, please—'

'Don't argue with me, Jez. I'm not strong enough. Let me do this. Should have had the sense to marry you years ago.'

'Very well,' she agreed, not wanting to agitate him further.

'Good girl.' He was silent for a time.

He relaxed and closed his eyes once more. Jessie thought that he might have fallen asleep, and wondered whether she would have to send the clergyman away again. As soon as the door opened and the thin, grey-haired cleric came in with a book in his hands, however, Raff opened his eyes. 'Good,' he breathed. 'What's your name, Parson?'

'I am the Reverend Percival Goode,' he said. 'You are Lord Ashbourne, I believe.'

'I am. I'm good neither by name nor by nature, but I'm dying and I need you to marry me to this lady.'

'Certainly; if the lady is willing.'

'I'm willing,' Jessie agreed, stepping forward.

It was a wedding ceremony unlike any Jessie had ever attended, or indeed any in which she had ever imagined herself taking part. Raff spoke his responses clearly, but in a weak thread of a voice, while Jessie spoke hers with a calmness which differed wildly from the turmoil which she felt within. The very thing that she had always dreaded concerning her wedding, namely, the need to state her real name, passed by without anyone even giving a sign of having noticed. Mr Hinder and Pointer were the witnesses and the only other people present. To Jessie's great surprise, Hinder brought out a ring of just the right size at the appropriate moment, then helped Raff to slide it on to her finger.

After the short ceremony was over, Raff sighed and closed his eyes. Jessie stood with Hinder and Pointer by the bedroom door after the clergyman had gone, and swore them to secrecy. 'I should so much dislike any word to get out before Lady Agatha and Lord Ilam can be told in person,' she said. Inwardly, she had already resolved that she would never profit from this hasty marriage. She had refused to marry him in life. She would not lay claim to his property once he was dead. Hinder and Pointer would, she was sure, keep her secret. As for the clergyman, she would never see him again.

288

*　　*　　*

The night began quietly, but later, his lordship went into a high fever. 'Perhaps we should have let the doctor blood him after all, miss,' said Pointer. 'My lady, I should say.'

'Oh no, pray do not,' Jessie begged. 'Remember that I said we should keep it secret. No, Pointer, I'm glad we sent the doctor away. It cannot possibly be good for a man who has lost so much blood to lose more.' Although she spoke so confidently, she still found herself a prey to doubt, especially when she was watching alone in the sickroom, Pointer having taken his turn to rest. Mr Hinder had gone back to Sloane Street in order to inform Mrs Machin of the current state of affairs. He had promised to return the next day to take a turn at Ashbourne's bedside. Neither of them had voiced the thought that was uppermost in both their minds: if he lived that long.

Shortly after Jessie had begun her watch, the earl started to become agitated, first of all simply turning his head restlessly from side to side, then pulling his arms from beneath the covers and tossing and turning with increasing violence until Jessie became afraid that he would dislodge his dressings. He talked in his delirium as well, sometimes muttering, sometimes shouting out loud. Occasionally,

289

Jessie would catch odd words. He spoke his son's name several times and sometimes her own, but nothing that he said made any sense. This was terrifying enough, but after a while, he suddenly became quite still and silent, and for a few dreadful moments, Jessie thought that he had died.

She leaned forward to listen for his breathing, hardly daring to breathe herself, and placed a hand over his heart. Then somehow, inexplicably, the nature of the silence appeared to change, and Jessie turned her head to discover that his eyes were open and he was looking straight at her, but without recognizing her, his eyes hectic with fever. 'Sweetheart,' he said, and placing one hand behind her head, he pressed her closer and kissed her full on the mouth.

Struggling was out of the question. For one thing, she did not want to do anything to dislodge the dressings on his wounds. More importantly, however, she heard a voice deep inside saying, this may be your last chance. Far from pulling away from him, therefore, or even simply staying passive in his embrace, she leaned into the kiss, giving all of herself into the caress, bracing herself with one hand beside him, whilst she cradled his cheek with the other. Then as they drew apart, and he lapsed once more into a fitful slumber, she allowed herself the luxury of lying beside him, her head on the same pillow. After all, he is my husband, she told herself, and the only husband that she would ever have. Whatever happened, she would not marry Henry Lusty now.

CHAPTER TWENTY

Lord and Lady Ilam arrived the following evening, accompanied by Lady Agatha. Jessie and Eustacia embraced one another warmly, the latter enquiring tentatively about the health of Lord Ashbourne, for she remembered how Jessie had confessed her love for the dissolute nobleman.

Lady Agatha greeted her companion sympathetically, but in a more restrained style, for she and Jessie had never been effusive in their relationship with one another. 'I take it my fool of a brother is still alive,' Lady Agatha said, her careless tone rather belied by the shadow of anxiety in her eyes. 'What the deuce did he do to get himself into this mess, anyway?'

'He was injured in a duel,' Jessie replied.

The earl's sister gave a contemptuous snort. 'Over a woman, I expect,' she said. Jessie prudently remained silent concerning the cause of the duel. Involuntarily, her fingers touched her wedding ring, which she had slipped off her finger and wore on a chain about her neck.

'Has the doctor been today?' Ilam asked. 'What does he say about my father's condition?'

'The doctor came this morning,' answered Jessie. 'He is surprised that Raff has held on for so long, but he still does not expect him to . . . to . . . ' She had been determined to be strong, but now that others had arrived who could share the burden, her voice gave way, and she burst into tears. At once she found herself gathered into Ilam's powerful embrace.

For a short time, the viscount let her have her cry out. Physically, he and his father were alike, although Ilam was a little more heavily built than Ashbourne. 'You have had to bear this alone, but we're here to help now,' he said eventually. 'How did you come to be called, by the way?'

Jessie had had time to think about an answer to this question. 'His second knew that I was a friend of the family,' she said, drawing back from Ilam with a word of thanks, and taking out her handkerchief.

'May we go to see him?' Ilam asked. Lest the sickroom should be too crowded, Eustacia stayed downstairs, whilst Jessie conducted Lady Agatha and Ilam to Ashbourne's room.

'Pointer is watching him at the moment,' said Jessie, as she quietly opened the door. The valet was sitting by the bed, but he stood up as the three of them came in. 'How is he?'

Jessie asked.

'Drifting in and out of consciousness, ma'am,' answered the valet. He dropped his voice. 'At one point, I thought that . . . that . . .' He did not finish his sentence.

Lady Agatha walked over to the bed and stared down at the still figure of Lord Ashbourne. He did indeed look as though he were barely alive. 'He is my brother,' she said decisively, 'and if *anyone* is going to decide that he will die, *I* shall do it, and not some scoundrel of a doctor with nothing but sawdust in his cockloft.'

From then on, life became much easier for Jessie. Logically, she knew that it was much better that more people should help with the nursing, but part of her resented the fact that she no longer spent so much time with him. He is my husband, after all, she told herself. Then she remembered that it was her own decision that no one should be informed about their marriage until Lady Agatha and Ilam knew, and she just could not think how to tell them. To do so whilst Ashbourne's life hung in the balance seemed wrong. The more time elapsed since his injury, the more she began to hope that he might actually recover. If he does get better, we will tell them together, she told herself. She dared not think about what his reaction might be. After all, he had been on the point of getting engaged to Lady Gilchrist.

As the days went by, the earl seemed set to

293

give the lie to the doctor's diagnosis. Lady Agatha, once she had met the physician and spoken with him, developed a greater degree of respect than she had had for him at first, and she took over the chief role in discussing the earl's condition. Jessie tried not to feel resentful. Until Ashbourne's sister and son had arrived he had been nearly all hers. At least no one had suggested that she should move back to Sloane Street. She was not sure how she could have borne it had she not been permitted to take an active share in the nursing.

For this mercy, she had Eustacia to thank. Ilam had indeed suggested that Jessie should go back to Henrietta, but his wife had said that she should not be expected to leave. 'It would be too cruel,' she told him. 'If your father dies, she should not be denied the chance of being with him until the last. Besides, I think that Aunt Agatha is glad to have her here.'

Ilam grinned ruefully. 'She and my father have never been close, but I think that his injury has made her realize how much she would miss him if he were not there.'

'She would have no one to accuse of dragging the family name through the mud,' Eustacia agreed.

So Jessie was allowed to stay, and day by day, as the earl's condition very slowly improved, she began to hope; but to hope for what? For his recovery, yes; but for anything more? She did not dare.

*   *   *

Ashbourne opened his eyes, his head feeling curiously light. A moment or two's inspection of his surroundings told him that he was in his bedroom at Berkeley Square. He could not remember how he came to be there, but it did not seem to matter very much. He tried to lift his head off the pillow, and found that he did not have the strength. That did not seem to matter much either. Cautiously, he turned his head to one side, and that seemed to be quite possible. A woman was sitting writing at a table in the window and, to his surprise, he recognized her as his sister.

'That's absurd,' he said out loud. 'She'd never cross my threshold.'

Lady Agatha turned her head at the sound of his voice, and got up to come and stand by the bed. 'So you've decided to rejoin the land of the living, have you?' she said.

'So it would seem,' he agreed. 'Disappointed?'

She raised her brows, so like his both in shape and in colour. 'Hardly. You would have no business to be dying without my permission.'

He chuckled. 'Are there any other members of my family in attendance?'

'Ilam is here. He's sat with you from time to

time. I must go and tell him that you have woken up.'

As she left the room, he frowned. He was sure that someone else had been sitting with him at times, someone who was very important to him. He was still puzzling over the matter when he dozed off again.

The next time he woke up, two men were talking in low tones at the foot of the bed. One of them he recognized as being his son. 'Good day, Ilam,' he murmured. 'At least, I assume it is day.'

The two men broke off their conversation, and the one whom Ashbourne did not recognize approached the bed and took hold of his wrist. 'Good day, my lord,' he said. 'I'm Dr Prentiss.'

'Have you been attending me throughout?' the earl asked.

'I have, my lord.'

'My thanks. Am I going to live, do you think?'

'More than likely,' the doctor replied. 'You have been ill for some days, however, and need to give yourself time to recover.' He turned to Ilam. 'Your father will need great care for some time.'

'It shall be done,' said Ilam.

'Will it? By you?' said Ashbourne quizzically.

'Only until I get the chance to smother you so that I can be Lord Ashbourne,' answered his son in much the same vein.

The earl chuckled. 'May I have a drink?' he asked. 'I'm feeling devilish thirsty.'

'I think Jessie is bringing some lemonade,' said Ilam.

'Jez!' Ashbourne murmured, his brow lightening. 'That's who it must have been.'

As if she had been summoned up by the speaking of her name, Jessie came into the room, a tray in her hands. Her arrival seemed to be a signal for the doctor to announce his departure. 'I'll be back in the morning,' he said, turning to Lord Ilam. 'In the meantime, my lord, I will give you more detailed instructions concerning his lordship's care.'

'Of course, it's nothing to do with me,' murmured Ashbourne as they left. He watched Jessie as she crossed the room holding the tray. As she walked, she glanced at him, blushed and looked down. He eyed her curiously. She was dressed in a gown of dull gold, which seemed to bring out the lights in her soft brown hair, which was gathered loosely in a knot on top of her head. As he observed her, a shaft of sunlight caught a few tendrils of her hair, turning them to gold. To Ashbourne at that moment, she seemed to be very pretty; no, not pretty—winsome was the word. He was also conscious of finding her very desirable. It was almost as though he was seeing her for the first time. 'Thank you,' he said, as she put the tray down on a table close to the bed. 'I'm not at all sure that I can sit up, though.'

'I can't lift you on my own,' she said, smiling. She looked a little self-conscious.

'Do you mean that you've tried? Jez, I have a feeling that you've been helping to nurse me, but I can't for the life of me remember anything about it. How do you come to be here? Did someone send for you?'

She had been standing quite close to him. Now, she turned away, busying herself with tidying the coverlet. When she looked back at him, it seemed that the rosy glow had gone from her face, leaving her looking suddenly much older.

'Do you remember anything about how you come to be here?' she asked.

He wrinkled his brow. 'I think I took part in a duel,' he answered slowly. 'I can't for the life of me remember why.'

'I don't suppose it was important,' she replied colourlessly.

He reached out and caught hold of her hand. 'Jez, have I hurt you, offended you by anything I've done or said? If I did anything to distress you whilst I was in my delirium, then I would be begging your pardon'

'There was nothing,' she answered. 'Please let go of me' At that moment, Ilam came back to help his father sit up. As Jez brought the glass to Raff and held it so that he could drink, he looked into her eyes, which now seemed so desolate, with tears not far away. For no reason that he could fathom, he suddenly felt guilty.

Guilt was not something that he was accustomed to feeling with regard to women. Now however, perhaps because he was forced to be inactive and, despite the kindness of those caring for him, often on his own, he found that as time went by he was thinking about Jez's feelings more than he had ever done before. Her withdrawal from him had been quite marked. Increasingly, he began to think that he must have done something to distress her whilst in his delirium; something that he needed to apologize for. Perhaps if he did so, that glowing smile would return to her face. To see it again was becoming an ambition with him.

As the days went by, he began to recall, first hazily, then in more detail, the events that had taken place in London after Jez's arrival. In particular, he remembered seeing her at the theatre, then accompanying her to Vauxhall. In his mind, he contrasted her elegant, restrained appearance with that of some of the other women he knew, who seemed determined to show off their charms or their jewellery, or more frequently as much as possible of both. How austere and incongruous, yet how arresting she had looked standing in the brothel.

His mind gave a start of surprise. A brothel!

299

What had she been doing in a brothel? Ah yes, she had been looking for her friend. What had happened then? It was no good. He could not remember, and he did not want to ask her for fear of hurting her. The need to protect Jez from hurt was becoming important to him. Slowly, he was remembering how his feelings for her had changed.

It was not long afterwards that Jez came to his room with a tray containing some tea and biscuits, both of which he was now allowed. He had noticed that since the others had arrived she came to his room much less frequently, and never unless she had some sort of errand to perform. He was already half sitting up, since now that he was slowly recovering, he did not like to lie down all the time.

Once inside the room, she hesitated, looking round. 'I thought that Pointer was here,' she said.

'I sent him out for some fresh air,' Ashbourne replied. 'You don't need him, do you?'

Jessie looked at him as he lay back against the pillows, his long black hair loose about him, his white night shirt with the top three buttons undone, so that a hint of chest hair was visible. He looked devastatingly attractive as always. He was her husband, yet he did not remember it, and he was as much out of her reach as he had ever been. In the circumstances, drawing closer to him was probably not the wisest thing; yet if he was to drink the tea that she had brought, she needed to put one more pillow behind him. She paused for a moment in indecision.

While she was still standing there, he spoke. 'If I'm to drink that tea, I'll need another pillow. Can you manage, or shall I ring the bell?'

'I think I can manage,' she answered. She approached with the pillow in her hand, then laid it down on the table next to the bed. 'Can you lean forward a little?' she asked.

He tested his strength for a moment, then said, 'I regret to say, not without help.'

She leaned towards him, resting one knee on the bed and, after a little hesitation, put her hand round and behind him, saying, 'If you would but lean against me . . . ' She felt him put his arm around her shoulders, then for a moment too his full weight, which was considerable, even though it was only the upper part of his body, and he had lost some weight by virtue of his injury. She knew straight away that she could not manage to put the pillow behind him as well as lift him, but it was dangerously sweet to feel him pressed close to her in this way.

'I'm sorry,' she said. 'I can't . . . ' He leaned back, but her hand was still trapped behind him, and for a moment, their faces were very close. Her gaze fluttered down to his lips—lips that had bruised hers just a few nights before when he had seized her in his delirium, and then fluttered back until their eyes met.

'Jez,' he said. 'Jez, did I kiss you when I was delirious?'

'It's all right,' she said, blushing fierily. 'You didn't know what you were doing.'

His gaze dropped to her lips before his eyes met hers once again. 'That's not very flattering to you,' he said. 'A man would have to be mad, not to want to kiss you; especially one who had tasted the sweetness of your lips.' There was a long silence. Then the door opened, and Ilam came in.

Jessie turned her head, her face aflame. 'I can't manage him,' she said, sounding breathless.

Ilam crossed to the bed. 'I believe a lot of women have said the same.'

In the past, Ashbourne would have made a smooth rejoinder. On this occasion, as much to his surprise as anyone else's, he snapped, 'Have some sense, Ilam. She's only trying to give me an extra pillow.'

After the earl had been propped up, Jessie left Ilam to give his father some tea whilst she retreated to her room to cool her hot cheeks.

'Thank you,' said Ashbourne, after Ilam had assisted him to take a few sips, the earl's hands still being too shaky to hold the cup reliably.

'I'm glad that I can be of assistance,' Ilam replied in an even tone.

'But you still wish me at the very devil,'

Ashbourne observed.

'Not sufficiently to smother you with that pillow,' Ilam pointed out.

'Ah, but then you had Jez as a witness,' the earl reminded him.

'So I did.'

'Not that I think you would have done it anyway. I appear to have fathered a man of principle. God alone knows how.'

'Doubtless it's because I never saw anything of you.'

Ashbourne raised his hand defensively. *'Touché.'*

The viscount got up off the bed where he had been sitting and wandered over to the window. 'Anyway, sir, to prove that I intend nothing but your good, I'm setting plans in motion to take you to Illingham.'

'Illingham? Why?'

'The doctor tells me that you will recover better in the country.'

'We could go to Ashbourne, then the expense and trouble would fall upon me and my servants rather than yours.'

Ilam looked at him, his face set. 'I would rather not go there,' he said harshly.

'Why ever not?' the earl asked.

'Some of the most unhappy moments of my life have been spent there, thanks to you,' said Ilam.

'And mine,' answered Ashbourne softly, 'but the place amounts to more than fleeting moments of unhappiness for you and for me. What's more, it will be yours one day; perhaps sooner than later, if you decided to smother me after all.'

After a pause, Ilam shrugged and said indifferently, 'Please yourself. Have you finished with that tea?'

'Yes, thank you.'

Ashbourne stared at the door after his son had gone. It was possibly the longest conversation that they had ever had.

CHAPTER TWENTY-ONE

They left London several days later, with every arrangement having been made for Lord Ashbourne's comfort. Their party formed quite a cavalcade. Ashbourne travelled in one carriage with cushions, footstools and blankets all provided for his comfort. Pointer, being well acquainted with his needs, likes and dislikes, accompanied him, along with Jessie. Lady Agatha travelled in the second coach with Lord and Lady Ilam. A third carriage followed, carrying most of the luggage, and the remaining abigails and manservant.

The arrangement of the different persons in the party had been the subject of much discussion. Naturally, Lord and Lady Ilam wanted to be together. There was not room for all the others to go in Lord Ashbourne's coach, and for him to be comfortable. Lady Agatha and her brother tended to irritate one another, so it was decided that Jessie should go with the earl. 'Jez never annoys me,' he said, making her blush with this mild compliment.

'If he hurts her, I really will kill him,' Ilam said, under his breath to his wife before they got into the carriage.

'I don't think he will,' Eustacia replied, catching hold of his arm and squeezing it. 'He's fond of her, I think. Oh Gabriel, wouldn't it be wonderful if that fondness became something more?'

He looked down at her glowing face. 'Very wonderful,' he answered. 'You look deuced pretty this morning, my love. Can't we make Aunt Agatha travel on the box?'

For the journey, Jez took with her several books to share with Ashbourne, as well as a travelling chess set and some cards. She also had with her the copy of Mary Wollstonecraft's book that Lady Ilam had given her. No doubt Ashbourne would become tired and need to rest frequently.

In fact, the very activity of getting ready and setting off proved to be too much for him, and he soon closed his eyes, leaving Pointer to his book—a copy of *Robinson Crusoe*—and Jessie to her own thoughts.

She had been to Sloane Street to see

Henrietta in order to bid her farewell. She had also told her, as gently as she could, that she had decided to end her engagement to Henry.

Although disappointed, Henrietta had not been completely surprised. 'I think you would have been very good for Henry, but I could tell that your feelings turned in another direction when you hurried off to Raff's side,' she said. 'I do hope that there will be a happy outcome for you.'

Jessie smiled. After loving Raff for so long without any prospect of a return she did not hold out a great deal of hope but she did not say so. 'I have written to Henry, but I do not like to entrust his ring to the postal service,' she said. 'Will you take care of it, please, until he can collect it from you in person?'

'Of course,' Henrietta replied. 'Although I fear he may not be very pleased with me.'

'Why is that?' Jessie asked.

'I have told Mrs Smales that I do not need her to return.'

'What are you going to do instead?' Jessie asked curiously.

'I have invited Miss Simms to come and live with me,' she replied defiantly. 'I hope you don't disapprove. She has told me about her connection with Sir Wallace Weary, and knowing what he is capable of, I believe that she is not to blame for her misfortune. We will find a tenant for her house and share the proceeds.' Then, to Jessie's great surprise, the other lady hugged her warmly. 'Thank you,' she said, with unmistakable sincerity.

Jessie returned her embrace but had to say, 'Whatever for?'

'For helping me to be more brave and daring,' was the reply. 'While you have been here, I have done things that I only dreamed of before.'

Jessie had to reply that the feeling was mutual, although she reflected privately that there were some things that she had done that might have been better left alone.

She had also taken a little time to say goodbye to Miss Simms, who was truly sorry to see her go. The dressmaker presented her with a shawl which she had made from a length of silk, and edged with a frill. 'I have really enjoyed the times when we have sat sewing together,' she said. 'Apart from the fact that you did a good deal of work for me, you made the time pass very agreeably.'

'I enjoyed it too.' Jessie confessed, trying on the green patterned shawl in front of the mirror.

'Not only that, but you have introduced me to some new friends. I don't know whether you have heard, but Mrs Machin and I plan to share a home together with Bryony.'

'I had heard it and I'm very pleased for you both,' answered Jessie. She only hoped that Mrs Machin would not lead her new companion into any scrapes in pursuit of ideas for her novel.

To no one did she divulge the fact that she and Raff were married. She was still trying to summon up the courage to tell him. No doubt he would then immediately seek an annulment.

Any doubts on that score were laid to rest after Lady Gilchrist had come to pay Raff a visit. Her ladyship had called on the same day when Jessie had visited Henrietta, and had been shown to the earl's room by Pointer.

'Penelope, my dear, this is very kind,' said Raff, as she walked gracefully over to the bed and bent to kiss him.

'Raff, how delightful to see . . . so much more of you,' she answered, glancing down at his half unbuttoned night shirt.

He laughed. 'I'm glad you admire my *décolletage*,' he said. 'It's only because Pointer needs to be able to get to my bandages.'

'I am glad to see that you are recovering so well,' she said. 'Rumour had it that you were on your deathbed.'

'Rumour had it about right,' he replied, 'But thanks to a good constitution and excellent care, I have been preserved.'

'And so you fought the wearisome Weary, who has now relieved us all by fleeing to the Continent,' she remarked. 'Thank you, Pointer, yes I would like a glass of wine,' she added to the manservant who had just come in. 'Are you allowed any yet, Raff?'

Raff looked at Pointer. 'Well, am I?'

'Perhaps a small glass, my lord.'

'Yes, I fought Weary,' Ashbourne agreed after Pointer had gone. 'There was always bad blood between us, you know.'

'Weary was his wife's second choice. He never forgave you because she preferred you. I suppose this duel was over a woman?'

'It was; but not over you, my dear.' He had remembered that much.

She smiled. 'I didn't suppose it for a minute,' she answered. 'Have you finally admitted to yourself that you are in love with her?'

He smiled ruefully. 'Yes I have; twice, I think.' Seeing her startled look he went on. 'Your words to me at the Cumberland tea gardens made me question my feelings for her. It was only when I thought I was losing her to Weary that I realized how much she had come to mean to me. Then, of course, I took that wound, and everything went hazy for a time. Penelope . . .' He paused.

'Yes, Raff?'

His voice, when it came, was quiet and hesitant. If it had been anybody else in the whole world who had spoken, she would have said that he sounded shy. 'Have you ever been in love?'

'I believe so,' she answered carefully.

'Then you'll know what I mean when I say that every new revelation about her is fascinating to me; her every movement a delight; her every word and opinion to be stored and remembered. I can't get enough of her, Penelope. I want her here all the time;'— he patted the bed—'preferably *here* all the time. I want to care for her, to protect her; but I burn for her as well, and if by my blindness and neglect I've missed my chance, well, I shall wish that Weary had been more lucky in his blow.'

They sat in silence for a while. At last, Lady Gilchrist said, 'You really *are* in love. My dear Raff, she has been in love with you for years. It cannot be that her love could just die. Wait until you are a little better and speak to her then.'

'But she is engaged to Henry Lusty,' he said, his dejected tone in marked contrast to the passion that had been in his voice as he had spoken about his feelings for Jessie. 'He's a far better man than I have ever been, or probably ever will be. She's even told me so.'

'But he is not you,' she answered. 'There isn't another man like you.'

He laughed softly. 'Is that a compliment?'

'It's the truth'

'We each have a glass of wine. What shall we drink to?'

She thought for a moment. 'To our happiness—and the triumph of true love.'

Jessie, returning from her visit to Sloane Street had decided to pop in to Raff's room with Henrietta's good wishes, and a copy of her book, *A Scoundrel in The Church*, which she thought the earl might find entertaining during his convalescence. As she approached the door, which was about a quarter open, she realized that Ashbourne was with Lady Gilchrist, and was just in time to hear the last five speeches. The faint hope that the earl might turn to her finally died. Sir Wallace had been right. Raff's happiness lay with Lady Gilchrist. She straightened her shoulders and walked to her room. Mrs Machin's book could wait until later.

*   *   *

As they were leaving, Mr Hinder came to Berkeley Square to wave them off. 'I haven't mentioned *you-know-what* to anyone,' he whispered to her, when no one was looking.

'Well don't,' answered Jessie. 'Pretend it never happened.'

'But—'

'Do as I ask, please,' Jessie implored him.

'Has he remembered? Raff, I mean.'

'No, not yet.'

'Well, tell him, and the sooner the better in my opinion. The longer you leave it, the harder it will be.'

Jessie knew it. The trouble was, that fact did not make disclosure any easier at the present moment. She would wait until they were at

311

Ashbourne and he had recovered more of his strength. She would also wait until they were able to speak alone. Then she would pretend that she still intended to marry Henry. That way, Raff would not feel obliged to remain married to her from any misplaced notion of chivalry.

They were obliged to take the journey very slowly, in order not to jolt his lordship, so they spent two extra nights on the road. When they arrived at an inn, Pointer, assisted by Lord Ilam, took Lord Ashbourne to his room to rest. Later, the party would meet for dinner, which the earl always insisted on attending, even though he looked exceedingly tired and drawn. Afterwards, he would retire immediately.

During the journey, Jessie shared a room with Lady Agatha, whilst Lord and Lady Ilam had another room and Ashbourne and Pointer a third. These wayside stops provided an exquisite form of torture for Jessie. During the day, closeted with Ashbourne and uninterrupted save for Pointer's unobtrusive presence, she was able to pretend that the marriage ceremony which they had gone through had actually meant something. She talked to the earl, made him laugh at some of Mrs Machin's exploits, read to him, played chess with him, and managed to forget about the other travellers, and her position with regard to the whole party. Once they had

312

stopped for the night, she remembered that she was just Lady Agatha's companion, unsought and now ruined, and that the man she loved was himself enamoured of Lady Gilchrist.

'For how long have you been living with my sister? Nine years? Ten?' he asked her one day when he had woken from a short nap and she had laid down her book.

Taking his cue, Jessie told him a little about Lady Agatha. She made him laugh by telling him about the lengths to which her ladyship had gone to keep the vicarage of Illingham for her own use long after she should have moved out.

'You make me sorry I don't know her better,' he remarked. 'We've never been close, and I don't suppose we ever will be.'

'Why was that?' Jessie asked curiously, then blushed because she had been rather impertinent. 'I beg your pardon,' she went on in a mortified tone. 'You'll say, and rightly, that it is none of my business.'

He shook his head. 'It's not a secret,' he told her. 'My father never encouraged closeness between us, and with eight years separating us—although Agatha would hate to hear me say so—we spent very little time together. As soon as I was old enough to understand that I even had a sister, she had been sent away to school. Then I went to school myself. Our lives ended up having very little in common. The one time we did spend any time together socially, the whole business ended disastrously.'

'Can I guess? Might it have been when you were in Bath in pursuit of Lady Hope?'

'How acute of you,' he replied, grinning derisively. 'Yes, it was my first truly determined pursuit of a female. I was less than twenty and must have been utterly tiresome. Agatha dressed me down quite publicly and it took me a long time to forgive her. By the time I had done so, she had ruined her prospects by her public championing of an actress, and wanted nothing to do with me.'

'How sad for you both,' Jessie murmured.

From his side of the carriage, Ashbourne observed her and thought how much a thoughtful expression became her. He was finding a pleasure in her company that seemed to increase with every day that they spent together. He discovered that she was an intelligent woman with a sense of humour, a pretty laugh which made her eyes light up and revealed the graceful shape of her mouth which he had remembered was rather kissable. The problem was that she was not his to kiss. Since Jessie had not told him otherwise, he thought that she was still engaged to Henry Lusty. When he thought about the matter, he was gnawed by jealousy. It was an unfamiliar and very unwelcome sensation.

Ashbourne Abbey was an imposing pile,

sharing one wall with a ruined Cistercian monastery, after which it got its name. Jessie had only visited it once or twice, and had found it rather gloomy. It always seemed to her, however, that the house itself wanted to be happy; it was the occupants who had made it a depressing place, chiefly because of the poor relationships that always existed between fathers and sons. Glancing at Ilam's rigid countenance as he helped his father into the house, Jessie gave a sigh. It seemed as if things would be no better with this present generation.

*   *   *

'What a gloomy house, my love,' Lady Ilam said to her husband, when they had retired for the night.

'Yes, I've always found it so,' he agreed, as he brushed her hair. Eustacia's maid, Trixie, and Ilam's valet, Sanders, had both been sent to their own beds.

'And yet I feel that the laughter of children and a happy family could transform this place.'

'I hope you are not thinking of our children,' said his lordship.

'No, ours of course will be brought up at Illingham,' she assured him. 'Actually, I was thinking of your father and Jessie.'

'Eustacia, my love, you are talking nonsense,' he told her, pulling her to her feet

315

and into his arms. 'Jessie has been in love with my father for years, but he has never taken any notice of her. Actually, to give the devil his due,' he went on grudgingly, 'he has never encouraged her.'

'No, but I have been watching him and I think that he has changed.'

His face hardened. 'By God, if he does play with her feelings, I'll kill him myself,' he said savagely, releasing her and turning away. 'I know what he can do, believe me.' In his mind he went back over five years. A girl with whom he had thought he was in love had come with her parents to stay at the abbey. It had turned out that she was really infatuated with Ashbourne, and she had been discovered in his bed. Gabriel had turned his back on Ashbourne, the man and the abbey, from that moment on.

Eustacia crossed the room to where he stood looking down into the fireplace, where a fire had been kindled earlier to air the room. 'Gabriel, it was a mistake. Your old tutor Dr Littlejohn told me before we were married. It was she who pursued your father, not the other way round.' He turned and looked down at her, puzzled. 'If it had been the other way round, would not *he* have been in *her* bed?' Gabriel grunted. Treating this as a promising sign, Eustacia went on. 'Besides, it has turned out for the best really. If all that had not happened, she would have been married to

316

you by now, and where would that leave me?' He grinned reluctantly, and she was encouraged to go on. 'When we first met, you accused me of being in pursuit of him. He is impossibly handsome. Even I can see that, and I am besotted with you. So surely some of the time—' She was destined not to finish this speech, for he caught her to him and kissed her hard on the mouth. 'Oh, Gabriel,' she breathed, knowing that before they were married, to sigh his name in this fashion would encourage him to bestow more kisses. She was not to be disappointed.

'Enough talking, now,' he growled, lifting her easily on to the bed, and proceeding to disrobe.

'Well, almost,' she agreed. 'It's just that we were talking about children earlier and, well, I thought you would like to know . . .'

She was not allowed to say any more.

CHAPTER TWENTY-TWO

Lord and Lady Ilam decided not to share their good news with the rest of the party just yet. The knowledge of impending fatherhood had such a mellowing effect upon Ilam, however, that he even offered to take Ashbourne out in the gig to show him some of what he had been doing on the estate. The ladies were unsure about the wisdom of this, but the day was warm, and Ilam promised not to take his father too far.

After the men had gone, Lady Agatha took Eustacia and Jessie around the principal rooms, for Eustacia had not visited Ashbourne Abbey before, and Jessie had not been for some years. It was a Jacobean mansion, similar in age to Illingham Hall, but much larger, and lacking the warm atmosphere that prevailed at Ilam's residence. Lady Agatha took them to the long gallery, in which hung portraits of monarchs and statesmen, but also pictures of previous Earls of Ashbourne, most of whom looked as if they considered all of these extra people privileged to be allowed to hang in their midst. The last picture in the line was one of the present Lord Ashbourne, portrayed in his velvet and ermine state robes. He looked imposing, handsome and also somehow desolate and very alone. Next to his picture hung one of a man dressed in the costume of about thirty years before. Like Raff, and all the other Ashbourne men, he was handsome; but there was a look in his eye which was downright malicious.

'He does not look very lovable,' Eustacia observed.

Lady Agatha sniffed. 'That was my father. He was a horrible man. He never forgot a grudge and he never forgave a mistake.' After they had looked round for a little longer, Lady

318

Agatha said, 'This place holds no happy memories for me. Shall we go in search of refreshment?'

'Very well,' agreed Eustacia. 'I wonder how the men are getting on.'

*   *   *

After he had exercised his husbandly privilege the previous night, Lord Ilam had lain awake in thought beside his sleeping wife. The idea of impending fatherhood excited him, but also made him a little fearful. His relationship with his natural father was distant. In order to discover what a father ought to be like, he would look instead to his foster father, Tobias Crossley, the local farmer with whose family he had been placed as a baby by his grandfather. He would attempt to be the kind of father who listened to his children, and gave them his time. He would take his son round the estate and show him what needed to be done. He would not blame him for things that were not his fault. Smiling at this agreeable picture, he drifted off to sleep.

His good mood persisted the following morning, and this resulted in his invitation to his father. The pleasant feeling continued until Eustacia said to him, 'Ask your father about the truth concerning that young woman—the one we were talking about last night.'

'Certainly   not,'   he   replied   shortly.

Nevertheless, the feeling of well-being continued, and he pushed his wife's suggestion to the back of his mind. After all, he reflected, what did she know about the situation? His father had blotted his copybook too publicly and too frequently for his son to be prepared to listen to him.

Then, as they drove off, he glanced down at his wife, and saw the breeze catch hold of her gown and mould it to the contours of her still slender figure. He remembered all that he had thought and planned the previous night. He wanted to be a father who listened to his son; but he had to face the fact that he was the kind of son who would not listen to his father. Impulsively, before he could think twice about it, he said, 'Tell me, without roundaboutation, what happened when Lucy Planter came to stay?'

*   *   *

The day was instructive for both men. Ashbourne had answered Ilam's question honestly, and Ilam had listened without comment to his father's account, which had tallied exactly with what Eustacia had told him. Afterwards, they had confined their attention to the land and the situation of the tenants.

They greeted a number of local people on their travels. Both of them were recognized,

Ashbourne with a kind of wary deference, Ilam with a mixture of informality and respect. The same thing happened when they stopped at a local farm for refreshment. Ashbourne was greeted warily, even fearfully, but Ilam was welcomed, consulted, and even gently teased over the amount of time that he would now need to spend dancing attendance on the new Lady Ilam.

While they were there, Ilam happened to notice the reaction of the farmer's two daughters to his father. Once they had overcome their astonishment that he was there at all, they began whispering, giggling, and trying to attract his attention. Eventually, their mother packed them off to the kitchen. Ilam had been keeping an eye on his father the whole time. He had done nothing to attract them. Eustacia was right: women were simply drawn to Ashbourne. He just couldn't help it.

For his part, Ashbourne watched his son's easy manner with wonder and, to his astonishment, some envy and a good deal of pride. When Gabriel had a son, the boy would have a far better model than Gabriel had had in his own father.

'Where the deuce did you learn all of that?' Ashbourne asked Ilam, when they were perched atop the gig for the last time setting out for home, the earl more tired than he was prepared to admit. 'It wasn't from me, I know.'

'From Tobias Crossley,' Ilam answered,

321

adding nastily, 'I didn't learn anything from you,' regretting the words the instant they were out of his mouth.

'I'm aware,' Ashbourne replied. 'My only excuse is that my father didn't give me the chance.'

There was a long silence. 'The one thing that I find it hard to forgive is the way that you gave me up so easily,' Ilam said eventually.

'It was not at all easy,' Ashbourne answered. 'Pressure was brought to bear on me which—' He stopped abruptly. 'Never mind. In any case, you should be thankful. You would have been far worse off left to your grandfather's tender mercies, believe me.' Ilam glanced curiously at his father's face, shadowed by memories which were clearly not pleasant. Misunderstanding the nature of his silence, Ashbourne said defensively, 'I was only a boy when you were born, you know, and still under my father's authority.'

'Eustacia said that,' Ilam replied. 'How old were you, exactly, when you married my mother?'

'I was sixteen years and ten months,' Ashbourne answered. 'When you were born, I was not yet eighteen.'

'You were too young,' said Ilam.

'I agree.' They were silent for a time. Then the earl said suddenly, 'Do you call him father?'

'Who?' Ilam asked blankly.

322

'Tobias Crossley.'

'I've always called him Uncle Tobias.' Another silence. 'If you want me to—'

'No.' Ashbourne interrupted him. 'You're far too old for me to insist that you call me father. But I should be delighted if you can bring yourself to call me Raff, as my friends do.'

*   *   *

It had been a very significant day for both men. Perhaps because of that, as well as because of the physical exertion, Ashbourne felt quite tired the next day. Although he did get up, he would not allow Pointer to arrange his hair or to tie his cravat. He went straight to the drawing-room after breakfast, which he shared with Ilam, the ladies not having yet come downstairs.

Ilam accompanied his father intending to sit with him for a short time before attending to some estate business. They had not been there long before the butler came in with a message that a clergyman had called and was asking to see Lord Ashbourne.

'A clergyman?' replied the earl. 'That's novel. Did he say what he wanted?'

'Only that he was in the area, and knowing that you had been ill, wanted to congratulate you on your recovery.'

'Then you had better admit him,' said

323

Ashbourne. He turned to his son after the butler had left the room. 'Did any clergyman attend me, thinking that I was on my deathbed?' he asked.

'Not to my knowledge,' answered Ilam.

The butler returned shortly afterwards, announcing the clergyman as Rev'd Percival Goode. The thin clergyman entered the room, wreathed in smiles. 'My Lord! This is a sight to gladden the eye indeed! How thankful I am to see that my prayers have been answered.'

'You are very good,' answered Ashbourne. He had risen briefly from the sofa on which he was sitting, but resumed his seat again almost immediately. 'You will understand that I am still very weak.'

'Of course, of course,' the clergyman agreed.

'Ah, my son, Lord Ilam,' said Ashbourne.

The clergyman bowed respectfully. 'Lord Ilam, you must be beside yourself with joy.' Ashbourne gave a low chuckle.

'Just so,' Ilam answered politely. 'It is a little early for wine, but may I offer you some coffee?'

'Coffee would be very welcome,' answered the beaming clergyman. Ilam rang the bell and gave the order when the butler came.

'How do you come to be in these parts?' Ashbourne asked, feeling his way.

'I am on a walking holiday,' Goode replied. 'Learning that your estate was very close to the area where I plan to walk, I made enquiries and heard that you were in residence and making a good recovery. I decided to call and offer you both my good wishes. How delighted her ladyship must be at your recovery. After all her devoted care, it must be a great cause of thankfulness.'

'My sister, Lady Agatha and my daughter-in-law are both staying here,' said Ashbourne, not at all sure to which ladyship Goode might be referring. At that very moment, the door opened and Lady Ilam came in. She was introduced to the clergyman, who showed every evidence of gratification at the introduction, but who then turned back to Lord Ashbourne.

'I am referring, of course, to your wife, my lord,' he said. As luck would have it, at that moment the door opened and Jessie was admitted. She halted by the entrance, her face the very picture of consternation. 'And here she is!' he exclaimed, and hurried over to take hold of both of her hands. In his delight, he did not notice how white she had turned. 'My dear Lady Ashbourne, what a joyful situation is this compared to that sickroom where I first met you! I must admit that when I joined your hands, I felt sure that you would soon be a widow, but now I see that your husband has made a remarkable recovery. What a fine constitution he must have! Although I am certain that much of his recovery must be due to your loving care.'

His attention was fixed upon Jessie, and therefore he did not see how his revelation had poleaxed the other occupants of the room. Lord Ashbourne was the first to regain his poise. 'Indeed, you are right,' he said smoothly. Then to Jessie he added, 'Pray come and sit next to me, *my love*. Please be seated, Mr Goode.'

Jessie was too stunned to do anything other than obey Ashbourne's instructions. The last thing that she had expected was that the clergyman who had married them would appear in Derbyshire. Indeed, he had looked quite frail when he had conducted the ceremony, almost as if he might be the next to expire.

As she reached the sofa, Raff put out his hand to take hers, pulling on it with surprising strength so that she found herself sitting so close to him that they were touching. To her further embarrassment, he held on to her hand, clasping it so that it was resting on his thigh. She knew she was flushing, but the clergyman, who clearly saw them as a loving couple almost parted by death, beamed on benevolently.

At that moment, the coffee was brought in and Lord and Lady Ilam, who had been standing rather like actors who had suddenly found that they had been given the wrong script, bustled about, making sure that everyone was offered a cup, and had somewhere to put it.

To Jessie's great relief, Ashbourne was obliged to relinquish his hold of her hand in order to take his coffee. She was still very conscious of where his body touched hers through the silk of her gown.

'Now, Mr Goode,' the earl said when they were all settled, 'you must tell us the story of that night, for my son and daughter-in-law have not yet heard it, and my own memories of that time are hazy, to say the least.'

'There is not a great deal to tell,' Mr Goode confessed. 'I was called upon very late by one Mr Hinder, who asked me if I would perform a marriage that was earnestly desired by a desperately sick gentleman who was not expected to last the night.'

'Hinder,' breathed Ashbourne. 'Of course. Go on.'

Jessie put her half-drunk coffee on one side. 'I . . . I think I might go upstairs,' she murmured, making as if to rise.

Anticipating her intention, Ashbourne put down his own cup and caught hold of her hand, imprisoning it once again upon his thigh. 'By no means, my love,' he said in an amiable tone, but with a hint of steel in his gaze which only Jessie could see. 'I well know your modesty, but I must insist that you stay.'

Jessie subsided uncomfortably against the back of the sofa, and wished that she might just disappear. What must everyone be thinking of her? All the occupants of the room, with the exception of Mr Goode, knew that she had adored Raff for years. No doubt they would now be thinking that she had acted the opportunist and taken advantage of a desperately sick man for her own advantage. She cast one more scared glance at Raff, then stared at the pattern on the carpet, barely taking in the words of the clergyman as he recounted the events of that fateful night.

Eventually, his recital came to an end. As it did so, he glanced round, colouring a little as if at last becoming aware of the exalted nature of the company in which he found himself.

'What a romantic story,' exclaimed Eustacia. 'Do you not think so, Ilam?'

'Fascinating,' replied her husband.

'It was very kind of you, Mr Goode, to furnish us with this story,' went on Lady Ilam, 'but I am sure that there is more. Let me show you something of the gardens here, and you can tell me the rest.' She stared at her husband pointedly.

Ilam looked at Jessie, unwilling to leave her alone with Raff if she did not wish it. It was Ashbourne who spoke next. 'Yes, pray take Mr Goode around the gardens, both of you. I would very much like to have a private word with *my wife*.'

CHAPTER TWENTY-THREE

'When were you going to tell me, Jez?' he asked her. He did not sound angry.

They had both stood up as the others had left. Now Jessie sighed and walked towards the window. 'I did not think that I would ever have to, to be honest,' she replied frankly. 'When Hector Hinder fetched me, he told me that you were dying, you see.'

'So you came in response to the request of a dying man.'

'Yes.'

'And only married me for the same reason?'

'I didn't want to agitate you,' Jessie explained.

'I see. How very lowering.' His usual society drawl concealed the hurt that he felt inside. Once she had loved him. Now, at best, she only pitied him.

'Lowering?'

'I have never before had a woman accede to my wishes because she did not want to agitate me.'

'You had fought a duel; you were gravely wounded . . .' It was a strange, stilted conversation that they were having, she thought to herself. But it was either that or be completely shamed by flinging herself down at his feet and begging him to give her a chance

329

to make him happy.

'Ah! The duel. I remember now.'

'I should thank you for your gallantry,' she said, looking across at him.

'Yes, I really think you should,' he answered. 'I don't remember putting myself to such trouble over a female before. By the way, did it occur to you what you might do if I lived?'

'It was not thought likely, to start with,' said Jessie. She paused as she remembered lying by his side, thinking that she might wake and find him dead. 'Then, of course, when you began to recover, I knew what I must do, as soon as you were strong enough.'

'And what might that have been?' he asked her, his head slightly tilted to one side, his tone quizzical.

She straightened her spine. 'The marriage is not a proper one. Neither you nor I desired it; it was forced upon us by circumstance. There should be no bar to an annulment.'

He drew his brows together. 'An annulment? Is that what you want?'

She could feel tears coming into her eyes but she refused to let them fall. 'Of course. It is the best thing. It means that . . . that another marriage would be possible.'

'Ah yes, Henry Lusty,' he murmured. 'You want an annulment because of him?'

She looked straight at him. She knew that she could never marry Henry, but it was not necessary to tell Ashbourne that. If he believed that she still desired the marriage, then he would be able to seek freedom for himself, which was what she was convinced he wanted. Then he would be free to marry Penelope Gilchrist. 'I am still engaged to him after all,' she said.

'And he is the better man. You said so yourself, I seem to recall.'

She did not answer this. 'We have both been placed in a very embarrassing situation, but at least it can be remedied, and the sooner the better. I will go upstairs now and pack. To stay here would only be awkward.'

'Jez,' he said. If Jessie had not been so distracted herself, she would have been able to hear the note of uncertainty in his voice.

'No, Raff, please; I do not think I can bear to discuss this any more.' He said nothing. She just managed to get out of the door and up the stairs before her tears started to fall.

*   *   *

After a brief excursion around the gardens of Ashbourne Abbey, Lady Ilam invited Mr Goode to stay for lunch, but he excused himself. 'I have promised myself a walk in Dovedale today and as the weather is fine, I ought to be on my way. Should I return to the house and say farewell to Lord and Lady Ashbourne, perhaps?'

'I think that might not be wise,' replied

331

Lady Ilam. 'They have a lot to talk about at the moment.'

'Every time I think he's gone his length, he finds another way to shock everyone,' said Ilam, staring after the retreating clergyman.

Eustacia did not make the mistake of thinking that her husband was referring to the inoffensive Mr Goode. 'Not this time,' she answered. 'He never appreciated her before, but now I think he is truly in love with her.'

'And what makes you say that?' he asked.

'The way he looks at her,' Eustacia replied.

'What of it?'

'It reminds me of the way that you look at me,' she replied demurely.

Gabriel caught hold of his wife by her waist and pulled her against him. 'Then he must be in love with her,' he replied, kissing her thoroughly, to the satisfaction of both parties. 'What now?'

'We go to the saloon and see what's happening,' she told him. 'Either they have kissed and made up, or . . .'

'Or?'

'Or you and I have some work to do.'

Gabriel sighed, and ran a gentle hand over his wife's still flat stomach. 'Do you suppose he will be this much trouble?'

She pressed his hand with hers. 'She's sure to be,' she said serenely.

'She? Are you certain?'

Eustacia smiled knowingly. 'You don't mind,

do you?'

Gabriel grinned, and took his wife's hand in a gentle clasp. 'Will I mind having a daughter as beautiful as her mother? What do you think?'

* * *

It was while Jessie was trying to pack her things through a haze of tears that there was a gentle tap on the door and Eustacia came in. 'Are you all right, Mama-in-law?' she asked. Then, seeing Jessie's face, and noting the activity upon which she was engaged, she murmured, 'Oh, my dear,' and took her in her arms. Although Jessie was taller than Eustacia, and her senior by eight years, it was still very comforting to cry on her friend's shoulder.

After Jessie's tears had subsided, Eustacia encouraged her to sit down on the bed. 'Now tell me what happened. Was he very angry?'

Jessie shook her head. 'No. He was kind, actually. He's always been kind. Look.' She took a linen-wrapped bundle out of her half-packed bag, and opened it to show Eustacia her figurine. 'When I was a girl, he found me crying over this and mended it, because he was sorry for me. That's how it's always been; I've been in love with him, and he's felt sorry for me. I used to hope it might change one day, but now I know it never will, and oh, Stacia, it hurts so much! When he was ill—dying as we thought—he married me out of pity, to save my reputation. But I don't want to be married to him because he pities me.'

'Did he say that that was his reason?'

'No; but he didn't say he loved me. And I love him so much!' Her voice caught on a sob, but she soon mastered herself. 'One night, when I thought that perhaps he might die before the morning I lay down beside him on the bed, with my head next to his on the same pillow. I would rather have that one memory than a whole lifetime with Henry.' She paused. 'I have told Raff that he may have an annulment. Then he can marry Lady Gilchrist.'

'Lady Gilchrist?' queried Eustacia. 'I don't think . . .'

'Stacia, I heard them,' Jessie replied. 'They were planning a future together.'

Eustacia had her doubts, but did not voice them. Instead she said, 'Are you going back to Illingham?'

Jessie nodded. 'For the present,' she agreed. 'I can't think further ahead than one day at a time.'

'I'll have the gig harnessed, then you can go straight away,' said Eustacia. 'I'll tell Aunt Agatha where you have gone when she comes back from spending the day with Dr Littlejohn. I'll send the rest of your things on later.' If I need to, she added silently to herself.

*   *   *

It took Ilam a little longer to find his father. Lord Ashboume had been gaining in strength every day, so the viscount was not entirely surprised to discover that the earl had had a horse saddled. He was rather disturbed, however, to discover that his lordship had gone alone. 'Do you have any idea which direction he may have taken?' Ilam asked, when he was in the saddle himself.

As he rode off in the direction that the groom had indicated, he was rather surprised at the anxiety that he felt. He had grown up blaming the earl for his neglect. Since Ashbourne's illness, he had had more to do with him than at any other time, and a few things had happened that had given him pause for thought. For one thing, he had been accustomed to thinking of Ashbourne as vain. To his surprise he had found that the earl, although beautifully turned out, never glanced at himself in the mirror.

On one occasion, Lady Agatha had said something outrageous, and Ilam had found his amused gaze meeting that of his father as the same thought ran through their minds. Then, only that morning, he had found a footman distraught over a bottle of wine that he had broken, and Ashbourne laying a hand on the man's shoulder and assuring him that he had never liked that particular vintage anyway.

335

Ilam was used to hating his father. It was rather odd to find that the man he had hated probably didn't exist.

Just as he was starting to think that perhaps he ought to return and organize a search party, he saw Ashbourne's riderless horse cropping the grass. Concerned that his father might have taken a fall, he sprang down, to discover Lord Ashbourne leaning against part of a fallen tree and gazing into the distance. Ilam walked over to him.

'Do you recognize those hills over there?' Ashbourne asked him, pointing.

Ilam looked, wrinkling his brow. 'I'm not used to this view,' he said eventually, 'but the formation looks a little like that to one side of Crossley Farm.'

Ashbourne nodded. 'I used to ride over here and take a look,' he said. Ilam stared at him. As if he had asked a question, Ashbourne said, 'I had two sons, remember; Michael, and you. My father's price for supporting Michael was that I kept away from you. I was only allowed to see you when he gave permission, and that was rarely.'

'My God,' exclaimed Ilam, as soon as he was able. 'But that was infamous!'

'Infamous, yes. I should have done something, but I didn't know what to do. Until I was twenty-five, I had no money of my own to support either of you. By that time, I was a stranger who meant nothing to you, and I didn't want to spoil what you had. You could say that it was my own stupidity that got me into that mess in the first place, and you'd be right. No one asked me to go to bed with Dora Whitton, did they? I was an adolescent and I was in love. Could there be a more explosive combination?' All this time, he had been staring into the distance. Now, he turned his face downwards.

Ilam was appalled. He did not know what he would do if Ashbourne wept before him. 'Dora was the mother of Michael?'

'My first love. I thought that she would be my last, as well.'

'You love Jessie?'

Ashbourne turned to look at him, then. For the first time, Ilam saw the likeness between them that everyone commented upon. 'Ironic, isn't it?' he said. 'Yes, I love her. I've been so used to having her in love with me, but now it's too late. She's tired of me and she wants an annulment. I've lost her, just as surely as I lost Dora.'

'She wants an annulment?' asked Ilam. 'Did she say so?'

Ashbourne wrinkled his brow. 'She said it was the best thing,' he said slowly. 'I assumed it was so that she could marry Henry Lusty.'

'Did she mention him by name, then?'

'No,' replied Ashbourne. 'I did.'

Ilam shook his head. 'I never thought I'd know better than you did in *this* area of expertise,' he said, grinning. 'Yes, you lost Dora Whitton, but you were a boy then. You're not a boy now, and Henry may want to marry her but she's your *wife*.'

'But . . . what if she won't have me?' Ashbourne asked uncertainly. 'I'm more than half convinced that she only feels sorry for me.'

Ilam gave a crack of laughter. '*Sorry* for you? My God, I wish the *ton,* and especially the female half that is so besotted with you, could hear you say those words,' he exclaimed. 'If you don't try, you'll never know, will you?'

An arrested expression spread across Ashbourne's features. 'God damn it, but you're right, boy,' he said, untethering his horse, and mounting. 'I'm going to claim what's mine.'

'Go to it, Raff,' called Ilam, as he watched him go. Then, rather surprised at what he had just said, he rode back to the Abbey to tell his wife what had transpired.

CHAPTER TWENTY-FOUR

Jessie entered the house by the garden door and wandered dispiritedly up to her room. She sat and wept for a little while, then eventually dried her tears and looked about her. This was the room that she had occupied since her

338

arrival in Illingham. It looked exactly the same as it had done when she had left. She was the one who had changed. Now, she wondered how she could ever take up the threads of her old life again. Oh, but it was too bad to be so near to her heart's desire and yet so far away!

She did not have very much time to spend in this kind of dispiriting introspection before there was a knock at her bedroom door. Surprised, because she had not thought herself observed, she opened the door to find Lady Agatha's butler Grimes on the threshold.

'Beg pardon, miss, but the gardener said he'd seen you come in. Mr Lusty is asking for you downstairs.'

She stared at Grimes for a moment in consternation. His announcement filled her with dread. She knew that she would have to meet Henry, but she had hoped that she would not have to do so until she was feeling a little stronger. The meeting was not to be avoided, however, and part of her thought the sooner the better. She could only wish that she had not left his ring in town. It would have been good to return it today and be done with the whole business.

'Thank you, Grimes, I will come down at once.'

Mr Lusty was waiting in the drawing-room, looking much as he always did, apart from the fact that he was perhaps a little more drawn. They greeted one another formally and Jessie offered him refreshment, which he refused, after which an embarrassed silence fell.

Lusty was the first one to break it, saying, 'I imagine you understand my purpose for visiting you today.'

'I do not believe I do,' Jessie answered steadily. 'I think I made myself plain in my letter to you.'

'The nature of your decision I understood,' he said, a little tight-lipped. 'Your reasons I fail to grasp.'

'My reasons?'

'Your circumstances are the same as they were. Your fortune has not changed. Pardon my bluntness, but you have not got any younger. I fail to see why you have changed your mind.'

'You may fail to see it, but that does not mean that it has not happened,' Jessie answered.

He rose to his feet. 'I blame your sojourn in London,' he said, with more than a hint of bitterness in his voice. 'It has turned your head.'

'It has done no such thing,' she responded indignantly.

'You cannot see it yourself, but believe me I can,' he replied, a little more aggression in his voice. 'Before you went to London, you conducted yourself becomingly. You dressed with modesty, attended only seemly entertainments, and treated me with respect.

Now look at you!'

Jessie looked at her reflection in the pier glass next to the window. Her blue gown was of a fashionable but decorous cut, and had a modest neckline. Her hair had become a little disarranged during her flight from Ashbourne Abbey, but she had tidied it before she had come downstairs, and now it was gathered neatly on her head, with a few tendrils escaping at either side of her head. 'I see naught amiss,' she said, honestly puzzled.

'No, I dare say,' he answered in a jeering tone. 'I declare I do not have far to look for the source of the bad influence upon you. It is that profligate with whom you choose to associate.'

'Indeed?' uttered Jessie, stiffening her back. 'To which profligate are you referring, Mr Lusty?'

'I think, perhaps, he is referring to me, my dear Jez,' said another voice. As both the occupants of the room turned their heads, they saw Lord Ashbourne on the threshold. Those who were accustomed to seeing him pay social calls would have been astonished to see him dressed thus. His black hair hung loose about his shoulders and he wore no cravat; but he walked into the room like a king. Paradoxically, although his faultless dressing usually made every other man look a little slovenly, on this occasion his very casual attire made Lusty's tidiness look finicky. 'You left

341

rather precipitately, my love; so much so that I found myself obliged to come in pursuit, *en déshabillé,* as you see.'

Mr Lusty stared at him in baffled fury. Aware that he had already gone too far in criticism of one who had power over his preferment, he nevertheless could not prevent himself from saying more. 'You address Miss Warburton in very familiar terms, my lord,' he said, his chin jutting out aggressively.

'Would you say so?' replied his lordship in tones that were deceptively soft.

'I certainly would,' answered the clergyman. 'Considering how greatly she has changed, and not, I may say, for the better, I suppose I should not be surprised at any familiarity that she is prepared to permit.'

'But then,' answered the earl, with the ghost of a smile, 'a husband is allowed to take more liberties than other men.'

'A husband?' echoed Mr Lusty, completely bewildered.

'Certainly,' answered Ashbourne, taking a pinch of snuff. 'Jez did me the very great honour of becoming my wife towards the end of her stay in London. I believe she will be prepared to receive your good wishes.'

Jessie stared at the earl in consternation. The last time she had spoken to him, they had agreed upon an annulment. Now, his words and actions were completely at variance with one who intended to take such a course. What was she to make of it?

'Jessica! How could you?' exclaimed Mr Lusty, with justifiable consternation. 'We were engaged.'

'You will have to excuse her,' said Ashbourne. She was thankful for the intervention, as she did not have the smallest notion as to what she might say. 'She was called to my deathbed, as everyone thought. In sympathy for a dying man, she agreed to marry me. Most unexpectedly I was spared.'

Lusty stared at them both. 'I cannot believe this,' he uttered. 'You both seem utterly devoid of any proper feeling or sense of conduct.'

Ashbourne's smile faded. 'You may say such a thing of me—indeed, people have been saying it for years—but if you speak of my wife in that manner, then you will answer to me.'

Jessie gestured for the earl to be silent, then stepped forward, seeing bewilderment as much as anger on the clergyman's face. 'Indeed, it is quite true,' she admitted. 'We would never have been happy together.'

'We might have been had you not gone to London,' he replied wistfully.

Jessie shook her head. 'We would have discovered too late that we were not suited, and that would have meant a lifetime of regret,' she told him.

The clergyman stepped back and bowed formally. 'I wish you both very happy,' he said stiffly, before leaving the room.

For a short time after he had gone, silence reigned in the drawing-room. Jessie wandered over to the window, whilst Ashbourne remained standing in the centre of the room. Eventually she said, 'Poor Henry. He should not have found out in that way.'

'He was unconscionably rude,' the earl replied. 'He must learn to take the consequences.'

A sudden thought came into Jessie's mind. 'In fact,' she said turning to stare at him, 'he should not have found out at all.'

'Discovery was almost inevitable, I would have said,' he answered calmly.

'I do not see why. If we had kept the matter within the family, then the marriage could have been annulled almost without anyone knowing. Now, he will probably tell everyone that we are married.' She began to wring her hands in distress.

He walked over to where she was standing until he was very close to her, then took hold of her hands, holding them still. 'They have to find out from somebody,' he said. 'If you simply moved into the abbey, I think everyone would be rather shocked.'

'Move into the abbey? But I thought you wanted an annulment.'

'Strangely enough, I thought that that was what you wanted.' She looked up into his eyes and was transfixed by their expression; amused, warm, and tender, and lit with some

344

other emotion too; something wilder and more passionate. 'As a matter of fact,' he went on, 'I'd much rather have a consummation.'

'Raff!' Jessie exclaimed, turning bright red.

'Would you prefer I pretended that I want the bloodless relationship that would no doubt have kept your erstwhile suitor happy?' he asked her, his voice becoming a little rough. He turned away from her, running his hands through his hair. She watched him in wonderment. She had never seen him like this before, with his mind obviously in such turmoil. 'When you first came to London, I still saw you as an acquaintance for whom I had a kindness. You kept getting into scrapes, and I found that I couldn't stand idly by because I wanted to protect you. Then I kissed you at Vauxhall, and I found that you were a woman who could make my blood burn in my veins. You know my reputation. It exaggerates a little, but not very much. I've enjoyed intimate relationships with a number of women, although I've kept clear of despoiling the young and the innocent.'

'Yes, I know it,' Jessie replied, laying a hand on his arm, her heart beating wildly as she listened to his words.

He lifted her hand to his lips, never taking his eyes from her face. 'I wonder you don't run away,' he said softly. 'After all, I'm dangerous.'

'Handsome, wicked and careless was how I described you to your daughter-in-law,' she

345

replied.

'Pretty is how *she* describes me,' he retorted. 'As for the rest, well, you just about hit the nail on the head. I'm evidently the kind of man to whom women turn for a thrill or two, but whom they would never dream of in a million years if they wanted a man they could depend on. You said it yourself.'

'Yes, but I didn't mean it,' Jessie protested. 'I was angry and I wanted to hurt you.'

'All the same, I am very well aware that by so inconsiderately not dying as I should have done, I robbed you of your chance of marrying a decent man.'

'But I don't want a decent man; I want you.' The words were out of her mouth before she had thought about how immodest they would sound.

'Oh Jez,' he groaned; then his lips were on hers, and she was held tightly in his embrace. The last time they had kissed, he had been delirious, dying as everyone had thought, and she had kissed him back, thinking that it would be for the last time. Now, the passion in his kiss offered a promise for the future, and in glad surrender, she returned his embrace with all her heart and soul. Their lips parted. He let go of her, but only to cradle her face gently between his hands. 'I fell in love when I was sixteen. When she was taken from me, I swore I would never fall in love again, and I never did, until I looked at you and saw you as if for the first time.'

'But I thought that you wanted to marry Lady Gilchrist.'

He smiled wryly. 'It was Penelope who made me confront my feelings for you,' he told her. 'I have known her for a long time, through Philip, but we have never been lovers. She has been my very good friend. It was she who encouraged me to hope that your love for me hadn't died, as I feared.'

She put her hands on his shoulders and looked into his eyes. 'I've always loved you, and I always will,' she said, 'But, oh Raff, are you sure that . . . ?'

'That . . . ?' He prompted.

'That I will be enough for you? So many women love you . . .'

'Ssh.' He placed a finger upon her lips. 'Sweetheart, I'll not deny that there was a time when female admiration pleased me, but it's been some years now since I've courted it. The trouble is that a reputation for raking once gained tends to stick.'

'What about the women that we saw at Vauxhall?' Jez asked. 'Lady Agatha says—' She broke off, colouring.

'Yes, my heart, what does Agatha say?' he asked her, his tone tender and amused.

'She says that they are the kind of pretty . . . pretty . . . females that appeal to you,' Jessie replied hesitantly.

'I doubt that Agatha called them females,'

he answered wryly. 'In twenty years on the town you get to know a lot of people. You must not imagine that I have been on intimate terms with every woman who greets me.'

She caught hold of his coat and shook him gently. 'Please don't treat me like a fool, Raff. I've loved you for so long, and to hear you say that you love me too is beyond my wildest dreams. But if you were to turn to someone else because you were bored, it would destroy me, I think.'

He was silent for a time. When he spoke again, it was in a voice that had the unmistakable ring of sincerity. 'I don't think I've ever felt really ashamed of myself until this moment,' he admitted. 'Since I'm being honest with you, I freely acknowledge that I have always enjoyed the thrill of the chase. The problem with that approach to life, though, is that sometimes, the chase becomes more exciting than gaining the quarry.' She was about to speak but he silenced her with a gesture. 'Jez, I have never seen you as quarry. To me, you were always a friend, someone to be cared for and watched over. Gradually, as time has gone by, you have become so much more, and the more that I get to know you, the more precious you become to me.' He paused. 'Jez, you're going to laugh at me.'

'Never,' she answered.

He laughed, a laugh that held a hint of self-mockery. Then he released her, stepped back, and went down on one knee. He looked up into her face, his own expression utterly serious. 'Jez, you are my lady, my treasure, my guiding star, and somehow, you have become my reason for living.' He paused. 'I suppose it's a little late to propose properly, but will you marry me?'

For answer, she tugged at his shoulder, and he stood and took her in his arms once more. After a long, very satisfactory interval, she said, 'In some ways, you have always been my gallant knight.'

'With rusty armour and a soiled tabard,' he said derisively.

'Perhaps,' she conceded. 'But remember that I have positive proof of your gallantry.' He raised his brows. 'My figurine,' she reminded him. 'I have it still.'

'And where is it?' he whispered, just before he kissed her.

'In my room, upstairs,' she replied, as soon as she was able.

*　　　*　　　*

'What made you come after me?' Jessie asked some time later, as they lay entwined on her bed. She had dreamed of him here so many times. Never had she thought that they would lie here together as lovers, as man and wife.

'It was a conversation that I had with my son,' he told her. 'He reminded me that if I

349

really wanted you, really loved you, then I should be prepared to fight for you. He made me wonder whether we were each agreeing to an annulment in order to make the other happy.'

'I *love* Ilam,' mused Jessie.

'Do you really, madam wife?' asked the earl, tipping her on to her back and soundly kissing her.

'Yes of course,' she answered, as soon as she was able. 'But not nearly as much as I love you. He's not pretty enough for me.'

He gave a shout of laughter. 'What *I* know,' he said, when he had stopped laughing and they were gazing into each other's eyes, 'is that I love you more than I would have believed possible.'

She reached up with her left hand to touch his cheek. He took hold of her hand, and turned the wedding ring on her finger. He had removed it from the chain around her neck after he had unfastened her gown, and put it on her finger before they had made love. 'I think that I am going to like being married,' she murmured.

'It has many benefits,' he agreed, his lips very close to hers.